The Creation of Kaitlyn Jones

By
Kathleen J. Shields

This book is a work of fiction. Places, events, and situations in this story are purely fictional. Any resemblance to actual persons, living or dead, is coincidental.

ISBN-13: 978-1-941345-06-1 Paperback
ISBN-10: 1941345069 Paperback
ISBN: 9781301010394 Smashwords eBook

Canyon Lake, TX
www.ErinGoBraghPublishing.com

Chapter 1

Darkness swarmed the area with such despair it seemed she couldn't breathe. She knew the small dank room would make her ill, and so over time, it had. Cold air seeping in through packed dirt and the walls made her shiver to the bone. As each shiver worked through her aching body the pain grew worse. As an evil orange light blinded her to the faceless ones, she knew it was going to happen again.

One by one the evil men came down to the tiny dank cellar where Janie had been held captive for so long. She heard heavy breathing. She smelled sweet liquor on their breath and heard the deep grumbles of their laughs as they shut the door behind them, locked it, and took advantage of her again.

She had learned months earlier her screams would never be heard so far under the ground, and she had also learned her screams excited them more. Like wild hyenas searching, hunting for food, they enjoyed the fight and the struggle. With that in mind, she just gave up. Let them do their will and leave her to her silence was all she could possibly want now.

She had prayed every silent second during the past eight months for someone to rescue her from this miserable existence. She knew she would be dead soon, but she didn't want to die in here. As her belly swelled, she prayed for serenity for her unborn child. The father didn't matter. According to her imagination it was the prodigal of every one of those men. Its fathers were six of the most horrible men on the planet; its mother was the prisoner in their sex-crazed dungeon.

They threw down a piece of bread every once in a while, but it wasn't enough to survive. It kept her alive, without strength to fight back. So she ate herself. She bit her fingernails and the skin around her fingers until they bled. Then she would drink blood for nutrition. It kept her awake at night wondering what this sort of treatment was doing to her unborn child. Their dirty deeds would soon kill the baby, disfigure, or deform it. She felt it would die upon birth if it didn't die before then, but she prayed it wouldn't.

If the baby did survive, she prayed it would be healthy and not deformed. She prayed it would be able to escape this place. That it would be raised by a good family if she wasn't able to go with it. Most of all she prayed it would be able to do all of this. If it were able to escape and survive to a better life that it would do one more thing. That it would have the smarts, the strength, and the power to keep itself and everyone from ever living such a horrific ordeal. She prayed it would be the savior of the unsaved.

She spoke prayers through thoughts, not able to open her mouth and actually speak now; she felt the child would hear her thoughts. Like a telepathic link between mother and child she spoke.

"I pray you will be strong. As strong as six men, those six men. I pray you will use that strength to help others in need, other women in this sort of predicament. I pray you will have every ability to do this, and so I give you all of my abilities. Take my sight from me, the sight that has grown so accustomed to the dark that I can now see no matter how dark it gets, no matter how black it is. Take my agility, the gymnastics that I learned as a child, I cannot use it now. Take my dreams, I give them to you. My fantasies of being able to see this before it happened, so I would never have gotten into this. Use my dreams to help others, see them before they get hurt and help them. Take my mind, the mind that I use to talk to you with and share it with someone special. Oh if only I could will the door to open. If only I could make those men fly off of me with the power of my mind. I may not have the ability to do so, but maybe my prayers will give it to you. The ability to move objects with your mind. I know you will be a girl, I can feel you

2

growing inside of me and I feel your strength and promise. You will be everything I want you to be, I just know it."

She prayed over and over again, never changing one word. Maybe the Lord would give this to her, her last request. She was certain now she would die. She could never recover from this abuse and torment. She held on though, everyday, only for her child, in hopes her prayers would be answered.

The day started like every other day had for the majority of a year, dark. The silence was so eerie, so different from mornings before, it led her to realize something was happening. She felt it in her bones that someone was watching, and as quickly as that feeling came to her, the silence broke and there was nothing but noise.

Wood splintered and cracked under the pressure. Then footsteps, enough to sound like ten or more large men. Men shouted, and then she heard gunshots and more pounding as if men were falling. She heard more shots and more screaming. Furniture crashed, dishes broke and then finally all went quiet again.

She knew something had changed. Maybe her captors had all been killed. Maybe she would be saved. She was too weak to stand. She wanted to call out, but she couldn't. She longed to see the sunlight, but had lost all will to move. She stayed on the floor, sniffing the moldy air, smelling the disturbance in the room, the new smells, the new people, even the smell of blood.

As she heard footsteps walk over the hidden entrance to the basement and walk away over and over again, she felt her hopes grow and shrink. She worried she would be left there alone. That maybe the good guys would never find her. And what of her baby? It would be due soon. How long could the both of them survive?

Finally, after contemplating the worst for close to an hour, and silence once again filled the house, she prayed for her salvation and her child's life. And as she finished this prayer she once again heard footsteps above. As the footsteps stopped above the secret door, her heart began to tremble. She heard them walk back and forth on the wooden floor. Different sounds came from over top the door and then the regular floor. The hollow sound as if there were something more beneath the rug. The echo of that sound filled her ears until it was all she could hear. She sensed the man bend over and remove the dusty rug to reveal the secret door. As blinding white light filled the room, she could tell the outside door was open to the sun.

Then a second blinding light came on, a flashlight, and she watched it sway from side to side on the creaky wooden stairs. As the silhouette of a man stopped in front of her, she slowly closed her eyes against the pain from the bright light, not able to look away.

"Oh, my Lord," the man said. He then called for help and an ambulance.

As the ambulance and paramedics raced down the stairs to help the officer, the shear sight of her must have sickened them. Her once beautiful face had shrunken around her skull and most of her hair had fallen out. She had been starved until she was just a frail skeletal structure with a baby inside of her. The baby moved around inside of her, its appendages nearly poking through her skin. It was the sight of death, giving the gift of life.

They carefully took the woman from the room and brought her upstairs. She remained silent as they carried her on the gurney outside, but she smiled when she saw the sky. A smile was all she had strength for as she was rushed to a hospital. The ride was bumpy but she didn't mind it no matter how painful. She knew she was safe now and her baby would be saved.

As they rushed her into the hospital she heard nurses scream at the sight of her. She was poked and prodded with needles and IVs where she felt nutrients fill her and shortly after the labor pains begin. They must have given her something to help the baby out as well. Before she knew it, she was in a delivery room where the doctor talked frantically with other doctors. Due to her year's worth of silent listening, even though the doctors talked in a separate room behind a pane of glass, she heard everything.

"We have to do a C-Section."

"It'll kill her!"

"If we don't take the baby now, the baby might die!"

"How do you know that the baby isn't the only thing keeping her alive?"

She knew her time was near and she knew the doctors would have to hurry if her baby was going to survive. She found the strength to speak to a nurse who was looking over her, and what she said touched the heart of that nurse.

"Save the baby."

The doctors had nothing else left to do except retrieve the baby and let God's will take care of the mother. Like she felt the breath of God on her face, the baby had been swept from her body and cleansed. The nurses and doctors kept talking, praising her.

"It's a girl!"

"It's a perfect, healthy and strong little girl!"

As they handed the baby to the mother, the first and last time she would ever get to hold and see her child, she took the baby in her frail arms and looked upon the face of her masterpiece. She smiled just a little as she looked upon the child of her will and prayers and like every great artist; her last deed was to name the baby. Her last airy breath that came from her body was a name: Kaitlyn.

Chapter 2

He just doesn't know of the love that I hold;
Deep down inside me, burning and bold.
But every so often I get a glimpse of his eyes,
And I imagine a love that he just can't disguise.
But just as quickly as that, the moment is gone,
And I'm left here wondering if this love will dawn.

Kaitlyn Jones looked up from her writing and sighed as she peered down the auditorium bleachers to Tom McKinney in the wrestling ring. His fight was about to begin, and his trainer rushed to gear him up. Most of the other guys on the wrestling team looked silly in the schools purple and yellow wrestling suits, the colors clashed with their skin tone and the suits hung on them funny. But not Tom. His muscular, tan body looked good in anything he wore. His dark brown hair and dark brown eyes seemed to soak up any color near him. Kaitlyn found herself completely infatuated in him most of the time, but this afternoon she was a little more preoccupied.

Kaitlyn stared back down at her English paper briefly and reread what she had just written. It was a great poem, but it wasn't one she wanted to turn in. She tore it from her book, crumpled it into a small paper ball and threw it towards her backpack. It missed the bag opening by a rim shot and fell under the benches where Tom's mother, Marge, sat.

Marge looked up from a book when she heard the bell ring for the start of Tom's fight and she stood and cheered for her son. Kaitlyn also cheered with the rest of the crowd. The fight didn't last long. Within moments after the bell tolled, both competitors had a half -nelson on each other, but Tom, using strength and speed, knocked the other guy's legs out from under him, pinning him to the ground. Three seconds later, Tom was

6

pronounced winner. The referee grabbed Tom's hand and held it high as everybody cheered his win.

Ten minutes later, the crowd had thinned and Tom was in the locker room changing clothes. Kaitlyn and Marge sat on the bleachers talking.

"So how is your junior year going Kaitlyn?" Marge asked of her favorite sitting buddy. No one else really knew enough about Tom to know this older lady was his mother, so as if she were as contagious as the plague, no one sat next to her. It wasn't cool to be seen with someone who was 25 years older than you and knitted in public.

Kaitlyn had found out simply by accident that Marge was Tom's mother one day during his workout about a year ago. Kaitlyn tried to sit with some of the more popular girls but they shooed her out of their area like an ant at a picnic. So Kaitlyn found an empty spot on the bleachers next to a middle-aged lady knitting a sweater.

"Hi, I'm Kaitlyn," she said, as she set down her books and began to settle down and prepare for the fight.

"Well, hi there, Kaitlyn, I'm Marge. How are you doing today?"

"Fine. So what are you here for? Do you know one of the wrestlers?"

"I sure do, Tom McKinney's my son."

Kaitlyn was shocked. "You're Tom's mom?" she whispered.

"Yep, you know you're the first person to ever ask."

"I don't doubt it. If those girls down there knew who you were, you wouldn't be all the way up here by yourself."

Marge gave her a sly smile. "Well, you won't tell them will you?"

Kaitlyn had made a point to be at all of Tom's wrestling matches. She really wanted to be a part of his cheering section and then celebrate with him afterwards. But she was never allowed to be part of the crowd who celebrated with him, she just wasn't cool enough. She had a secret crush on him, but it seemed the whole school knew about it. It was hard for Kaitlyn to hide her feelings. Each time she looked at him, she got lost in his eyes, whether he was facing her or another girl. Every time he brushed against her, she'd likely melt right there in the hallway. Tom never knew. If he did know, he didn't seem to care enough to show it.

Kaitlyn lacked the courage to go up and talk to him. The few times she did find the nerve, she'd say something off the wall about a stupid math quiz after he had just won a wrestling match and wanted to celebrate or worse. One most embarrassing time she had actually said,

"I Kaitlyn, you Tom, " completely ruining the well-planned sentence she had prepared to say the entire afternoon.

But Tom didn't laugh as she thought he would have. Tom smiled at her, shortly before Susan spoke loud in front of everyone gathered around them.

"Sorry but Tom doesn't do the Tarzan and Jane speak, but Munce over there plays a good monkey."

Everyone around them burst out laughing as Kaitlyn looked over to the slightly chunky class clown squirting milk from his nose through a straw. Feeling hurt and embarrassment growing, Kaitlyn ran off through the crowd and prayed silently for a very large rock to fall on her and end her misery.

"School's good, Mrs. McKinney. How's your quilting class going?" Kaitlyn asked today as she slid her notebook into her bag and gave her full attention to Tom's mother. The gymnasium was very quiet now that the crowd had dispersed.

"Wonderfully, they're going to use my design for this years quilt bazaar."

Kaitlyn smiled as she talked with Marge. She liked her a lot; they thought the same about many things, and sometimes she got to hear stories of Tom as a young boy. Marge and

Kaitlyn only had the occasional meeting at the gym last year, but last summer when Kaitlyn's mother passed away their relationship changed. From that day on Marge had taken Kaitlyn under her wing. She had done all she could to be a good friend to Kaitlyn and to her father during their time of grieving. It had brought Marge and Kaitlyn's relationship closer and to Kaitlyn, Marge was now like the mother she didn't have any longer.

This particular afternoon Kaitlyn had had a bad day. She had been trying to write her feelings down in poetic form for English class but everything seemed to be wrong. She tried to write something about her mother, but it was too hard to complete and she felt guilty if she began to write anything about Marge. Kaitlyn tried to write about something not so close to herself, like flowers or bunnies but she hated those subjects even more and every time she tried to write something happy, it turned out that she was writing about Tom. Yet although the poems about Tom were great, she knew she couldn't turn those in. What if the teacher liked it and wanted her to read it for the entire class, including the man of her dreams? She just couldn't turn anything in about Tom; it would be way too embarrassing.

Shortly into their conversation, Tom walked up the bleachers to get his mother, which interrupted Marge and Kaitlyn's conversation.

"Mom, I'm ready."

"Tom, honey, have you met Kaitlyn?" Marge asked her handsome son. Kaitlyn looked from Marge over to Tom in absolute shock because she hadn't seen him coming. To her surprise he admitted he knew her, which amazed Kaitlyn.

"Well, good, I wanted to make sure before I invited her to dinner tonight."

Kaitlyn's heart jumped for joy and then she nearly choked on it. To be invited to Tom's house! To eat dinner with Tom! But to be invited by his mother and not him, was a real downer.

Kaitlyn began to decline but something even more surprising happened.

"Sure mom, that sounds nice..." Tom began. Kaitlyn thought her life was about to change. Tom didn't mind at all that she'd be coming to his house for dinner. "But I can't be there, I already promised the guys I'd go out with them tonight."

"Oh," Marge said, obviously trying to hook her son up with Kaitlyn.

Kaitlyn tried not to show her complete disappointment. "That's okay, Mrs. McKinney, I actually have a bunch of homework to do tonight."

"Okay, sweetheart, I'll take a rain check, but you and your father must come by for dinner sometime soon okay?"

Kaitlyn smiled wide. "Sure thing, Mrs. McKinney." She then bolted down the bleachers, feeling so much like a fool she didn't even want to look at Tom. Marge stood up, reached below her seat and picked up her purse, grabbing a crumpled piece of paper with it. As she saw the paper she opened it and read it, gaining Tom's attention.

"What's that mom?"

"A beautiful love poem." She smiled as she watched Kaitlyn turn the corner and leave the gym in a hurry.

Tom laughed just enough to show surprise. "Someone wrote you a love poem?"

"No, honey," she sighed as she started down the stairs. "It was directed to a guy who doesn't even know it." She handed the note to Tom and started walking down the stairs. Tom read the poem briefly, noticed Kaitlyn's name at the top of the page and then crumpled the paper and followed his mom down the stairs. As he passed a trashcan he almost threw the paper inside, but something made him keep it. He slipped it into his pocket and then opened the door for his mother.

The next day in English class Kaitlyn stared at Tom, her head resting on her hands, her elbows on her desk. Nothing could have been more obvious, and when other students began to notice and point at her, Kaitlyn quickly glanced elsewhere. She felt so alone at times. No one ever seemed to give her a chance; no one ever seemed to understand what she was about. She wasn't as weird as everyone made her out to be, and yet, she was treated like an outcast. Sure she had stopped smiling when her mother had been fighting with the cancer. Sure she hadn't really talked to anyone after her mothers passing, but did that make her a bad person? Was that really a reason to spread rumors and joke about her being weird?

Kaitlyn used to always go out of her way to try and make friends. She'd be as nice as she could to people. She'd help them if they needed it and she'd listen if they wanted to talk. All she wanted out of all of this was friendship, someone to hang out with, to talk with, and someone to like her. Some people she had thought were friends were only friends as long as she gave out free lunches and money handouts. She soon learned that all that turned out to be was a bribe, instead of the intended help she thought they needed. She went out of her way to listen to a few other people; they'd tell her everything, and she thought they were really connecting. Until she told them a little about herself and her life, but they weren't interested and quickly changed the subject back to themselves.

But this would never stop Kaitlyn from trying to make friends before. The problem she had after her mother's passing was she just didn't care anymore. It was just too difficult to put on a smile and pretend to be happy for the sake of friends. So when people left her alone she didn't mind. However now that she had taken the time to grieve, now that she wanted a friend, or to try to make friends again, she found it down right impossible. Now that she was trying to regain some form of popularity and find a group to hang out with, she simply couldn't remember what it was she used to do to make herself a friend. Or maybe she had never truly been successful at those attempts in the first place.

This made for a very upsetting and disappointing sophomore year of high school. And now as a junior, her teenage mind rang with alarm since she only had two more years to get this right. After that it would pretty much be tattooed on her soul what kind of person she was and everyone in the world would be able to see it. Kaitlyn needed to do something big this year, but she didn't know what. The only thing she seemed to care about more than making friends was Tom, and for now he seemed a lost cause.

As the teacher called her name that day during English class, to ask why she didn't turn in her poem, Kaitlyn felt perplexed. She had been writing poems all night long, but they all seemed to be about Tom, and they all seemed to express a pathetic attempt to get noticed by others. It was all too embarrassing to turn in and chance another person reading or hearing about it. As Kaitlyn began to explain why she didn't have it, the old dog ate my homework bit, Tom stood and spoke for her.

"Miss Periwinkle, it seems Kaitlyn dropped her poem yesterday at the wrestling match. I found it but didn't get a chance to give it back to her before class began." He walked up to the teacher's desk and handed her the wrinkled paper, smoothed out flat. The teacher looked at the poem and read it over and then spoke.

"Okay, I'll give this to you this time, but next time Kaitlyn, you turn it in with the rest of the class or you get an incomplete." Mrs. Periwinkle glared as she looked over at the shocked Kaitlyn sitting at her desk.

"Yes, ma'am." Kaitlyn said, as she looked over at Tom with her bright green eyes opened wide with shock and surprise. Tom didn't look back at her. She wondered why he helped her and as the bell rang to release the students from class, Kaitlyn rushed to gather her books and find Tom in the hallway to thank him.

"Hey Tom," she said to get his attention and have him wait for her to catch up. "I just wanted to thank you for what you did for me in class. I really appreciate it."

"Don't mention it." Tom said. Kaitlyn stared up into his eyes, a smile spreading across her rosy heart shaped face. Tom looked back at her and then rolled his chocolate brown eyes.

"I mean it! Do not mention it... ever," he said as he turned and walked away. Kaitlyn's smile turned into a frown almost immediately as she heard giggles behind her from Susan and her cheerleader friends. Kaitlyn quickly ran off the other direction not quite sure what to think of it all. She felt like she had stood there like a loving puppy, waiting expectantly for the praise and love from her master, only to be shot down and scolded instead. She wished she could understand what she was doing wrong. She wished she were more popular; that she had some way to stand out in the crowd in a good way, but that didn't seem to be happening. She thought she had tried everything but nothing so far had seemed to work. She began to wonder if something really was wrong with her, and she just didn't know it yet.

Kaitlyn took her time getting to her history class; she took the long way around because she wasn't in too much of a hurry to sit in front of Susan, the blue-eyed goldilocks blonde bombshell and head of the cheerleading squad. Ever since Kaitlyn had tried out for the cheerleading team and was laughed off, she had a cold feeling Susan wasn't going to ever be friendly to her. Kaitlyn also had a sinking feeling if she let her guard down in class, she would walk out with gum in her hair. It seemed like the thing for Susan to do to finally get back at Kaitlyn for what she said that day at tryouts.

Two months previous, the day of cheerleading tryouts, there were girls that looked as if they hadn't exercised one day of their life. Girls that looked as if they had no fashion sense,

13

girls doing this to get their mothers off their back, and girls like Kaitlyn who wanted to be a part of this tremendous high school experience, had the gymnastics ability, and the will to give it their all.

Kaitlyn had been stretching and preparing for the cheer she had planned out when the girl before her tried to do a cartwheel and landed on her knee and limped off crying. Nervous, Kaitlyn was called in next and was prepared to show them all just what she could do. She walked out in front of the rest of the cheerleaders, got into pose, and waited for the music she had picked to cue up. Finally, she heard the beat begin and started to dance.

A little toe tap for eight beats, then hip shakes and then Kaitlyn started shouting out her cheer. She had rhythm and rhyme. She danced like a pro and towards the end of her cheer she did a triple flip cartwheel that ended in a twisted back flip. Kaitlyn looked at the judges and saw open mouths and wide eyes. She knew she was in. She was flying on cloud nine for the next hour just knowing she was the best person to try out that day. When they posted the list of winners, Kaitlyn took her time getting to it, knowing her name would finally be on it, that all of her hard work and practice this summer would finally pay off and she would finally belong to a group.

She made it up to the list, skimmed down it once, not seeing her name, knew she had missed it and then went over the list again. As her finger slid down the list to the bottom again, her stomach ached. She went over it one more time reading every single name slowly and when her finger reached the bottom of the list for the third time another girl behind her said it all.

"Look, you're not on the list! You mind if everyone else still waiting here gets to check?"

Kaitlyn looked behind her at other girls still waiting, and as she realized she wasn't chosen, her heart began to crumble and she found something in her that she never knew was there. Anger. She stormed up to Susan, tapped her on the shoulder, and spoke to her in a way she had never dreamed possible.

"I want to know why I wasn't picked."

"You just weren't quality material darling," Susan exclaimed with a wicked sneer.

"No! You know I was good. I was better than anyone else who tried out today. I'm even better than you are. And I'm starting to think that I wasn't chosen because someone may find out you're not all you're cracked up to be and shun you like you've had them shun me."

"How dare you," Susan said as she flipped her curly blonde hair over her shoulder. "Look, just because you didn't make the cut doesn't mean…"

One of the other cheerleaders spoke. "Susan, I thought she was good, why didn't she make the cut?"

"Darlene? Butt out," Susan yelled at the overly tall red head. Then she turned back to the fuming Kaitlyn and spoke in a growl. "We didn't pick you because you're not a team player and your outburst just now proves it! You can't be a part of a team if you think you're better than everyone else."

"You know what," Kaitlyn said too angry to think straight. "I don't know why I wanted to be a part of such a snobby, arrogant group of girls. I have more personality than you and all of your pathetic little followers put together." Kaitlyn then turned and walked towards the door.

"Pathetic?" One of the other girls screamed, ready to begin a fight, but Susan stopped her by putting up her hand. When she spoke, her cheery voice carried enough sarcasm in it that Kaitlyn could hear just how much she would never fit in.

"Let her go. The poor thing just realized she's a nobody with nothing and she'll never be as cool as us."

As Kaitlyn walked up to the door of her next class, a voice caught her attention and she stopped just shy of going inside.

"She really is pathetic. She tries way too hard to belong, and looks needy. She spends way too much time mooning over a guy who's completely taken..."

"You only wish Tom was taken," Darlene laughed.

"Hey, he will be when he realizes I'm the best thing for him," Susan said with a giggle. "Anyways I was trashing Kaitlyn, not talking about Tom and me."

Kaitlyn had heard enough. With a slow glance over to the side door leading to the outside and the pathway to freedom, Kaitlyn made the run for it, and didn't turn back that day. She knew in her heart one of these days she would belong. The only thing she didn't realize was that day was quickly coming and she just didn't see it yet.

It was a beautiful summer day without a cloud in the sky and the breeze blew every so often, just enough to keep it from getting too hot. Kaitlyn had come over to Tom's house per Marge's request; she wanted to give Kaitlyn a casserole she had made for Kaitlyn and her father. Marge knew Kaitlyn's father was still very much depressed over the passing of his wife last summer, and she wanted to help. Marge knew how it felt to lose a loved one, especially a significant other.

When Tom's father was killed on the job three years ago, she had a hard time mourning and then getting back to her life. She blamed his partner and the rest of the police force for not watching her husband's back. She knew how she felt then and knew that though Kaitlyn and her father, Harold, had time to prepare for her mother's passing, since she had been struggling with the cancer for so long, it was still a tough thing to get over. So once a month, Sunday afternoon after church, Marge called over to Harold and Kaitlyn's home and would have Kaitlyn come over and pick up a freshly baked casserole. Marge knew from their talks during Tom's wrestling matches that Kaitlyn did the cooking for her and her father and every little break helped. Kaitlyn appreciated Marge's caring and she also appreciated the open ticket to Tom's house.

Kaitlyn sat inside the kitchen at the breakfast room nook across from Marge who would tell Kaitlyn tales of Tom as a kid, wild, crazy, and a little bit kooky. Kaitlyn would then tell stories about her mother, she had definitely been old enough to remember her mother, but as Marge always said, telling the stories was a wonderful way to remember, to keep her mother alive. So Kaitlyn would share memories of her mother, and when it became too difficult to go on, Marge would share stories of her late husband.

While she listened to Marge, Kaitlyn peered out the kitchen window at Tom who was out on the driveway washing his car. Tom's red mustang was his pride and joy. A car he and his father bought and rebuilt one summer. After his father's death the only thing that seemed to brighten his spirits was the car, washing it, waxing it, sitting in it and driving it. It gave Tom a sense of freedom, like everything was going to be all right just as long as he had this car. As Tom slaved over the mustang in the hot sun beating down upon his body, he began to sweat. And as the calming wind that was due to come, never came, Tom needed relief from the heat. He tore his white shirt off over his head and tossed it to the ground. It landed in a puddle of soapy water, then Tom went back to his work, scrubbing the hood of his red mustang with the cool soapy water and a soft towel.

Kaitlyn watched the sun light him up like an angel. She watched as if in slow motion, him ripping his shirt off, exposing his rippling muscles shimmering like diamonds as the sun's rays reflected off of tiny beads of sweat. He turned the hose on just a bit and let the cool stream of its water trickle down his face and chest, and she watched as one droplet of water slid all the way down his chest, over his rock hard abs and seemed to disappear into the darkness of his jeans.

Kaitlyn sighed as she watched him, completely forgetting Marge sitting across from her. Marge had stopped talking and was now simply watching Kaitlyn watch Tom. She smiled at Kaitlyn's sigh. Tom had his father's good looks, Marge thought as she too looked out the window at her son, but she also knew that her son was still very much a loner. After his father's passing, Tom had stopped living. His attitude towards life became a mere existence. He was sad, but never cried, and Marge worried about him, praying and hoping one day he would snap out of this depression and actually start living again. She hoped at the very least Kaitlyn might be able to help since the two of them already had the death of loved one, a parent, in common.

Marge finally offered a suggestion. "How about you take a glass of lemonade out to him?"

Kaitlyn loved the idea, and thought it could be a great conversation starter, a reason to go out and talk to him and be next to Tom. Then, Kaitlyn realized it was Marge's idea and Marge was looking at her, looking at Tom.

Kaitlyn snapped out of her daze. "He's probably thirsty and he's hot." Kaitlyn paused thinking about how great a description that was for him, hot. But liking the idea that it could have two meanings.

Marge got up, poured a glass of lemonade and handed it to Kaitlyn. "Let him know there is plenty if he wants more." She hoped maybe her son would say something to the effect of keep them coming. Then maybe as Kaitlyn stood out there with him they would strike up a conversation.

Kaitlyn walked outside. "Thought you would like some lemonade."

He ignored her words for just a moment as he finished buffing one side of the back panel with wax, then he stood up straight, throwing the towel on top of the trunk lid and looked at Kaitlyn. He had never paid her much attention, had known of her visits with his mother and he knew of her mother's passing with cancer, but other than that he hadn't made any other initiative in getting to know her. He just didn't care about anyone else. But as he saw the tall glass of lemonade, he smiled. He watched Kaitlyn stop just feet away from him, close enough to be personal, yet not invade his space.

"Thank you." He took the glass from her hand, his fingers brushing hers just slightly. The touch was a spark to Kaitlyn and sent shivers straight up her arm to her neck and tingled her entire body. But as she watched him gulp down the liquid, wipe his mouth with the back of his arm and then hand the glass back to her, she knew that would be the end of their conversation and their encounter. Tom picked up his towel, crouched down and began waxing his car again. Kaitlyn turned and walked back inside, thanking Marge for the idea.

Then, with a small frown on her face Marge would hand over the casserole dish to Kaitlyn, give her directions on how to warm it and send her on her way. No matter what Marge felt like, or how she acted, she always had the best intentions for other people and always went out of her way to help them. Kaitlyn walked away that afternoon holding a dish, but as her imagination took over she realized, returning the dish was a good reason to come back.

Chapter 3

Two nights later, Kaitlyn had a dream about Tom. He was driving his car over Sabine Pass, a very dangerous mountain top road with steep inclines, sharp turns and cliffs. Knowing if someone ever went over them, that person would surely die, Kaitlyn paid extra close attention to her dream not quite sure what to do if anything should happen.

Kaitlyn felt in her dream that something bad was going to happen, but she was powerless to stop it. She watched, as if she were in the passenger seat as Tom passed a yellow caution sign showing dangerous curves ahead. She watched as he came in and out of sleep. As the second right turn approached, his eyes closed and the car went flying off the cliff and landed nose down in a patch of bushes, holding him and the car from falling hundreds of feet to his death. Kaitlyn looked over at Tom from the passenger seat but he was out cold, his head on the steering wheel, blood dripping from his forehead down over his eyelids. Kaitlyn was unable to do anything in her dream state so she woke up.

Sitting up from this dream, fear filled her. Sweat poured down her face, and as the moonlight swept into her room allowing her eyes to see through the darkness, she noticed she had fallen from her bed and it helped her remember the dream crash. It was three in the morning, way too late to call over to Tom's house. What would she say? Kaitlyn then quickly jolted to her feet and ran to her bookshelf, flipping on her lamp as she approached. She scanned the shelves for a book her mother had given her some time before. Finally she found it. Covered in dust, it was a dictionary of dreams. She blew off the dust, eight years worth since she had thought about it or needed it. Remembering that her mother had gotten it for her many years ago, when she saved her father in the forest one day.

Kaitlyn kept claiming she saw her father step into a bear trap in a dream, but her parents just waved it off. So when Harold and her were walking through the field making their way to the far end of town that day, Kaitlyn somehow recognized the area and warned her father about the trap. He was just about to step down upon it when he saw it. He was so excited; so proud of his daughter for having such keen eyesight that he totally forgot she had talked about it earlier that morning. But her mother went to town that day and bought Kaitlyn a dream book to open her imagination about her dreams, to find out exactly what they meant.

Kaitlyn opened the book and flipped the crisp pages through her fingers, first looking for the word car, as in car crash. But the only reference to cars it showed was streetcars, like trolleys or train cars. Deciding the car wasn't the important part but the crash was, she looked up the word crash. Not there, she looked up the word wreck next. It said to dream of a wreck denotes sudden failure and harassment from peers. She had enough harassment from her peers as it was, and failure was a word she had hoped would not appear so early in her life. Why was Tom in her dream? Was it her deep caring for him making her imagine being in his car? Did the car ride mean anything symbolic, or was it just hope that one day they'd be together? The more Kaitlyn thought about it the less sense it made and the more she thought it was all a big mistake. She then wrote the story down in her dream journal. The book was partially full because she didn't dream much, but everything she wrote in it seemed to hold some importance to her.

She wondered why Tom had fallen asleep. Was it a message that their relationship would be boring? Why did he crash? Was it a symbolic meaning that trying to join him along the same path would hurt her? Did he die in the dream? Was it a subliminal message that their love would never be, and Kaitlyn should just let the hope of dating him fade away and die?

Kaitlyn finally decided the dream meant nothing. She would never get together with Tom, and if she mentioned her dream to someone it would get to the "in" crowd and they would harass her for dreaming nonsense. Exactly what the dream book had told her. She had already lost an hour and a half of sleep over this nonsense. She turned her lights off, crawled back into bed and fell asleep.

The next morning she woke up remembering the dream. With an odd urgency to find out more, but more of a fear of having her feelings hurt by the kids at school, she once again, pushed it away, ate breakfast and went to school. She didn't see Tom in the hallway that morning, but that was usual. By the end of her first class, she had all but forgotten about her horrible dream, and was trying to figure out how to get by Sam "the spike" Gordon, one of the meanest girls on the Volleyball team. She was like a one -girl team, tougher than most all the girls combined, and no one ever wanted to get in her way when she played. Sam had forgotten the meaning of team, and no one dared tell her. As long as the team won the coach wouldn't interfere because she wanted the pennant. Kaitlyn was the brunt of this girl's attention outside the gym. Her locker was right above Kaitlyn's giving her the upper hand, but she was also a bully and knew Kaitlyn would be a ready victim.

As Kaitlyn walked up to her locker, praying Sam was in a good mood, she took a big silent gulp and leaned in to do her combination. Everything seemed to be going well. Sam hadn't noticed her. Kaitlyn straightened her back up after bending into her locker but hit her head square into Sam's locker door that wasn't open just two short seconds earlier. The bump and pain made Kaitlyn drop her books, one of them fell open and papers scattered everywhere. Everyone laughed, making her angry. She bent down to grab her books. "Damn girl and her damn locker." Kaitlyn mumbled.

"Whatcha say, girl?" Sam asked.

When Kaitlyn looked up, Sam stared at her with fire in her eyes. Trouble followed Kaitlyn and everyone enjoyed watching it. Kaitlyn looked up at Sam.

"Were you talking to me?" The world famous start of any hallway brawl.

"Yeah, I asked you what you said." Sam said again.

"I didn't say anything."

"Oh I think you did, girly. You calling me a liar?'"

"No!" Kaitlyn flinched, expecting to be struck.

"Well, I think you are." Sam turned to the crowd of students. "What do all of you think?"

"Kick her ass!"

"She's asking for it."

Kaitlyn never wanted to be called chicken; she never wanted to run from a fight. She wanted to be strong and independent, but she didn't have it in her just yet. So she ran away like she always did, hearing others call her a chicken and a woosie. She hated backing down, but knew she would never find a boyfriend if her face had been rearranged.

Kaitlyn was just settling in to her second period class, ready to forget about Sam for an hour, when she noticed that Tom was missing. Last nights dream popped in her head, but she quickly pushed it back, forcing her mind to consider he was just running late from wrestling practice. During roll call he was named absent and she thought it odd that Tom be out sick on a day there was a wrestling match, and again she thought of her dream but she pushed it back again, knowing it could be the flu going around.

After the class as she walked past the principal's office she saw two male cops and a woman crying. When Kaitlyn took a closer look, she recognized Marge McKinney, Tom's mother. Kaitlyn had talked with Marge enough to know that Marge had no love for the police force anymore. Tom's father had been a police officer, and one night he tried to stop a bar brawl between a young girl and a drunken guy, who swore he was her husband. Dave, Tom's dad was shot. Tom had taken his father's death very hard, and almost seemed to have never gotten over it. Marge never seemed to get over it either. She blamed the other police officers there that night for not watching Dave's back.

Now, as Marge stood in the principal's office crying and begging the police to help her, Kaitlyn knew something serious had happened. Curious, Kaitlyn walked in the office.

"Marge what's wrong? Is everything okay?"

"Tom's missing. He never came home last night."

Kaitlyn's dream rushed back, pleading to be heard but Kaitlyn put it aside again, afraid of the truth.

A rude cop spoke up first. "Young lady we can handle this, why don't you just scoot along to your next class?"

Marge ignored the cop and continued to speak to Kaitlyn.

"He was supposed to drive up the mountain to Cloudy City to drop off some food I had made for old Mrs. Garrison. When he never came home last night I assumed he stayed the night at her house, but when I called her this morning, Mrs. Garrison said Tom left early last night."

Kaitlyn's legs became mush and she nearly toppled over, realizing every bit of her dream could very well be true. Knowing every square inch of that mountain road because of her fathers' weekly jaunts to the junkyard, she spoke out with honest certainty.

"I believe I know where he is."

By now the cops had had enough of Kaitlyn's meddling. "Young lady we are handling the situation."

"Yes but if you'd just listen..."

"Miss Jones," the principal said. "I'm sure the news of Tom's disappearance is a little hard to swallow but you're just going to have to go to class...."

"But Principal Sweeney..."

"No buts, Kaitlyn, the police have already sent a car up the road and back again and they saw nothing of Tom or his car."

"Have you checked just off the road on Highway Ninety? Where the sharp turns are? Because I had this really vivid dream and…"

"A dream?" One of the officers almost laughed.

Kaitlyn tried to explain, but the cops and even the principal smiled.

"Look Kaitlyn, " the cop said. "I'm sure you may have thought you dreamed something but this is real life."

The cops had just asked Mrs. McKinney if there had been any arguments between her and her son. Their questions did nothing to ease her worries or lead her to believe they were ever going to find her son. They decided she was a distraught mother who didn't know anything and they treated her as such. So when Kaitlyn spoke so certainly about finding Tom, Mrs. McKinney had to hear her story.

"Please, Kaitlyn, tell me what you dreamed." Mrs. McKinney suggested.

The principal spoke up. "Mrs. McKinney, I'm sure you are upset about your son being missing but some young girls pranks won't help us find him any quicker."

"Kaitlyn, you said it was off of Highway Ninety. Would you be able to show us where?" Mrs. McKinney asked.

"Marge, are you really going to listen to this girls ranting about some dream?" the principal asked.

"I apologize for intruding," Kaitlyn said fast. "But I did have a dream about this, and it very well could be false. But if it is true and I do know where to find Tom, don't you think it would be important to find out for sure before he bleeds to death from the wound on his head?"

The cops were stunned as Mrs. McKinney spoke up. "He has a wound on his head?"

"In my dream as we went over the cliff and landed in the bushes, he hit his head on the steering wheel and was knocked unconscious."

Marge stood. "Well, then officers, let's stop wasting time and go find my son!"

Kaitlyn sat in the back seat, one cop drove, and Marge sat in the front. Two police cars followed, and Kaitlyn heard one radio that they may need an ambulance and a tow truck and to stay on alert. Kaitlyn sat up and searched for the yellow caution sign she had seen in her dream and prayed selfishly that her dream was true so she could show these cops once and for all. Never once did she consider realistically what she would do if it actually was true.

Kaitlyn broke the silence in the car. "That's the sign we passed. He's just up ahead." Marge sat up and looked carefully at the road for clues.

"If my dream was right, he should be right over that cliff in some bushes."

The cop stopped driving and everyone got out. Kaitlyn ran to the side of the road and saw the red Mustang.

"Tom!"

Without thinking, she started down the steep incline. One of the cops followed, yelling up to the other,

"Call the ambulance!"

Tom's mother stood at the road edge looking down, her hands over her mouth, her eyes blurred with tears. Kaitlyn continued down the dangerous cliff to Tom's car, nearly tripping over a couple bushes and loosening some rocks. When she reached the car, he was unconscious on the steering wheel. She reached through the open window and placed her hand over the forehead cut to stop the bleeding, when he began to stir.

"Tom, don't move! You've been in an accident." He opened his eyes and looked at her.

"Kaitlyn?" was the only thing he said before the cops arrived and took over.

As Kaitlyn stepped back and let the paramedics do their work, she was amazed at the truth of her dream and shocked at the courage she found in getting down to him. Kaitlyn was even stunned because Tom had said her name. She watched as the paramedics lugged Tom up the side of the cliff and into the ambulance.

"Very impressive, Miss Jones," the officer began once everyone was safely back at the top of the cliff.

"Sir?" She looked up at the officer next to her.

"Tell, me again how you knew exactly where to find him?"

"I told you, my dream."

"That's right. But you kept saying, we were driving down the road and we drove over the cliff."

"He drove over the cliff." Kaitlyn corrected.

"Yes, but earlier you said we, as if you had been with him."

"Well," Kaitlyn said, choosing her words carefully. "I was in the dream, but no I was not with him physically in the car last night. He was alone, or else I would've been unconscious in the car with him."

"Yes, I'm sure. Still, maybe you should come in for questioning. I think it would be a good idea."

"Kaitlyn, would you please join me and Tom." Mrs. McKinney interrupted the officer and moved in, wrapping her arm over Kaitlyn's shoulder and walking her to the ambulance.

Kaitlyn was grateful Marge had pulled her away from the questioning cop. She got a weird feeling this officer wanted to blame her for the crash, or somehow fit her into it as being involved, or worse yet, responsible.

A few hours later, Tom woke up in a hospital bed. He looked around slowly, then over to Kaitlyn. She looked at him, then stood and walked to his bedside.

"Hi, you're looking better," she said.

His voice remained weak. "I feel like crap."

"We'll you don't look it." An awkward silent moment followed.

"So you found me?" He asked changing the subject.

"I did."

"How?"

"I dreamed about it." Kaitlyn said, with just a little too much emotion and pride for Tom to understand completely.

"Yeah? Okay." He almost rolled his eyes.

"Hey, don't you go and think I'm a wacko, too. I saved you're life."

"You're right, and I owe you mine."

"Nah, I don't want that." Kaitlyn said, looking away.

"But you do want something?" He asked with a smile.

"No, not really."

"Not really? So you do."

"Kind of."

"What?"

"I'd like to learn how to fight." Kaitlyn said.

"Wrestle?"

"Well, I suppose, but just some sort of fighting."

"You want to wrestle with me?"

"Yes."

"I feel sick." Tom turned his head on his pillow.

"Should I get the doctor?"

"No, just go get some help."

"I don't understand." Kaitlyn spoke with confusion.

"I don't have a girlfriend because I don't want one." He grumbled as he thought about all of the shallow girls he had tried to date at school only to find that they just couldn't understand him the way he needed to be understood. All of the girls in school were more concerned with popularity, clothes and their hair. They could care less if Tom was still mourning the loss of his father. Tom had seen them attempt to care but their attitudes just didn't express the kind of compassion he was longing for. He didn't want them to feel sorry for him, he just wanted them to be aware that he might have off days in memory of his father and for them to give him a break.

"Well I see you've got your attitude back." Kaitlyn growled, annoyed with his rudeness. She had known him to blow girls off, completely ignore them and she wondered why he acted this way at times, but she had also seen him, known him before his fathers passing and she knew the real Tom. A sensitive yet fun loving guy who knew how to party, to celebrate and to live life. Before his fathers passing she had wanted to know him just because knowing him would be fun. After his fathers passing she had wanted to know him to show him she cared, to hold him when he was upset, but after her own mothers passing, she felt she could know him better than anyone because she had experienced the same sorrow and grief he had. She knew they would have so much in common, so much to talk about and to share if only he would give her the chance. But she had also seen his annoyance and anger after the loss of his father, and that, she didn't like at all.

"What's that supposed to mean?" Tom countered.

"You're back to acting like a jerk." Kaitlyn scowled.

"I am not a jerk!"

"Could've fooled me!"

"Why are we fighting? I'm in the hospital and you're picking fights with me."

"You're right, you are in the hospital, so that means you won't have to go far when I wring your neck!"

"I thought you couldn't fight?"

Kaitlyn paused then smiled. "I can't but I'm really good with threats."

"Threats won't get you anywhere, if you're up against an opponent that is ready to fight you."

"What?"

"You want me to teach you how to fight, right?"

"Yes. Protection, defense, something like that."

"Right now?"

"No, when you're better."

"You've already tried to pick a fight with me."

"I did not. You did!"

"Tell you what. I'm going to teach you how to defend yourself."

"You are?"

"Just tell me this isn't some lame attempt to get a boyfriend."

"Lets just say if you treat all the girls like this you wont ever have to worry about getting a girlfriend."

Tom smiled. "Touché."

Two days later as Kaitlyn was heading to second period a familiar voice called to her in the hallways.

"Hey, Kaitlyn, wait up."

Kaitlyn turned around and saw Tom walking up to her. A slight feeling of tables being turned swept over her, but she let it go and found a smile larger than anything. She hadn't noticed yet that his arm was in a sling.

"You're back. Do you feel better?"

"I don't feel like crap anymore, but my arm is pretty sore."

"You're arm wasn't in a sling before."

"They didn't know about it until I tried to use it. It's just a sprain, but it hurts pretty bad."

"Need some help with your books?"

"Nah, I'll be fine."

"No, really, I can get them." Kaitlyn took the books from his hands.

"Okay, if you want to help."

So Kaitlyn carried his books to second period, then third. Then, she carried his books every day until his arm heeled and it was out of the brace. Then she continued carrying his books, which began to annoy her because he should have been carrying her books if anything.

That all was about to change.

One day, right before lunch, Kaitlyn was holding Tom's books and hers when she cracked under the mental strain. A pretty black haired journalism student, smiling like a Cheshire cat while waving her hair around, stood in front of Tom asking him about his car wreck. After a short conversation that quickly turned to coffee, Tom turned toward Kaitlyn and spoke.

"Hey, take down this number for me." He hadn't meant to sound rude, he had only hoped that by writing down the phone number would get the girl out of his face, but Kaitlyn blew like a stick of dynamite.

"Take down a number? One, I am *not* a secretary! Two, I am *not* your backpack. Carry your own books, and the next time you decide to use someone, you had better hope I haven't learned how to kick your ass yet!"

She threw his books down onto the floor and stormed off.

"Kaitlyn," he yelled, starting after her immediately feeling guilty for treating Kaitlyn like that.

"Leave me alone," she yelled as she walked down the hall.

"Kaitlyn, stop, please."

She spun around to face him; he stopped dead in his tracks just shy of bumping into her nose.

"You know the next time you're in a deadly situation, I sure hope I'm not involved."

31

"Thank you." He said.

"For what? Being your slave?"

"No, for saving my life. I never said thank you."

"Oh, great. I'm glad your conscious is clear. Can I puke now?"

"I'm sorry. I just wanted to see if you were truly willing to learn."

Kaitlyn's brow arched. "To learn what?"

"To fight. I wanted to see if you had the spark."

"Oh, you were testing me? Good try but it's still not an apology."

"Okay, I'm sorry."

"No you're not!"

"I am. I just said so didn't I?" Her lip curled up in disappointment. "Okay, I'm not sorry, but I had to make sure I wasn't going to waste my time on a girl who wasn't going to learn."

"What makes you think I wasn't going to learn? I asked didn't I?"

"That's the point. Many girls have asked for fighting lessons, if only to find themselves in a clutch in my arms, then that so-called kiss would happen, and wham, they think we have something."

"Oh, give me a break. If that's not an ego trip I don't know what is."

"It's not ego, it's the truth."

"Oh, so you've gotten girls through that fighting, thing. So I had a bad idea, okay? Why don't you just leave me alone now?" She sensed the tears coming but didn't want to cry.

"But I don't want to leave."

"What? You want to hurt me some more? Is that what this is?"

"I never wanted to hurt you."

"So using me wasn't an intentional hurting device?"

32

"No. Well, yes kind of, but I've been hurt before, too."

"Oh, poor baby. So you know how to hurt people through experience. Good for you." She turned to walk away.

He grabbed her upper right arm to stop her from walking away.

Angry, she swung her free arm at him to slap him, but he grabbed it. Now with both arms constrained, Kaitlyn tried to kick him where it counts, but he blocked her kick, and with one swift move he knocked her to her knees, spun around her and held her from behind. In his grasp with nowhere to go, and nothing to do, she yelled out.

"I'm going to scream!"

"Great! What are you going to scream?"

"What?" She was caught off guard but still angry.

"If you just scream a noise, nobody will pay attention or help."

"I - I'll scream rape."

"If you're being attacked that's the last thing you'll want to scream."

"Why? People will come to help."

"No, people will come to watch, if anyone shows up at all."

"That's sick!"

"Yeah, it's sick but it's the truth. Scream out fire. It involves everyone. When the people are evacuating their homes, searching for the fire, there will be too many people as witnesses for the attacker to continue his attack."

Tom still held Kaitlyn on her knees, her arms crossed in front of her.

"So do I need to scream fire, or are you going to let me go?"

Finally, he let go and helped her stand. She slapped his hand away. Once to her feet, she fixed her skirt, and peered up at him with hate in her eyes.

"You are the rudest guy I have ever met!"

"But you learned you're first lesson."

"How to get attention, great. What I want to know is how to prevent myself from ever getting into a mess like that in the first place."

"I'll teach you that in good time, if you're still willing to learn from me."

"I asked didn't I?"

"Then, we'll continue."

"So should we shake hands on it or something?"

"Sure." Tom held out his hand to Kaitlyn,

As Kaitlyn shook his hand a simple vision popped into her head. Nothing of danger or life or death, but she envisioned herself shaking Tom's hand, and then spinning and flipping him over her shoulder on his back. The idea of her knocking him on his back, and teaching him a lesson made her smile.

"What's so funny?" Tom asked.

"Funny? Nothing of importance right now." She smirked savoring the idea.

As they walked to lunch, picking up their books along the way, Kaitlyn felt the dawn of something new approaching her. Things were changing in her life. Some things she couldn't wait for, others she didn't know about, but could feel their existence. She was about to change, and so was everything she ever knew to be true.

Tom walked Kaitlyn to the lunchroom; she smiled at him, still slightly angry. He seemed to enjoy the negative attention. When he smiled, Kaitlyn's curiosity got the better of her.

"What?"

"I like you, Kaitlyn."

"What?" She questioned him curiously.

"Not as a girlfriend, but you've got spunk."

"Oh, thank-you." She winced.

"No, I mean it. I'm looking forward to teaching you," He admitted.

"You sure have a weird way of showing it."

"I admit we got off on the wrong foot..."

"Wrong foot? Try the wrong sidewalk, in the wrong side of town, and in the wrong state!"

"Are you done?" He asked with exasperation.

"I suppose."

"When do you want to start your second lesson?"

Kaitlyn thought about it for a moment. "This afternoon, after your practice?"

"Fine, I'll meet you in the gym."

"For real? You won't stand me up?"

He half laughed. "Why ask something like that?"

"Because when you're done teaching me, I'll be able to kick your butt."

Tom laughed out loud. "You'll never be that good."

Kaitlyn's lips curled up as her imagination soared. "We'll just see about that."

Chapter 4

Each afternoon after Tom's wrestling practice, he would meet Kaitlyn in the gym to practice different fighting techniques. Tom taught Kaitlyn something new about fighting every single day. They started with Karate, then after a couple months moved on to Tai Kwan Do, and about a month later kickboxing.

Kaitlyn became good with spinning kicks, Karate chops, punches, double kicks counter attacks, and even a few aggressive maneuvers. Tom taught Kaitlyn how to defend herself, and as she practiced at night and came back the next afternoon, ready to move on, Tom couldn't help but be amazed. Tom spent each night trying to learn more himself to keep from being left behind and to keep their classes flowing smoothly in a forward direction. Kaitlyn felt pride, often wondering where she got the strength and stamina to learn all of this. She knew, in part. She just hadn't realized the truth yet. That afternoon Tom and Kaitlyn learned a new martial Art.

"It's called Aikido. It's the way of having harmony with your life force; also referred to as Zin-art. What I'll teach you about this are ways to escape the rage of attackers, redirecting their attack and moving them out of the range of fire through defensive throwing maneuvers. Like if I'm the attacker and I'm coming at you with a knife, you would want to reach forward, take the hand with the weapon in it, and then with the shear force of my forward motion turn me past you so you wouldn't get stabbed. So let's try it, let me show you what to do."

So they worked for an hour and a half on this new martial art until exhausted. When they decided they had finished their daily practice, Tom took Kaitlyn home. Kaitlyn really enjoyed this part of the day because she could walk home, but lived over a mile away and never really wanted to walk after the gym. She worked so hard with Tom because she wanted him to be proud of her, to know when she says something she follows through with action. It was also something else. She worked this hard out of necessity. Whether it was important to her future, or the future of another, something in her soul told her she had to learn. She also felt slightly that when she was with Tom, practicing seemed right, like finding your destiny, but Kaitlyn never thought that far in advance. That feeling always took her back to her desire to belong and thus find her path in this world.

Tom enjoyed training Kaitlyn. She never once disappointed him, never once did he think he was wasting his time on her. Everyday she'd show up ready to learn and everyday when they tried out older, already learned techniques, she did them correct and on cue. Tom always looked forward to their afternoons together, but there was something nagging him that kept him from passing the friendship point with Kaitlyn, and he just didn't know what. He didn't want a girlfriend right now, and that was what he understood least. Sure most of the girls in this school were the same, mindless shoppers with nothing better to do than spend money on clothes, but Kaitlyn was different. She was everything he'd want in a girl, but a nagging sixth sense kept him away.

As Tom pulled up in front of Kaitlyn's house that afternoon, she did something unexpected, she asked him if he wanted to come in for a while. She had never done that before, but today for some reason it just came out. As Kaitlyn waited to hear his reply, worried he would say no and immediately wanted to take it back, she heard his answer and froze.

"Sure."

Had he really said that? Did he really mean it? She was just about to ask those questions when he added.

"But just for a little while, I have to be getting home."

Kaitlyn went straight to the kitchen and asked if he wanted something to drink. As she got him a soda, he looked around her living room, noticing pictures on the wall. When she walked out of the kitchen with two sodas in hand, he was staring at a picture of her and her parents.

"My mom and dad."

"You're mother for some reason looks familiar. Does she work in town?"

"Not for a while. She had been too ill to work, and passed away last summer."

"Oh, I'm sorry. I forgot. What was her name?"

"Allison Jones."

"Allison sounds right the name goes with the face but not the Jones. What was her maiden name?"

"McFarrel. Why?"

"No reason, just curious." Tom stated, beginning to figure a mystery out but not believing it could be true or that he could have found the missing link. He accepted the drink and when they sat on the couch, an awkward silence followed.

Kaitlyn broke the ice. "So how about that English exam?"

"Yeah, that was a killer! What did you get for the last answer?"

"Oh, I had to guess on that one I put D."

"D? I was drawn between that one and A."

"I think it was a trick question."

"You know, me, too."

At least, they were talking. That conversation led to other discussions and before long to jokes. Then, Harold, Kaitlyn's father came home.

"Honey I'm h… Oh, hi, I didn't realize you had company."

"Daddy, this is Tom, my friend from school."

Tom stood to shake Harold's hand. Slightly nervous about being there now, he wondered what Harold thought about some guy alone in the house with his daughter. Harold did seem cool about it though.

"Tom is it? Nice to finally meet you I've heard so much about you."

"You have, sir?"

"Yep, Kaitlyn can't stop talking about you."

"Daddy." Kaitlyn squirmed.

Harold laughed. "I'll leave you two alone now. I've got things to do in my study."

Tom had a better answer. "Actually, I have to be getting home. I've got homework."

So Tom left, and Kaitlyn thought it had been a rather good afternoon.

That night as Kaitlyn slept she had dream after dream, all of which she couldn't remember when she woke up the next morning, except for one that wasn't really a dream but a bunch of words. It had seemed very familiar to her and very scary. Kaitlyn remembered having a feeling that this dream meant something, life and death. She always woke up panicked about the dream, wondering who this person was, where this person was if there was anything she could do to help. But even though Kaitlyn had always seemed to have dreams of something that was currently happening or about to happen, this dream just seemed to be old, like it had already happened and remained in the past. Kaitlyn would always write her dreams down the best she could recall and pray that one day she would be able to make sense of it all. It simply said;

"I pray you will be strong. As strong as six men, those six men. I pray you will use that strength to help others in need."

Kaitlyn then looked back upon her journal for a few moments, finding some more of those weird dreams she read them aloud.

"Take my dreams, I give them to you. My fantasies of being able to see this before it happened".

Kaitlyn found another voice dream and read that one.

"Take my mind, the mind that I use to talk to you with and share it with someone special."

Like the others Kaitlyn couldn't figure out the meaning. She wondered if it was code; a poem or riddle she had heard some time before but had all but forgotten, except the one little section lost in her mind until she slept.

"If only I could will the door to open. If only I could... (something) ...with the power of my mind."

Was there something missing from that message or the last one she had written down?

"Use my dreams to help others."

That one always caught Kaitlyn off guard. She had dreams all of her life, dreams that had saved her father, dreams that had recently saved Tom. It was the one dream that had always made her wonder if she was special somehow. She always ended this thought with a laugh. Hero comics always seemed to be able to bring normal people into the imaginary super hero world, but this was real life.

How could Kaitlyn possibly consider she was born to be a super hero? How crazy she might sound if she ever mentioned it. Kaitlyn rolled her eyes, stood from her desk, closed her journal, and placed it back under her bed mattress before getting dressed for school.

That day at school Sam was back to her old tricks but Kaitlyn managed to avoid her all day. Kaitlyn knew she had to go to her locker to change her books for science class, but she ended up going to class without them. When the teacher asked everyone to pull out their books, Kaitlyn excused herself, saying she forgot her book. Sure the teachers didn't like it, but it was better than an unscheduled visit to the nurse's office.

In the past couple of weeks, everyone had opinions about Tom and Kaitlyn. Susan had told the cheerleader squad that Kaitlyn was doing this to gain popularity. Susan made a big show of saying it in front of everyone.

"Kaitlyn, just because you're hanging out with Tom McKinney doesn't automatically put you in the popular group. You have to actually be popular to start out with and I'm afraid you just don't have it."

Kaitlyn had heard the comments and the following laughs, but she wasn't angry about that, she was angry because she had stopped thinking of Tom that way. Since Tom had started to teach her, she wasn't concerned with what people said to her or about her; she just wanted to learn.

Tom had heard the rumors and laughs and he was still curious about Kaitlyn's intentions. However, each afternoon without fail he would forget about what everyone had said. He started spending more time with Kaitlyn during school, meeting her at her locker before a class they had together, but almost always striking up a conversation with someone else once arriving there. He tried to meet her at her locker after the last class of the school day so they could walk to the gym together, if he didn't have practice first. That afternoon he didn't have wrestling practice and as he walked up to Kaitlyn's locker he noticed a confrontation already in progress.

"So rumor is you're learning how to fight." Sam sounded truly interested. Kaitlyn bit.

"Yeah, that's true."

"You think you'll be able to beat me up then?"

"The thought never occurred to me." Kaitlyn said. She had daydreamed about the day she would teach Sam a lesson about picking on people smaller than her but now was not that day. Sam hadn't believed Kaitlyn and egged her on more.

"So if I pushed you, you wouldn't push back?"

Sam waited for a reply for only a fraction of a second before shoving both hands on Kaitlyn's shoulders and knocking her backwards two feet. Kaitlyn didn't fall as Sam had hoped she would, but she did glare at Sam. She really wanted to take her on but knew she couldn't win yet. She did want to try though but Tom had perfect timing. He laid both hands on top of Kaitlyn's shoulders while steering her away.

"Come on, Kaitlyn, we've got things to do."

Sam stepped aside as they walked away. Kaitlyn still fumed as they entered the gym, but once her and Tom got started, she quickly forgot her anger.

That afternoon, Tom expressed his amazement.

"You sure you never knew any of these techniques?"

"Sure, I'm sure. Why?"

"You're learning them much faster than anyone I've ever known."

"I guess you're just a good teacher."

"And your strength, I must sound like a moron but when I see you lift weights and work out... oh, never mind."

"No what is it?" Kaitlyn urged, wondering if he had fallen for her.

"It's just that it seems you have the strength of six men," Tom said, as he flipped a page in a new martial arts book. Kaitlyn paused. She had heard that before, somewhere. She thought about it as Tom continued. "I must admit, I'm curious."

"About what?" Kaitlyn asked, as she leapt down in front of him from the balance beam.

"Why are you so intent on learning all of this?"

"I just thought it would be useful."

"I dunno. Seems like there's more to it."

Kaitlyn paused for a moment then spoke carefully. "Truth?"

"Yeah, of course."

"Well, it's difficult to explain." Kaitlyn trailed off.

"Try me." Tom sat on the mat ready for a story.

"Okay. Contrary to public belief I'm not here to get a date from you, grow my popularity or kick Sam's butt back into the prehistoric age, although, I'd really like to do it." She watched Tom's mouth curl up in a smile.

"So why are you doing this?"

Kaitlyn sighed. "Honestly, I hadn't thought about it much, but if I had to take a guess it could be because of Jed."

"Who's Jed?" Tom said, wondering if Kaitlyn did have a boyfriend on the side that no one knew about. As Kaitlyn smiled, trying to explain about Jed, the thought escaped Tom's mind.

"Now, Jed's a story." About two years ago something happened to me..." Kaitlyn stretched her arms over her head. "I was walking down the hallway to my choir class. It was located in one of the back halls of the school, with the band hall, so that way the noise wouldn't disrupt other classes."

Tom shook his head knowing the layout well.

Kaitlyn continued.

"No one ever went back there unless they were in band or choir because it was so out of the way, but it wasn't out of the way for me. I really enjoyed choir, so much so that I went in during lunch when no one else was there, just to practice. It's not like I missed much at lunch, the few friends I had, had a different lunch schedule. So, I'd leave quickly after eating and spend the time in the choir room, alone.

"One day as I walked down the hall, a guy followed me. He was actually a boyfriend of a good friend of mine and we were just friends, I guess. He walked up to me and began talking. I didn't mind because he was cute, and I enjoyed the company, but... well, like I said before, he was a boyfriend of a friend of mine, so my imagination never went any further. Anyways, I was leaning against the wall, trying to look cool, my pathetic attempt at getting any form of attention."

Kaitlyn began to mumble, hating to say it but knowing it was the truth.

"He kind of leaned against the wall next to me, facing me, with his hand holding him up. Then he leaned in closer to me." She demonstrated, but Tom shook his head again, relaying he understood.

"I forget exactly what we were talking about, but he took his fingers and kind of walked them up my stomach to my chest."

Kaitlyn paused recollecting the maneuver and the sick way it made her feel.

"I was a little nervous about him touching me there, but I liked him and knew him. I didn't worry enough, I guess." Kaitlyn didn't realize where she was going with this she hadn't thought of that day in so long that now, as it came back to her, all of the emotions came with it.

Tom knew where this was going though and he began to feel uncomfortable. He almost wanted to stop her from telling the story but he was too curious to speak. He allowed her to go on through his silence.

"He leaned in to kiss me and I kind of wanted it, but I knew he was dating a friend of mine so I tried to stop him. I tried to push him away, but he pushed in closer. I really liked it; I guess I was really desperate for someone to like me, but I soon realized I didn't want him to like me that way. My friendship with his girlfriend was more important. I told him to stop, but he wouldn't and as I began to panic he began to get more pushy. He grabbed my arm and pushed me into the choir room, closing the door behind him. I tried to slap him, to knock him away from me, but I was too weak to do anything useful. I didn't know how to fight back. He threw me to the floor and mounted me..."

Kaitlyn paused, her mouth slightly open from her last words as they trailed off into the empty room. Then she began to really remember that day. She remembered how she felt, so vulnerable, so weak. How she struggled with him but it did no good; he overpowered her so easily. He took both her wrists into one of his hands and held them on the ground above her head. She just didn't have the upper body strength to pull away. She tried to kick him but he stuck his knees in between her legs and then spread her legs open. She tried to scream but he took his other hand and covered her mouth. There was nothing she could do. She remembered crying, feeling fear rise through her body as he spoke.

"Come on, I know you want it."

Kaitlyn couldn't breathe, and as her body began to tremble, he grew more excited. Then somehow, and Kaitlyn to this day can't explain it, she slipped her wrists free and knocked him off of her. She didn't know she was free, but suddenly like a ton of bricks hitting her, she realized she could run. She ran to the door, threw it open and ran down the hall and into the girl's bathroom, the only place that seemed safe at the time. There she collected herself and her thoughts and figured out what to do next.

Kaitlyn looked over at Tom who was still sitting there waiting for her to continue. She had stopped speaking so he hung on those last words, wondering how she escaped or if she did at all. Kaitlyn then realized she had stopped speaking and at that moment she suddenly became too shy to speak. Tom wanted to say or do something but he didn't know what to say. Finally, Kaitlyn spoke again putting up a false sense of strength.

"Nothing really happened. I actually left a couple of broken fingernails in his cheek near his eye and as he backed off grabbing his face. I ran away."

Kaitlyn reached down, picked up a 20-pound dumbbell, and pumped her arm up and down. She was trying so hard to not think about those emotions. Tom stood and walked closer to her.

"So what happened? Did he get in trouble?" Tom realized it wasn't the right question to ask because Kaitlyn's eyes filled with tears and the dumbbell fell back to the floor. A loud clang reverberated around the gym, and the sound of Kaitlyn's words seemed to be of such a high pitch Tom didn't know what to do.

"You know, I told my friend what her boyfriend tried to do to me and she didn't believe me? She even told everyone I knew that I tried to steal her boyfriend and I couldn't be trusted. I became an outcast that day for the rest of the year. I even told the school principal, and do you know what he told me? Do you? He said Jed is a senior and in less than a month he's going to graduate and if I file charges he'll get kicked out of school and he won't graduate. He asked me to forget about it so Jed could graduate. Can you believe that? "

Kaitlyn turned away. Tom walked to her and placed a sympathetic hand upon her shoulder. She wiped her eyes and quickly turned to face him, knocking his hand away as she did and spoke with more control.

"It was tough for me to get over, but I did. I don't want pity, I never got any, anyway, but that's why I wanted to learn how to protect myself. I never want to be in that situation again. There's just something about me, I guess. I think it was supposed to happen to wake me up to something, so I could avoid that sort of situation again."

"Okay." Tom said, not sure what to say.

Kaitlyn glanced at him, sensing his discomfort. She had ruined this afternoon with her story, for herself as well as Tom. Her stomach churned, she felt shy and sick all at the same moment. As she looked into Tom's eyes, the pity she saw made her feel worse. "Um, I just remembered something I have to do, so I'm going to go now." She quickly walked away, grabbing her bag as she did.

"You don't have to leave." Tom called out to her.

"I'm fine. I just remembered something important." Before she walked out the door, she turned with a smile and waved to Tom.

"I'll see you tomorrow?"

"Tomorrow."

That subject was never brought up again. Tom was still concerned, even curious as to how she was doing, but he never brought it up again. He didn't want her to think he was prying and he didn't want her to feel uncomfortable around him. He did check out old yearbooks. He looked for seniors named Jed, but never found any. He wondered if Jed was a nickname, or if his picture just hadn't been available for the yearbook. He gave up his search, wondering briefly what he planned on doing if he had found out what Jed looked like.

Kaitlyn proved to be a quick study, a hard worker, and an outstanding fighter. The way she learned and took over, seemed to Tom that she was made to be a fighter, destined to use this information and her extreme ability towards something. Like destiny had found her, Tom could tell, that all she needed was someone to teach her and give her guidance, and she'd somehow, miraculously know the rest.

As the months passed, Tom was thankful girls weren't allowed on the wrestling team, or his position as captain could be short lived. Kaitlyn was getting very good. He was proud of her. Her ability to learn, practice, try-out and perfect every move he brought to her was outstanding. She lifted weights every night, strengthening her muscles and bones. She was a virtual fighting machine.

Still, beautiful, not the muscle man type with the biceps out to the moon, she looked exactly the same, but something about her had changed. Her personality had gone from lonely and disengaged, to someone who walked down the halls, proud of herself, holding herself up right and sure. Someone who smiles, and knows she is someone to reckon with, and was acquiring the attention of those who had evaded her before.

Sure her spending time with Tom after school helped her position, but Tom had seen her change. He found himself mystified by her transformation. One sunny afternoon after practice, he invited her for a burger and fries at the Mac, a local hangout after school, he just couldn't help himself. He wanted to spend more time with her.

When the two of them walked in the restaurant that night, it seemed everyone stopped to stare and mumble. Kaitlyn ignored it, totally forgetting her once childish desire to one day be Tom's girlfriend. Her strength, her agility, her newfound pride in herself had taken over. Other meaningless tasks seemed to be trivial. The idea of one day getting on the cheerleading squad, seemed ridiculous. She felt prepared for anything. Except for the only thing she couldn't imagine ever happening. She was about to be thrown a supernatural loop that would change her former belief system forever.

Chapter 5

Tom and Kaitlyn bought burgers and went outside to sit down. They were about half way through dinner when Kaitlyn got tired of the silence and began to confront Tom about his lack of conversation.

"Is your burger all right?" Kaitlyn asked, noticing Tom hadn't touched it.

"Fine."

"You haven't even taken a bite."

"Hmm? Oh, yes, I'm sorry. My mind is drifting."

Kaitlyn spoke low. "I guess us coming here together was a bad idea."

"It's not that. I've had something on my mind lately and I can't seem to shake it."

"Anything I can help with?"

"I'm afraid not."

"Oh." Kaitlyn looked away, stuffing another french-fry in her mouth.

They had decided to eat on the balcony, above the lake, a romantic place for most, but for the two of them a place away from the crowd. It seemed to Kaitlyn that he didn't want others to know of their friendship, that it could embarrass him and she tried not to let it bother her. She hoped after all that they had done together, he would at least acknowledge they were friends. But he didn't. She took a sip of her chocolate shake as Tom spoke again.

"I'm sorry I'm not good company tonight."

"I didn't expect you to be, seeing we're around other kids from school. We really should've gone to the Sloppy Joe house or the Bar-B-Q joint. At least, you wouldn't see people you know there."

"That's not it." He looked up at her almost upset.

"Oh, isn't it? You made it very clear when we first started our little gatherings that you weren't looking for a girlfriend..."

"What does that have to do with it?"

"...And if you'd let me continue. By being seen together outside of the training gym, it gives others the perception of the two of us being together."

"That's not it." Tom sighed.

"Deny it all you want, I don't care. Next time you invite me to dinner, either be more communicative or don't invite me at all. I get ignored enough at home to want to go *out* and be ignored."

Kaitlyn was about to leave when Tom stopped her by placing his hand over hers.

"Don't leave."

"Careful, others might get the wrong idea." Her green eyes flashed to his hand. He didn't move his hand away. He left it there.

"Don't leave."

"Why should I stay?"

"I apologize for not being very good company tonight."

"And you're good company otherwise?"

He smiled, knowing she was joking. He finally removed his hand and Kaitlyn sat back down.

"I guess I ought to try this burger before it gets cold."

"I guess." Kaitlyn shrugged. She had totally lost interest in this night.

As he began to eat and Kaitlyn ate another fry, she looked off over the lake, where the moon shimmered on the water. The night was romantic. She noticed movement in the bushes not far away, but she couldn't see it well. She looked harder, focusing in better with her eyes. She saw the silhouette of two people, one walking away and the other following. She wished she could have heard what they were saying because the stance of the person in the back displayed anger and the person in front showed fear.

Kaitlyn watch the person behind who look more like a man. He grabbed the girl in front of him by the arm, spun her around, and then slapped her down to the ground. Kaitlyn almost stood to get a better look, but realized low tree limbs would block sight of them all together. She sat and continued to watch as the man bent down and gathered the girl into his arms. Kaitlyn couldn't tell what was happening until they moved again. It seemed he was helping her to her feet, then he gave her a hug, and they started walking this way.

Kaitlyn looked forward to finding out who they were, when she was distracted by Tom's words.

"I love you."

Kaitlyn smiled at that, suddenly forgetting what she had just watched. Having heard it she responded without thought.

"I love you, too."

She looked away from the woods after that to look at Tom, but something wasn't right. As she looked up into his confused chocolate brown eyes, she knew by the half chewed hamburger in his mouth that he had not said anything out loud. She had totally caught him off guard with her response and as he swallowed his food, he was frantically trying to come up with a rebuttal.

Kaitlyn felt foolish. "Oh, my, God. You didn't say that." She stood, crumpling her napkin in her had. "I feel so... stupid."

Tom tried to finish his bite and swallow, when Kaitlyn, embarrassed beyond all control, started to leave, for sure this time.

"Kaitlyn, don't leave." He spat and choked on the remainder of his burger.

"I think this time I really should leave."

"No, I should." Tom spoke quick.

She turned around. "You? Why? I obviously overheard another person's conversation and simply reacted. You finish your dinner, I'm finished all ready. Really I am." She thought as she considered the ramifications of what she had just done.

"Kaitlyn you heard someone say I love you?"

"Yes, and even though it really sounded like you, I know now that it wasn't you. In fact, it was all a big misunderstanding. I just said it to say something back to you and not hurt your feelings. But now that I know that it wasn't you, I, um, I don't have to continue on with this lie."

"Lie?" Tom inquired curiously.

"Yeah, I didn't want you to put yourself on the line and fall in, you know, but you didn't so that's it."

"You just said that to be nice? You didn't mean it?" Tom asked almost looking hurt.

"I don't think so." Kaitlyn stumbled on her words confused as to why Tom actually looked upset.

"Do you mean it or not?" Tom insisted.

"Mean what? That I love you? It was a simple mistake." Kaitlyn tried to rationalize.

"Oh." Tom sighed.

Kaitlyn grew even more curious now from his questioning and response. "You didn't really say it did you. I mean it didn't sound like you said it with a mouth full of food."

"I didn't say it with a mouth full of food."

"So you said it?" Kaitlyn urged.

"No, I did not *say* it." Tom corrected.

"I'll uh, see you tomorrow at school then." She exhaled as she started to leave.

"Wait!" Tom stood.

"Nope, this time I'm leaving to go crawl under a rock for awhile. Goodnight." Kaitlyn spoke so low she felt as if she could pass out.

As she walked away, Tom was scared and excited. Not because he knew she really liked him, but something more. The something he had been preoccupied with for so long seemed to be making more and more sense. Something that he had known all of his life but chose to forget seemed to be showing itself again. He finished his burger in a hurry and ran out of the Mac towards his house. Towards the book that would answer all his questions.

"Tap...Tap..."

Kaitlyn rose from her pillow and looked at her clock. Two a.m., and someone was throwing rocks at her bedroom window. She slid the covers off of her body, grabbed her robe, and slipped it on as she walked over to her window. She looked outside and saw Tom about to launch another stone.

She pulled away from the window, before he would see her and she leaned against the wall. She had made quite a fool of herself tonight. She couldn't figure out why Tom was here, but decided finally to answer his tapping before he broke her window. Besides, she had to get whatever this was over with so she could return to bed.

She pulled back the curtains and opened the window.

"What are you doing here?" she whispered.

"Come down, we need to talk."

"It's two in the morning."

"I know, but this is important."

Kaitlyn pulled away from the window and sighed. What was he up to? Was he going to let her down easy? Was he going to laugh in her face? Was this some awful prank made to bring her self-esteem back down again? She hesitated.

"Kaitlyn?" Tom called up to her. She spun and spoke out the window.

"Okay, I'll be right down." She didn't know what he was up to but she was glad he wasn't going to do it at school in front of everyone.

As she walked out of the back door, she watched as he put down the rest of the rocks and bent down to pick up a book.

"Let's go someplace private." He looked around and behind him. "I can't tell you here, someone might hear."

"God forbid someone hear you talking to me." She gripped.

"This is too important. Is that gazebo over there secure?"

"Secure? Like will the roof cave in?"

"No. Secure like in safe to talk, preventive, vindicated."

"I suppose so. Why?"

"Lets go."

He started to walk there and Kaitlyn followed. There were so many questions forming in her head she wasn't sure how to organize them, maybe because she still felt like she was asleep.

Once inside the gazebo, Tom leaned over the railing to check the grounds and then under the seats. He placed the book on the bench.

"Sit down."

"No, thank you."

"I promise I'm fine, and everything is okay, but I do need you to sit down for this." Tom urged.

"If everything is okay then why did you check the gazebo like a spy?"

"Would you please sit down?"

"Remember, I can kick your ass." Kaitlyn voiced as she reluctantly sat down.

"I know."

Kaitlyn was confused by that last remark. Under any other circumstance he would have denied it. He would have said, you only wish you could or something just as cocky. He actually admitted she could defeat him, and that bothered her.

"So what's going on?"

"Tonight when you heard me say that I love you..."

"You did say it?" Kaitlyn sat at attention.

Tom paused but then continued his sentence without even taking a breath. "I said it with my mind. Telepathically."

"What?" Kaitlyn felt like the brut of a joke coming on.

"Telepathically, accidentally, only another telepath would have been able to hear it."

"Uh-huh?" Kaitlyn's jaw dropped and her eyebrow rose. She couldn't believe what he just said. Did he think she was a fool?

"It was intended to be one of those thoughts that never got out of my mouth...."

"And apparently it didn't." She said jokingly but more annoyed now.

"Look, this is going to be really hard to understand, but you have to believe me. By hearing my words tonight, you showed telepathic abilities. Only one of the many abilities you will come to know."

"Oh, boy, there are more?" Kaitlyn smiled with this annoyed tiredness that was showing on her face more now that she felt like she had gotten out of bed for nothing.

"This isn't a joking matter."

"Tom, I'm sorry but you're acting too weird to not take this as a joke."

"I realize this is something that you've never heard of before..."

"I've heard of Telepaths; people who can send and receive messages through brain waves. There was a movie about it once. I forget exactly what it was about, but it was pretty good."

"No, about being who you are."

"Who am I?" Kaitlyn exhaled in exasperation just wanting to get this over with.

"You are making this way too difficult."

"Then just spit it out. I'd like to get back to bed."

"Fine. Short story? Here it goes."

So for the next five minutes she listened in silence to this supposed short story that never seemed to get to the point and left her with more questions than answers. When he finished, she had so many questions, but those all had to begin with a laugh; a hysterical laugh.

"What's so funny?" Tom asked.

"I'm sorry. You think that I'm a telepath. I understand you're wanting to take back what you said, but trying to make me believe you didn't actually say it and that I heard someone's thoughts, is ridiculous."

"Not someone's thought. You heard mine."

"So you really did say it? Did you mean it?"

"That's not the point. We share something that few people do."

"Is that better than actually going out? Because I'm still confused."

"Look, it's obvious you're not ready to hear this, but I do want you to read something for me if you would."

Kaitlyn's eyes rolled back as she exhaled roughly. She looked as if she was being given homework on a weekend, and Tom grew impatient.

"Kaitlyn, my father told me all about this privilege. He taught me everything I needed to know about being a telepath, and even practiced with me all of the time to perfect my telepathic abilities, so I would know how to tell when another telepath was in my presence. My mother never knew we communicated telepathically behind her back. Well, actually right in front of her. Don't you see? You're the one I was meant to find."

"This is all a very creative trick to get me to fall for you, but I'm more of a direct kind of girl, you know."

"This is not a trick or a lie and I can prove it. According to this book, some telepaths even have the ability to see into the future, some even through their dreams. The dream that saved my life is just one of the many gifts you will find you have!"

Kaitlyn didn't believe him. "Oh, boy, should I make a list?"

"You're mind is obviously not open to this just yet, and it might take you awhile to absorb all of this new information. I'll leave this book here for you to review. Please, don't show it to anyone. Please. I'll see you tomorrow."

Tom didn't bother to mention the rest of the information he had. She wasn't ready to hear it. He hoped if she read some of the book tonight it would open her eyes to the possibilities and maybe allow her the option of asking him more.

Full of strange emotion, Kaitlyn watched him walk away. She looked at the book and slowly picked it up, feeling the old soft leather wrinkle between her fingers. She opened it up, and read the first page.

<u>January 5th, 1876</u>

I've known for quite some time now about my special ability to talk with my six-year-old son in the most silent way possible. I fear trying to find out more about this for fear of my life and what the other townspeople would think of my family and me. I've said things to my wife this way, telling her with the sheer force of my mind how much I love her and want to share this with her but she doesn't hear me, either that or she doesn't want to answer. So I've decided that it is the bond, the connection with my son that gives us this ability. I pray this connection will never fade because just the ability to talk with my son about anything in the world without worrying about other people hearing is just more exhilarating than I can explain with trivial words.

I am taking a trip with my son soon; a father and son trip and we will bring new foods and trades home for my family to survive on. I will write more after we return in a few months.

Although tired, Kaitlyn turned the page to read the next passage.

April 25th, 1876

Although our trip was almost unsuccessful in the bringing of valuable trades into the colony, we did find something more valuable to us than anyone else. During our trip as my son and I communicated telepathically we heard another voice speak to us in our heads. It was faint and brief but what it said sent us on a journey we could never have planned for. The voice said, "I hear you. Can you hear me?"

My son and I both stopped communicating that moment as we wondered if we had just heard the same thing, and as we spoke about it using our own tongue, we realized we had heard it together. So I spoke back to the voice with my thoughts, saying I hear you, where are you? And the voice answered back, "do not look, but I am sitting at a table behind you. I didn't mean to eavesdrop, but when you find someone else communicating like this you have to learn more." So I answered back that I agree and then we decided we must meet somewhere and talk more about this. He answered back, "my tribe is over the great valley and I would be pleased to meet with you in person." So we went and found the man who spoke to us and learned much of our talents that we didn't know.

"It takes great strength of mind to communicate this way, a strength not many people in the world possess." He explained and he worked with us for a week, training us how to better ourselves and how to share this ability with others like ourselves. To teach the ones with the possibility how to control it, how to use it and most of all how to keep it secret. He was very aggressive on that matter, saying how his tribe believed that silent speech is the way their God's communicated and to take that ability from them was evil and will be looked down upon. But he went on to explain his view on the subject, how his new tribe, not the tribe he talked about because he was banished from them, but his new tribe who all had the ability made their own memories from their own experiences.

He explained that there were many possibilities to the earning of this privilege. Maybe a gift from the Gods. Maybe they were Gods, or descendants of the Gods. He didn't stay on that thought long though because another tribe member approached and communicated with him silently about a new adoptee. So he had to say his goodbyes to us for it was time to crown a new leader. He explained that only the strongest silent communicator could teach the tribe, and so they trained, studied, and tested each other until the strongest was found, and when he was found he was crowned the King and his name was engraved on the sacred stone. His name was Telipaothees.

Kaitlyn looked up from the journal and said that name out loud.

"Telipaothees? Telepath? Whoa." Just then a chill came over Kaitlyn.

Kaitlyn stood, book tight in hand and walked back to her room. Once safely in her room, she turned on her light, closed and locked her door, and sat Indian style on her bed. She opened the journal again, this time resting it in her lap, and flipped to the next page, to read another entry.

June 30, 1878

It's been a while since last I wrote and not much has happened since then. That is, not much has happened in the world of mind communication. But last week I read an article, an article, which caused such disruption in our town and towns around us that it actually was brought to the courts to decide upon and they decided to ban the writer from the city forever!

I'm not too happy about the outcome for it only shows me the danger if my son or I were to be found out, but this writer knew exactly what we have been going through.

You see, in his article, he wrote about a tribe. I can only assume it was the same tribe my son and I met for he mentioned a word, so similar to the name of the newly crowned King that it had to be the same. He called the man Telepathies.

Tomorrow I will make up a story to tell my wife and I will travel to find this writer and find out more. I must find out more if I'm going to teach my son properly so that he may pass this knowledge down to his own son and so on. I hope I will return soon.

Kaitlyn stopped reading for a moment to gloat. Telepath, I was right. They just simplified the name down to the one we use at present day. She closed the book and looked at the cover again. Was this the first account of telepathic abilities in this nation? Was she really reading the journal of the man who first discovered the telepathic abilities and how to control them?

Chapter 6

As the sun rose over the mountains, Kaitlyn was dressed and ready for school, way before she normally would have been up. She walked to school, continuing to read the journal until she made it there. She found Tom's locker and sat down in front of it, having to move once for the morning crew sweeping the halls before they actually opened the school.

Kaitlyn kept reading. She read up to January 15, 1892. She had read all night. She read about how this man was found out, and how the townspeople found out he had the unnatural ability to talk to others through mind control. They believed it to be satanic. This put him in the same classification as a witch.

They stoned him, ignored him, put him on a horrible trial, putting him, his wife and his son in the circus ring. But he pleaded with them that his wife and son were innocent. How they hadn't acquired the ability, and it was only his curse. They finally believed him. The court decided he must leave the town and never return, and, although, the punishment was the harshest thing he had ever heard, the hardest part was leaving his wife and son alone.

He knew his time here was done. He had to journey back to that tribe and learn all he could, and so he said goodbye to his wife and son and then he left. He did telepathically communicate with his son where he would be, and that he would still keep in touch with him. His son was happy about that, and even swore that when he was of age, he would travel out there with him to learn about this ability as well.

January 18, 1882
A break through!

A breakthrough for our tribe! The head master has found another tribe nearby with the same telepathic abilities. He has succeeded in sending out a telepathic message over great distances.

Kaitlyn looked up from her reading and saw Tom walking down the hallway. Even though she wanted desperately to read the next passage, she closed the book, stood up, and waited for his approach.

"Sleep well?" Tom asked.

"Not at all."

"I see." Tom was ready for a pause of this conversation already, but Kaitlyn had other plans.

"I have questions."

"I have answers, elsewhere."

"Can we talk?"

"Have you read the journal?"

"Most of it, I've gotten up to January 18th 1882."

"Oh, you're almost done."

"What do you mean almost done? I'm only half way through the book."

"Then you haven't noticed that he stops writing after..." Tom paused.

"After what?"

"Look, just continue to read until it's over and then I'll explain the rest."

Kaitlyn stopped her questions and changed the subject.

"So about last night." Kaitlyn began but was stopped.

"I don't really want to talk about last night."

"You don't want to talk about what you said, or actually what you didn't say... about love." Kaitlyn prodded.

"That was a mistake." He almost turned away but actually looked in a different direction when he said it.

"Oh, it was?"

"You shouldn't have ever heard it."

"But I did, and besides that, you wouldn't have thought about it if it wasn't true."

"How do you know? How do you know what I'm thinking can you read my mind?"

"Not yet, but give me time."

"That is not funny!" Tom growled.

"Chill out a little. This is exciting and interesting and you treat it like a disease."

"You've read about how they treated him, what do you think."

"I think it was a long time ago, and things have changed."

"Have they? You ever watch TV? Sci-Fi's? Ever see how the government reacts and treats people who are different?"

"That's Hollywood. Nothing more."

"Well, you may think that, but I'm a little more cautious. And if you don't mind, I'd like to stay cautious, and not get found out and taken to some government agency that will poke and prod me like a guinea pig. If you're smart, you'll do the same."

Tom walked away leaving Kaitlyn alone with the book and her thoughts. So with fifteen minutes left until class, she sat and continued to read. She read about some of the many things the father had found out during his travels and life with the Teleotribe. He liked that name the leader had chosen. It described them and their ability without actually exposing the truth. The leader taught the other tribe, and found that not many people in this tribe had this ability. After a year or so the leader announced a replacement leader for the tribe and he took the people with the silent ability into the forest to learn more together. He heard everyone's story. How they first found out they had this ability, how they worked on perfecting it and using it, and then he taught them how to control it.

He taught them how to control their feelings, so that way another telepath wouldn't be able to read more of their mind that was allowed. He gave them strengthening exercises for their mind and had them keep track of their problems and miscommunications and he worked with them to fix those problems to become experts. All of this he wrote in his journal.

He named the ability, after himself, and called it telepath. Then sent each man or woman on his or her way to a different part of the world to seek out and find more people like this and train them to this art. It was his last dying wish to see this miracle of God was not lost.

<u>August 18th, 1803</u>

The illness I have contracted is slowly killing me. I have tried contacting my son and am not sure if he has heard. According to my calculations he is now thirty-three and I haven't heard from him since that day in the courtyard when he said he would find me when he was old enough. I figured he wouldn't, that a decade after, he would have forgotten about me, or moved on with his life, but I pray he has not lost this ability all together. I feel that this may be my last journal entry for my body has grown very weak. So I will leave the rest of this book open for my son.

Kaitlyn turned the page and then found a letter that looked as if it had been moistened and dried, over and over again. She paused before reading it. Knowing it was a letter written from a dying father to a long lost son, and as she hesitated reading someone's private words. She finally decided she should read it. And with one deep breath, she read on.

Dear son,

I know that it has been a long time since last we talked and I hope you haven't forgotten about me. I have taught you a lot, and then learned much more that I hope will be of use to you. Over the years I have found out many things about this ability that lead me to realize that it is not a curse and you should not feel ashamed of it.

With work your ability can become strong. So strong that not even I want to believe, but evil can take advantage of it. I know you are good. I know that you would never use this ability towards harm, and so I leave you with this journal. All of my notes, all of my teachings, all of me. My abilities have grown so that I now have the ability to see great distances. I've seen your wife in my dreams, and I saw the death of my own wife. I know that if you are reading this then you heard my message and so I know then that I have succeeded in transferring a telepathic message over the greatest distance of all: twenty-two thousand miles. For I know you will not reach me in time to say goodbye, but in your journey to find me it will bring you to the greatest land of all, America. Here you will not be judged for your ability, and you may find many other people here with the same ability as yours. And you will prosper in life and be well.

I pray you receive this for you are family and of all the people I have met in my journey's you are the only one I know who would appreciate this gift as much as I. Who knows maybe this ability is transferable into the afterlife and I may be able to answer all of your questions then. I love you son and always will. Take care of yourself and my daughter in law. She carries the next generation of telepaths even today.

Your Loving Father,

Jeremiah Solomon McKinney

Like time was on her side, she read that last part right as the bell rang for her first period class. As Kaitlyn got up and walked there, she looked forward to seeing Tom, despite knowing he wouldn't want to talk about the book. Kaitlyn was curious about the last name; this man must have been Tom's great, great ancestor, the first in his family with the ability, and this book had probably been in Tom's family for many generations. Kaitlyn wondered if Marge knew of the book, or if the family's telepathic ability only ran through the males. She was beaming with questions when she bumped into Cindy Rogers in the hallway.

Cindy was a friendly girl who had always kept to herself, especially now, that she was dating Jake Jersey. Jake was a bully. Driving to school on a motorcycle, wearing the heavy black leather jacket and posting sunglasses on his face during class, he was the kind of guy that not even the teachers wanted to discipline. Kaitlyn bumped into Cindy as she turned the corner of the hallway and the both of them fell over. Kaitlyn offered an apology and her hand to help Cindy up when Cindy looked up at Kaitlyn and smiled.

"It's okay, I'm fine."

"Cindy, what happened to your eye?" Kaitlyn asked, noticing the fresh blue shiner around her left eye.

"Oh, this? I fell into a doorknob. You can see how clumsy I am." She half laughed as she lifted herself off of the floor.

"Have you had that eye looked at? It looks bad."

"Its fine, Kaitlyn. It doesn't even hurt." She smiled again and walked away without even saying goodbye.

For a half second Kaitlyn had a flash back to last night at the Mac and the couple fighting in the forest. Then she remembered she had passed Jake and Cindy in the parking lot as she was leaving. It was dark outside so she didn't see them well, but she didn't think Cindy had a black eye at the time. Kaitlyn told herself it was nothing, but as the warning bell rang, she ran towards class and put her thoughts in the back of her mind.

Tom sat at his desk reading his textbook. She had many questions for him: like when did the son get the book, who is Tom to this man, grandson or what? Did Marge know about the ability? Or did it only run on the male side of the family? Why weren't there any other accounts of this happening, and why was the knowledge known but not talked about? The teacher spoke up before Kaitlyn could ask and told everyone to sit down and prepare for class.

After class, Tom seemed to know that Kaitlyn wanted to talk to him and he avoided her. He rushed out of class being the first one out and tried to get lost in the crowd but that sassy blonde cheerleader whose voice was as loud as a banshee failed his attempts.

"Tom McKinney! I didn't hear from you last night."

"I beg your pardon, Susan?" Tom said, looking around to see if Kaitlyn had heard. She had.

"Did you forget to call me last night?" Kaitlyn walked up to the side of them and listened.

"I don't remember telling you I'd call." Tom stammered.

"Oh, but you did, at the beginning of the baseball season. I asked you to call me and you said, you'd call when the Tritons made it to the play-offs."

Kaitlyn had to hide her smile, as Tom stumbled into her trap.

"And the Tritons made it in last night's game?"

"Sure did!" Susan smiled as she twisted her curly blonde locks in her fingers.

"I see."

"So I'm guessing you forgot, but that's okay..."

"Susan, I'm sorry..." Tom began but again was interrupted.

"It's okay, Tom, I understand."

"No, Susan, I'm sorry because I seem to have led you on. You see when I said that I'd call you when the Tritons made the playoffs; the Tritons were the worst team in the league. I figured they would never make it to the play-offs."

"Oh." Susan slowed and then suddenly perked up. "I understand. My cheering for them made them the best, and now you feel you're not good enough for me. It's okay, I'll still give you a chance."

By now Kaitlyn was laughing so hard she nearly fell to the floor. Slapping the walls to release some of the pressure on her diaphragm, she couldn't help but express her feelings. Tom really wanted to join her, but he stayed neutral, too neutral though, because Kaitlyn's outburst had just turned Susan from naive to angry.

"What are you laughing at loser?" Susan growled at Kaitlyn.

"You're so gullible you can't even see when you're being let down!"

"At least, I'm not making a fool of myself over someone who will never give you the proper time of day."

Kaitlyn at first didn't realize Susan meant Tom and her, but she countered with a good come back anyways.

"And you're not?"

"Everyone knows your pathetic attempt to have Tom teach you fight is just a ploy to get in his good graces."

"Oh, really?" Kaitlyn said, standing back up again. "You want to see how well I've learned how to fight?"

"Hey, Tom's right here." Tom interrupted, trying to get the girls to stop this verbal assault upon each other.

"Butt out!" Came the response from both girls, ready to pounce into the ring like wild cats.

"I happen to know Tom would never date someone as shallow as you, Susan."

"And I happen to know that Tom is only trying to teach you fight because you helped to find him at that car crash. He's only trying to be nice."

"And he's been a hell of a lot nicer to me than he has to you or any of your sniveling followers."

"No, I haven't." Tom cut in, but again was shot back. "Butt out!"

"Kaitlyn, you are a joke in this school!"

"Not as much of a joke as your face is going to be in a minute!"

Kaitlyn raised the leather bound journal in her hands, ready to smack it against Susan's pale face when Tom intervened.

"Kaitlyn."

Kaitlyn knew she had the ability to thrash Susan, but that would only cause more problems. She lowered the book, and as her mind reeled from the adrenaline pumping through her body, she came up with a better solution. She smiled when she spoke.

"You know, Susan, speaking of pathetic attempts, wasn't it you in that rumor, who worked her way to the popular group backhanded by the football team?"

"What are you talking about?" Susan growled.

"They say your name and number still to this day remains a shrine on the bathroom walls in the boys' locker room."

"That is not true! Where did you hear that?"

"In fact wasn't Jeremy Talbert one of your so-called boyfriends?"

"Yeah, so?"

"Well, I overheard a conversation between him and the school nurse and she was giving him medication for his rash."

"What rash?"

"Susan, if I were you I'd get checked. You know how these things spread."

"What things?"

"In fact wasn't one of the side effects hair loss?" Kaitlyn added, noticing again how much Susan cared so much for her curly blonde locks.

Susan ran off screaming. Angry at the guys, angry at the girls who spread such a rumor, angry at Jeremy who didn't tell her first, and scared to death of what she could possibly have. As her pom-poms flew down the hallway, Tom looked at Kaitlyn.

"That lie about Jake was mean."

"It isn't a lie."

"You don't believe that he's got...." Tom began.

"He really does have a rash. It's just on his arm, and it's from his laundry detergent."

"That's cold. But what about the hair loss?"

"Simple. She messes with me again, and I'll rip her hair out."

It seemed that Tom wanted to laugh, but he stayed strict. "You know you can't fight with people. You would win hands down and that would be unfair."

"Spoil sport."

"Kaitlyn..." He started to scold.

"I realize that. Mouthing off makes me feel better."

"To do what? Put people down?"

"When they start by putting me down? Yes!"

"I didn't know you could be that way."

"Everyone can be that way."

"Yeah, well I didn't expect you to be like everyone else."

"And what's that supposed to mean?"

"You use a lot more of your mind than most people. I thought you would use some of that to make yourself different, not to blend in."

"Wasn't it your idea to stay hidden? I do so and now I fit in too well with everyone else in the world?"

"I'm different, and yet I fit in but I don't follow their lead. What does that say about me compared to you?"

"That you know who you are and I don't. I can't just stop doing what I need to do because you say to stop. You don't control me, Tom. And you never will!"

Tom nodded then turned and walked away. Kaitlyn watched him for a second trying to figure what went wrong when the next bell rang and she realized she was late for class. As she ran down the hall to her next class, she realized she hadn't had a chance to run by her locker and pick up her next book. And she realized she still held onto the leather bound journal that seemed to just stop without ever letting her know what the son did. It reminded her of all of her questions she had wanted to ask, but hadn't had the chance because of Susan. As she walked into her next class, she made a mental note of questions to ask Tom the next time she saw him.

Chapter 7

Two hours later during lunch, Tom sat down with Kaitlyn.

"Funny, I figured you wouldn't be talking to me for a while."

"I wanted to answer your questions."

"What, here? Now?"

"They're pretty simple answers. But I have a feeling you didn't read the last page." Tom took the book in his hand and flipped it over.

"I did. The letter from the dying father to his son?"

"No, the back page." Tom said, as he opened the back cover and exposed a very small section of upside down writing on the backside of the back page. Tom flipped the book around and placed it in front of Kaitlyn.

"A telepathic ability is a very specific, highly trained and very powerful ability to have. You must keep a strong mental shielding in place to avoid a constant barrage of thoughts from those around you. You have to deliberately make the effort to mentally reach out, in order to scan another being's mind. That scan can vary from the superficial level (to get a quick reading on whether someone is telling you the truth), to a precise plucking of one small bit of information from a whirlwind of mental impulses, to a highly detailed examination of the individuals innermost thoughts, history and basic nature, right down to feelings and memories they no longer realize exist. While a superficial scan is something that can be performed instantaneously with the minimalist amount of effort, a more detailed scan requires careful concentration during which one needs to remain undisturbed and undistracted."

Kaitlyn looked up from the book. Her green eyes held questions but her mind hadn't analyzed and absorbed everything she had just read. Tom seemed to know and explained.

"The son found the book four years later. It had taken him that long to find the directions, gather the money and wait for his own son to mature enough to make that trip across the seas with him. As for what he did with the knowledge, he went on to publish many novels about it, however, his and his fathers research was deemed classified by the American government. He and his son however went on to realize they had this same ability and they worked on it together.

"After many long years of scientific research on the subject he wrote that insert on the back cover and passed it on to his son with the explicit instructions that everything he needs to know is in this book, and everything else is in his head. Then he left never to be seen again, or so the story goes. Rumors that he sought out and joined the tribe that his father had spoke so much of still are mentioned in my family, but all of the work he had done was never shared. This is all we have of his existence." Tom paused and then continued.

"The rest of your questions are pretty easy as well. It does seem to run on the male side of the family, my mother Marge does not know and will not if you get my drift. And I would appreciate it if you wouldn't mention it to anyone else either. I took a big chance in telling you about it, one that I'm not really willing to take and I hope that I can trust you with this knowledge."

"Wait a second. How did you know my questions?"

"They were the same questions I had for my father when he told me."

"So you are answering questions you think I should have?"

"I am answering the questions you telepathically sent to me during second period class today."

"I didn't send you any telepathic message."

"Didn't you? You thought simply this is what I want to ask Tom and then you thought about me. That's all there is to it."

"Then why didn't you telepathically answer me?"

"I was in the middle of a test." He answered, shoving a French fry in his mouth. "You really didn't mean to send the message?"

"Yeah, I just thought about the things I wanted to ask you and then the teacher started talking."

"You may not realize it, but you're very close to learning it."

"I am?"

"Yeah. Today after school I'll teach you a little bit about it if you want?"

"That'll be great. Thanks."

"Hey, this is a selfish act you know."

"Selfish?"

"Yeah. I'll finally have someone to practice this with again. Since my father died I haven't, you know, and I started to think I had lost it. It always helped me express myself better and it'll probably be good for our training as well."

"Oh." Kaitlyn said, remembering how his father died but not sure if she should bring up the subject. She grew excited at the thought that this ability would help the two of them grow even closer and she looked forward to discussing it more when the subject was ended by an outburst between a couple across the cafeteria.

"Slut!"

"Jake, I didn't do anything!"

"I saw the way you were looking at him. You think I'm blind? That I can't see how attracted you are to him?"

"Jake, I'm not!" Cindy pleaded, but Jake grabbed her arm and pulled her out the side door so they could fight in private.

Everyone else seemed to go back to their lunch and their other conversations, but Kaitlyn couldn't help but be curious.

"Tom do you know Jake?"

"He's pretty much a loner."

"Is he abusive?"

"What?"

"Okay, this may be completely off the charts, but last night at the Mac's I saw a couple out in the woods fighting."

"And you think it was Jake and Cindy? Kaitlyn there are thousands of other couples in this town."

"I know but I passed Jake and Cindy in the parking lot as I left and Cindy didn't look too happy."

"Are you sure you're not exaggerating."

"I hope that's all it is. But like this morning I saw Cindy in the hallway and she had a black eye, in the same place the man in the woods struck the lady."

"Did you ask her about it?"

"Doorknob. But I know she was lying about it. Or I think she was, and besides the outburst just now? Jake sounds like the jealous type and those kind of guys can get abusive."

"I'll go check on them okay?"

"I'm going with you."

Kaitlyn and Tom got up and walked over to the side door. As they walked outside they realized Jake and Cindy were gone. There was no one around to ask which way they went. Tom turned and looked at Kaitlyn.

"You know where her next class is?"

"Not really, but I can find out. Maybe..." But Kaitlyn stopped speaking when she noticed Tom bend down and look at something on the ground. "What is it?" He dabbed his fingers in a dark puddle and lifted his fingers to his nose.

"Blood. Go check the clinic."

"What are you going to do?"

"Find Jake. And I think I know where to find him." As Tom ran off, Kaitlyn started towards the clinic. She wondered if Cindy was okay, if Jake was really capable of doing this, if it was even Cindy's blood. Then she wondered where Tom was going. As she entered the clinic she was immediately aware that Cindy was there.

"May I help you?" The nurses' assistant asked, but Kaitlyn walked right by her and into the other room. Cindy sat on the examination table, a towel to her nose.

"Cindy! What happened?"

The nurse turned around and started to shoo Kaitlyn out of the room but Kaitlyn would have none of it. She pushed past the hefty woman and up to Cindy.

"Did Jake do this to you?"

"No, of course n…"

"Cindy, I saw you two in the cafeteria just now. I saw him yank you out of there by your arm."

The nurse then spoke up. "Is he abusing you child?"

"No, he's not. I did something to anger him…" Cindy began to defend him but was stopped by the nurse.

"You did nothing to deserve this girl." The nurse continued. But Cindy kept trying to explain.

"He pulled me, but then I fell, I tripped over my own feet and hit my nose on the ground."

"Why didn't you catch yourself? Block your face with your hands?" Kaitlyn asked.

"I just didn't react quick enough is all. It wasn't Jake's fault. Honest."

Kaitlyn had her reservations and although she was about to say just that, the nurse took her out of the room and spoke quickly.

"Thank you for bringing this to my attention. I'll handle it from here." She went back into the room and closed the door behind her.

As Kaitlyn walked out of the nurse's office, she wanted to beat Jake senseless. She realized then, that was exactly what Tom was doing. She ran toward the parking lot, knowing if Jake had just hit Cindy, he would head toward his motorcycle.

As Kaitlyn ran through the hall, Sam stepped out in front of her ready to start some commotion.

She blocked Kaitlyn's path. "Always running away aren't you?"

Kaitlyn didn't have time for this nor did she feel like dealing with it right now. Just as she thought that she spoke and acted as well. Without thinking, she pushed Sam out of the way, knocking the large girl off her feet and heard as she fell to her butt.

"I don't have time for this right now." Kaitlyn said as she kept running down the hall. Sam must have been shocked into silence because she said nothing back.

Tom was heading back from the parking lot just as Kaitlyn arrived.

"Where's Jake?"

"He's gone. So is his bike."

"Cindy has a busted nose."

"What does she say happened?"

"She fell."

"That's bullshit! Did you tell the nurse that?"

"Oh, she knows. But Cindy's in denial, she's even protecting the bastard!"

Tom sighed and shook his head. "I don't know what to do. I don't know where to find him. Maybe the nurse will be able to talk some sense into Cindy."

"I seriously doubt that. You should have seen how persistent she was that Jake was innocent."

"That's the first sign that she's in an abusive relationship."

"I know."

"Hello?"

"Jonathan?" Cindy asked, almost in a whisper.

"Cindy is that you?" Jonathan asked gripping the telephone tighter with concern since he hadn't heard from her since they broke up.

"Yeah. How're you doing?"

"Fine. College is a lot harder than high school. But how are you?"

"Fine."

"Good. So what's going on? Why did you call?" Cindy started crying over the phone. "Cindy? What's wrong?"

"Jonathan, I'm so scared."

"Scared of what? Tell me everything."

"I'm not sure if I can."

"You have always been able to talk to me, even after our break up. Now tell me, what's going on?"

"Tom can you hear me?" Kaitlyn asked telepathically as she sat in her room that night concentrating on Tom's face in her mind. She waited a moment and tried again. "Tom? Can you hear me?"

"I can hear you. What's up?"

"I did it! I did..." But the transmission stopped. Tom got on the phone and called Kaitlyn.

"Hello?" Kaitlyn answered normally.

"I think you lost the signal."

"I was just so excited."

"I could tell. Pretty impressive for your first real try."

"I still lost the signal."

"Tell you what. Let's get together tonight."

"To practice?"

"To celebrate. Where do you want to go?"

"How about the drive-thru? Haven't been there in a long time."

"Sounds good. You mind meeting me there, though?"

"Not a problem I'm closer than you are."

Kaitlyn hung up the phone and changed into a tight pair of jeans and tank top. She felt good. She had successfully sent a telepathic message to Tom and he wanted to celebrate. The guy who didn't know the meaning of relax wanted to celebrate. Kaitlyn was really excited.

Kaitlyn only lived a couple blocks away from the drive-thru and she knew there were always picnic tables all around for those who didn't drive yet. So she walked, enjoying the night air and thinking about the possibilities. When she arrived there the place seemed to be jumping. Music played over the loud speakers and everyone danced and laughed. She saw football players and cheerleaders, they must have won the game against the Panthers tonight Kaitlyn concluded.

While waiting for Tom, Kaitlyn noticed Cindy at a table towards the back of the lot, then she noticed Cindy was with someone other than Jake. Curious, Kaitlyn approached them.

"Cindy, hi."

"Hi, Kaitlyn, this is Jonathan."

Kaitlyn leaned over to shake Jonathan's hand. "Nice to meet you."

"You know me, last year's chem. class."

Kaitlyn thought about it for a moment. "Oh, yeah, you graduated early. That's right, you were Cindy's old boyfriend." Kaitlyn remembered; Jake was jealous over another guy today. Could it have been Jonathan? Cindy stood up, whispering to Kaitlyn.

"I called Jonathan tonight, and told him the truth about Jake. You were right, and I'm tired of being afraid. I needed someone to talk to, you understand?"

Kaitlyn did understand. She was happy that Cindy realized the truth so early into the game.

"You want to join us?" Jonathan asked.

"I am meeting someone here in a little while." Kaitlyn hesitated.

"Well, until they show up." Jonathan stood to give Kaitlyn his seat, and as she sat down, Jonathan took Cindy's hand into his and they began to sit down together. Jonathan sat Cindy first, then was about to sit down himself when Jake rushed up behind the two of them, spun Jonathan around, and punched him in the face, throwing him across the table and to the ground on the other side. Everyone stopped talking and turned to watch.

Jake grabbed Cindy by the arms, pulled her over the chair, making her stumble and then slapped her across the face.

"What did I tell you about cheating on me, slut! You asked for this!"

He was about to hit her again, but without a single thought, Kaitlyn made her way to the other side of the table and took the brunt of Jake's punch into her hand. She then sent the punch back to him with her free hand with as much power as she could muster. Before she knew it, Kaitlyn was in the middle of a ferocious battle... with a guy.

Jake tried to take her head off with another punch, but she blocked it and sent him a spinning high kick that knocked him down flat on his back. Jake was stunned and in shock.

"You ever touch Cindy or anyone around here again like that and I'll personally rearrange your face with my fist! You got me?" Kaitlyn yelled loudly and in total charge of herself. Kaitlyn then turned to check on Cindy. Jake looked around at the staring or amused faces in the crowd staring at him. He grew angry. He stood up quick, grabbed a metal chair, and was about to slam it down upon Kaitlyn's back when someone from the crowd yelled a warning.

Kaitlyn turned just in time to see the chair coming at her and she threw up her hands to block it. The motion of her hands mixed with the fear and adrenaline in her body seemed to mix inside of her like a blender on high speed. It collected like a tornado and then shot out from her hands, through the tips of her fingers like a whirlwind. Like she had just hit him without touching him, Jake and the chair flew backwards a good twenty feet. In seeing this happen, knowing full well she had not even touched him, she freaked. She looked at her hands in shock and then over to where Jake lay comatose, and then a few feet farther to Tom's car. Tom had just gotten out of the driver's side door and was staring at her wide eyed and shocked.

Everyone in the crowd seemed to be cheering, and Kaitlyn wondered if they saw what really happened or if they were just happy to see Jake out. As everyone started to gather around her asking questions, she soon realized they had seen what they wanted to.

"That was so cool, taking on Jake like that."

"You were so fast I didn't even see you push him!"

"You just beat up Jake the snake! That is so cool!"

Kaitlyn was beginning to enjoy the praise when Tom walked up to her through the crowd and whispered into her ear.

"We have to talk."

Kaitlyn and Tom walked away just as the police arrived. Everyone pointed towards Jake and no one seemed to mention Kaitlyn. That was a good thing because Kaitlyn and Tom had a lot to talk about, including Kaitlyn's newfound Telekinetic ability; the ability to throw objects with your mind.

Chapter 8

The next morning Kaitlyn was walking toward class when Susan approached her. Not feeling up to another verbal assault Kaitlyn immediately positioned herself ready to ignore her.

"Kaitlyn, you have to do it."

"Do what?" She asked completely caught off guard. Just then Beth, another cheerleader, ran up to her.

"Is she going to do it?"

"I'm not sure yet." Susan answered anxiously.

"Do what?" Kaitlyn asked curiously.

Before she knew it the entire cheerleading squad had gathered around her followed by Principal Green.

"Kaitlyn, I just wanted to congratulate you on an impressive job well done yesterday and grant you permission to use the gym after school for your classes."

"What classes?"

"The girls here all wanted you to teach them self defense after school, and I think it's a wonderful idea."

"You do?"

"So will you do it?" Susan asked again, making all the other girls quiet down.

Kaitlyn was shocked. All of these girls were looking at her expectantly. They all had these smiles and open eyes that seemed to be begging for something, and they were asking for it from Kaitlyn. What did they want? Classes? Self defense? They wanted to be taught. They wanted to defend themselves. And why shouldn't they? Every girl needs to know how to protect herself. Kaitlyn could do it. That's why she wanted to learn. And she had learned. She had learned a lot. Was she ready to teach? She wasn't sure about that but she was ready to do something with this knowledge. She wanted to help. She wanted to be there for these girls. She wanted to be here.

Kaitlyn was enjoying the attention when she realized that what the girls were asking would intrude in her afternoon time with Tom. Moreover, she realized that Tom was so intent to keep their secrets secret she wasn't sure if he'd be okay with her doing this. After the telekinetic episode last night he was very weary about Kaitlyn accidentally using that power in public.

"What did Tom say about it?" Kaitlyn asked of the girls assuming that they had to have gone to him first. I mean why learn from Kaitlyn when they could have Tom teach them, one on one?

Thinking of nothing more than the stress-filled discussion the two of them had last night, Kaitlyn got lost for a moment. Tom walked up behind her and placed his warm hands atop her shoulders.

"I think it's a wonderful idea."

"You do?" She asked looking into his eyes curiously.

"It's for a good cause. I can't think of anything better to do with your time right now."

"You can't?" Kaitlyn muttered with disappointment.

"So what do you say Kaitlyn?" Principal Green asked.

Kaitlyn looked at the girls who never gave her the time of day before but now wanted her help. Although, her first instinct was to walk away, she couldn't help but smile.

"I'll do it."

Everyone cheered as the warning bell for class sounded and the Principal told everyone to get to class.

The girls all patted Kaitlyn on the back, and she was smiling brightly when Tom pulled her to the side of the hall to talk.

"You okay?"

"Great. Why?"

"Are you sure you want to do this?"

"Do what?"

"It's still a shock huh?"

"Big shock." She chuckled. "They're all being so nice to me...."

Principal Green cut in. "So I was going to mention this over the intercom during announcements. When do you want to start your first class?"

"When?" Kaitlyn asked needing to hear herself say it, then she answered herself just as quickly. "This afternoon?" Kaitlyn said, not even realizing what she was saying.

"I'll spread the word." And he walked off.

Kaitlyn looked into Tom's eyes, still overwhelmed by the whole morning." I don't know how to run a class Tom. What do I do? What do I say?"

"Teach them how I taught you."

"Oh, you mean make them carry my books and be my personal slaves for as long as I want?"

"I thought we were past that."

"We are. I was just caught off guard today. I mean, none of those girls ever paid any attention to me before, well, anything positive at least."

"Now you're not sure if they really want to be your friend or just use you?"

"Exactly."

"You'll be great." Tom said.

"Will you come? To at least watch?"

"Are you sure you want me there?"

"Definitely!" Already feeling some of the nervous tension escape her. She knew she could do anything... if Tom were there.

During the day, many girls confronted Kaitlyn with questions. Stupid questions like what to wear, and should they pull their hair up. Exclaiming that this was going to be a lot of fun and so on. These comments got Kaitlyn thinking, and when it was time for her first class, she had figured out exactly what to say.

The girls had all gathered on the bleachers when Kaitlyn entered the gym with Tom. Tom gave her a kiss on the cheek for good luck and went to sit on the bleachers. Kaitlyn walked to the center floor where the girls had gathered and stood in front of them. She looked up at the expectant faces of her new class and found a sense of pride. Even when she saw Sam she didn't begin to worry. Kaitlyn remembered why she was here and began to speak.

"What I will teach you here is self-defense. I will teach you how to avoid dangerous situations first and foremost. Then I will teach you how to get out of one. I will not teach you how to start fights or defeat the attacker. I'll teach you what to do, what to say, where to go, and who to get if something ever happened.

"Secondly, this class is cutting into my free time; so I'm setting down one rule right now. Don't waste my time. This is not a slumber party, a fun get together; make up party or gossip shop. My time is very valuable, so if you're here to play around then leave right now. If you are not interested in learning then I urge you to leave." Kaitlyn waited but no one left.

"Okay then. Um, I've been asked if you all should change clothes before class. That's up to you, but let me say this. If you are attacked at a club, or in an alleyway, most likely you will not be in gym-wear. You'll be in street clothes, constricting dresses and skirts and off the shoulder tops, and you'll need to know how to protect yourself. So you are more than welcome to learn in gym clothes, but you are not required to change. I actually suggest you learn in your regular school clothes."

After a few minutes of verbal explanation of what Kaitlyn was going to teach the class, Kaitlyn finally decided it was time for a visual example. She thought about the first lesson Tom ever taught her and it became clear what she needed to do.

"Okay, first basic lesson. What do you do if someone grabs you from behind?"

Many girls raised their hands to answer, but Kaitlyn called on Susan, since she knew her name.

"Fight him off!" Susan said.

"How?"

"Kick him."

"Okay, but if he grabs you from behind, how will you kick him? Do you still believe you should fight him off?"

"Yes, of course."

"Okay, come here." Kaitlyn waved for her to come down and she did.

Kaitlyn turned Susan and then took both of Susan's arms by the elbows and pulled them behind her back loosely.

"Okay Susan, get out of this."

Susan squirmed and pulled but she couldn't get out of Kaitlyn's grasp. Uncomfortable at the thought of being held back by Kaitlyn, Susan decided to fight back her way. She squirmed harder, kicked in the air, tried to kick backwards, but instead lost her footing and fell to her knees. Kaitlyn still held her arms loosely, making sure not to hurt Susan but proving her point that it didn't take much to constrain someone. Embarrassed and slightly angry, Susan finally gave up and she spoke.

"Let me go."

"You really think an attacker would do that?"

"Okay, Kaitlyn how do I get out?" Susan growled.

Kaitlyn could tell Susan was embarrassed, and Kaitlyn enjoyed it, but kept her mind on the task at hand. Kaitlyn let go of Susan, who now faced her, and began to explain a few techniques while staring directly into Susan's eyes showing the cheerleader how sure and direct she could be.

"You could use the heel of your foot and stomp on his foot. Use your head to butt his face, or you could scream. You can sit back down, Susan."

Kaitlyn waited a second before continuing.

"You see, it's not something that can easily be picked up. If you don't know what you're doing, or if the assailant has a weapon, there is absolutely nothing you can do to stop him. However, during these classes I will teach you as much as I can to keep you safe. Any questions?"

"Is Tom going to help teach us?" someone said. All the girls turned towards Tom; some even giggled. Kaitlyn wanted to scream. Tom could tell by her face that she didn't know what to say so he stood up walked down next to Kaitlyn and spoke to the class.

"I will at times come in and check on the class, maybe even help out if I can, but this is Kaitlyn's class and I, like you, do exactly as *she* says."

"Thanks, Tom." She smiled and looked up at him with shock and surprise that quickly changed to happiness and pride. He placed his hand on her shoulder and squeezed it gently, relaxing her. She spoke again to the class.

"Now lets get some practice in before we leave today. Everybody on the floor for your first lesson."

Kaitlyn got the girls paired and started on a particular hold then she walked over to Tom.

"Did you mean what you said?"

"Every word of it…. What did I say?"

"That you'd do exactly what I say?"

"Anything you want"

She winked. "Anything?"

"What did you have in mind?"

"Nothing." She confirmed, smiling just a bit. Things were beginning to get really good. Her life was beginning to have meaning and substance. She was beginning to fit in to the crowd she had always wanted to belong to, and she loved every minute of it. Tom was also loosening up around her and the kiss he gave her on the cheek, in front of everyone, proved it.

The next few weeks went about the same way, each day, each class, Tom and she worked together. They talked and relaxed together in front of everyone. They were beginning to act normal, like boyfriend and girlfriend, and everyone had seemed to forget or just not care anymore about the previous month with the big fight with Jake. Every afternoon Kaitlyn and Tom would get together after her class and practice their moves together. Tom was still very much interested in training Kaitlyn more forms of fight; he enjoyed learning, and this way he had a partner. Tom also kept working with Kaitlyn on her telepathic abilities. He'd talk to her and she would hear him, but she'd lose the message when she spoke out loud saying, "I heard you!"

He trained her how to control her thoughts. That when she heard his message she had to clear her mind to everything but the person she wanted to communicate with, then send the answer in a form of meditative thought. Kaitlyn found this very difficult at first, but in less than a month's time she had pretty much mastered her thoughts. She wasn't as good as Tom, but she was determined that with daily usage she'd pick it up and be as good as Tom.

She did have one problem for quite sometime. When she'd send a thought to Tom, she'd send current feelings as well. Like one time as they practiced a new fight move, Tom accidentally knocked her back with a kick stance and she fell about five feet backwards. At the same time he was sending her a telepathic message warning her that it was coming and to prepare for it. They had been working on telepathic teamwork; something that would look to anyone watching that they were so good they could have been reading each other's minds, which of course they were, but the person watching would never know.

It had been working well; Kaitlyn had blocked every trick he shot her and she was doing it through his warnings. Problem was, after one neck gripping pin-down, Kaitlyn had a quick flash of how handsome Tom was and it made her mind wonder just a moment to a sexual nature. They hadn't gotten that far yet, but she thought about it at times. The idea he could read her mind and do whatever she wanted to please her while they were making out just sent shivers up her spine.

Tom telepathically warned her about the high kick, and since she wasn't paying much attention, she got kicked hard and fell backwards. Tom ran up to her to see if she was okay, asking telepathically if she was hurt and she answered back the same way that she was fine. The problem? She sent the thought she had been thinking with that message, and by the look on Tom's face she knew he had seen it.

He half smirked, half blushed, and she wondered if he wanted to say something about it but he didn't. He offered her a hand to help her up and she thanked him the old fashioned way.

"Thanks, I needed that."

"You sure you're okay?"

"Yeah, just a little shook up but that's what I get for not paying attention."

She had wondered if Tom would say anything about it, do anything, but he didn't. He let that last statement float away pretending that he hadn't seen it to keep things between them safe, and then he decided that it was getting late and they should go home. He drove Kaitlyn home and they talked about other things, school, news, and the weather. Suddenly, she did change the subject to something that had been bothering her for a while.

"Tom?"

"Yeah?"

"Why haven't we practiced the other thing?"

"What thing?"

"Well, the day that I threw Jake, the day he just flew away from me without my ever actually touching him."

"What do you want to know?"

"I'd like to learn how I did that. You know? Maybe learn how to use that in the future?"

I think it's a bad idea."

"What's a bad idea?"

"You learning more about your telekinetic abilities. It's not a good thing."

"What's not good about it? I could learn how to kick ass and never break a fingernail."

"Do you remember my reason for not wanting to discuss our telepathic abilities with others?

"Yeah, you're worried about the government finding out and…" Kaitlyn paused, realizing where he was going with this. "You think if someone sees me doing it I'll become some governmental guinea pig."

"I worry about you. You're strong, talented. You have telepathic and telekinetic abilities, and in the wrong hands you could be used for evil."

"Okay, I get it. But I'm not going to tell someone all of that. The only way they'd find out is from you, and I don't think you'd tell them since you're always trying to protect it."

"They wouldn't have to hear it from me. It's not as easy to hide as the telepathic stuff. Besides, I just worry about you. I don't want to see you get hurt."

Tom had pretty much summed it up. She wanted to learn, but didn't know how to start. The night after Jake, Tom pulled her aside and told her he saw what she did, and that it was potentially dangerous. After she got home she tried to do it again, but failed. She couldn't tap into that ability again and figured maybe in a small way she shouldn't.

As Tom pulled up to Kaitlyn's house, a black Chevy Camero with tinted windows pulled away. Kaitlyn noticed her father was home from work early so she thanked Tom for the ride, gave him a quick kiss on the lips and got out of the car, walking up to her house and waved bye to Tom as he drove away.

Kaitlyn walked in through the door, dropped her keys on the side table, and walked into the kitchen where she saw her father sitting blank-faced at the kitchen table.

"Daddy?"

He came back to reality. "Pumpkin how was your day?"

"Great. Yours? Everything okay at the firm?"

"Another divorce case, but other than that non-eventful. Tell me about your day, why was it great?"

So Kaitlyn told him about the self-defense classes she had been teaching and what she had taught them today. When she finished, he suggested they celebrate with ice cream for dinner, so they went out to the local ice cream shop and filled up on banana splits. They enjoyed the night together like they hadn't in a long time, laughing joking, and simply enjoying each other's company.

Ever since Kaitlyn's mother, Allison, had died of cancer last summer, her father had seemed to lose all connection with reality. He had lost all emotion. All he had now was his work at the law firm; he had seemed to even forget he was a father. He always seemed like he was preoccupied, always worried about something else but he never wanted to talk about it. Kaitlyn and he had a trusting silent relationship. He'd ask her how she was and she would tell him something other than fine. As long as she shared with him a little about her life he was okay with her doing what she wanted, as long as it wasn't illegal. For a while there Kaitlyn thought it was cool, not having to worry about a parent always holding you back, giving you constricting rules and telling you what to do and not to do, but tonight it all changed. Tonight, Kaitlyn had her father back. Tonight he showed a true interest in her life and they shared and talked with each other as if they hadn't talked in years. It was a wonderful night.

Chapter 9

Tom had become very outgoing and forward. He talked with people, laughed and joked, and when he was around Kaitlyn he didn't hold back one bit of emotion. If he wanted to kiss her, he would, and in every case, she had absolutely no problem with it. They had grown so close to each other these past weeks that they seemed inseparable. And each day they were together, talking, hugging, kissing, they grew even closer than they realized. They were about ready for a turning point that one of them was not prepared to accept.

About two months had passed since the beginning of Kaitlyn's class and while the girls didn't learn as quickly as Kaitlyn, she enjoyed every minute of teaching them. It felt like her nitch; like she was made to teach girls how to defend themselves, and it made her feel good about herself to share with others. And speaking of sharing something special with others, she was really getting excited about Tom. He still seemed to try to keep his emotions in check, still trying to keep things platonic, which Kaitlyn didn't understand since he let himself slip enough to kiss her all the time. Kaitlyn had decided to not make things easy on him though; she wanted more of this relationship and she would let him know it each time she could.

One day, about a month later, before wrestling practice, one of Tom's wrestling buddies chimed up. "Tell me about Kaitlyn. You two an item or not?"

"Not." Tom answered quickly, still warming up for practice.

"So you wouldn't mind if I made a move on her?"

"I don't care what you do, Shawn." Tom answered, trying to pay attention to the coach and not the tall, skinny, polo shirt wearing, rich Country Club going, daddy's perfect little guy with his own spare key to daddy's liquor cabinet and X-rated video collection guy standing next to him.

"Good. The guys and I've got this bet going that she would be great in the sack."

"What? Who?" Tom asked in shock finally paying attention to Shawn.

"Kaitlyn is so hot. Yeah, that girls got strength. All the guys are talk about it."

"Talking about what exactly?"

"Her on top and totally in charge. Makes me drool just thinking about it."

Tom's teeth began to grind, "Well, that's all you'll be doing is thinking about it because you're not laying a hand on her, buddy."

"Hey, what do you care? You two ain't even dating."

"She's my friend, and I wouldn't even let you date my enemies."

"What's that supposed to mean? You got a problem with me?"

"Yes, I do. Where do you get off talking about her that way?"

"Hey, I'm not the only one, and for someone who's not involved you sure are getting defensive. Maybe you've got something for this girl and don't know it."

"I told you, we're just friends."

"Whatever, man." Shawn finished up as the coach came in and began pairing up teams. Practice went smoothly for the next ten minutes or so; Tom had almost forgot about Shawn's ranting about Kaitlyn until the two of them were paired up to fight.

They stood in a fight stance; legs spread, arms open, crouched down ready to attack, waiting for the bell.

"I'm still going to ask her out. Rumor is sweet things like that'll put out quicker than cheerleaders."

Before Tom knew it, his fist flew towards Shawn's face, ready to teach this punk a lesson, and before he could think to stop himself, Shawn was on the ground, his hand covering a bloody nose.

"What the hell is your problem Tom?" Shawn yelled just before the coach stepped up and told Tom to hit the showers.

Kaitlyn had been in the process of teaching her class when Tom walked in to watch. He hadn't spent much time there lately because of wrestling practice, but today he got there early. Kaitlyn was in the process of teaching punching to the girls. They'd throw out their fist, twist, shove, and yell at the same time. The yelling was something used to catch the attacker off guard. When she saw Tom, she forgot everything for a moment. She found herself getting lost in him. He looked so good. His hair was shower wet and hadn't dried yet; his shirt kind of clung to his chest to expose his rippling muscles. Something in her body switched and she found herself thinking improper thoughts she was usually able to control. Today, she couldn't. Today, her emotions were on a rampage.

Tom walked over to the side of the bleachers to put his bag down, and Kaitlyn walked up to him. Today, he noticed her stride. As he watched her walk, he noticed her hips swaying more, he noticed her long brunette hair waving behind her, and he noticed her bright emerald green eyes focus in on him, tearing into his soul. It made him want to whimper like a puppy. She greeted him with a quick kiss on the lips, and he soaked it in like sugar. But when she began to pull out of it, she found his hand on her back, slightly holding her there, massaging her closer to him so the kiss could last a few seconds longer. For some reason, Tom just wanted more today.

She melted in his arms and her body seemed to burst with emotion. She wanted to do things to him she hadn't even considered in her wildest dreams and before she even realized it, she accidentally shot Tom a telepathic picture of one of those things. He stepped back slightly, looking into her eyes, wondering if that was actually his thought or hers. And he suddenly came up with a thought to follow hers and sent it to her telepathically. She smiled wickedly at him, but then turned to look at her class watching them. She walked away from Tom for a moment, getting after her class to start a new move. Tom walked over to stand next to her and was amazed at how well she taught and how well the other girls followed. He then sent another message to Kaitlyn telepathically reminding her of that kiss just a moment ago. She remembered it well. She leaned up and whispered something in his ear. He nearly stumbled on his feet then he spoke quietly and incredibly alluring.

"Do you want to let the class go early?"

Kaitlyn wasted no time at all. "Great work girls. Practice that move tonight and I'll see you tomorrow after school."

As the girls grabbed their things and started out the door, Tom stepped back to allow Kaitlyn time to answer any questions and say goodbye to everyone. Once the gym was empty she looked at Tom leaning against the wall.

"How you doing?" She approached him curiously.

"As well as can be expected." He avoided her eyes. She knew exactly what she wanted to do to him, and she telepathically shot him a vision. A vision of her taking him by the shirt collar, throwing him down on the mats, mounting him like a cowboy to his horse and kissing him like a lust craven mad woman.

He couldn't stand the visions any longer; he felt he had to have her. He met her halfway, grabbed her by the forearms and pulled her into a passionate kiss. She nearly melted into his arms but stood strong. He wrapped his hands around her torso and lifted her into the air just slightly. She wrapped her legs around his hips and held on tight. He slowly rubbed his hands up her back spreading his fingers out so his hands could touch every inch of her skin.

The kiss became more intense than they ever could've imagined. Emotions and feelings flowed through Kaitlyn like she had never felt before. She wanted him more than she had ever wanted anything in her entire life, and it scared her to have such strong feelings on the matter. But she was powerless to stop it, unwilling to allow such an intense emotional climax end without feeling everything there was to feel.

Tom held her tight, as she began pulling his shirt from inside his pants with her fingernails. As she lifted his shirt just slightly, uncovering his muscular abs, she tickled his sides with her fingertips, sending more shivers through his body, making him want her even more. He let go of her for just a second to rip his shirt over his head and throw it to the floor, but she held tight with her throbbing thighs gripped securely around his hips. As he came back to her he grabbed her arms by the wrist and thrust them against the wall so he could have full attention of her body. He began kissing her on her neck, kissing her around her collarbone, tickling her with his tongue.

She moaned as she felt his hands slide down her side and begin collecting the hem of her shirt. They were getting into it wildly. Kaitlyn had started undoing his belt buckle and she could feel that he wanted her just as much as she wanted him. She was ready for anything, she didn't know where the feelings were coming from, she knew that she was in love with Tom but she had no idea she wanted him this badly. She had no idea how close they had gotten to actually getting into it when she heard a familiar voice ring out from inside the locker rooms: the voice of Principal Green.

"Kaitlyn, Tom, you two still in there?" He called out as he began to walk out into the gym.

Kaitlyn did not want to be caught making out in school with Tom by Principal Green because he would surely cancel her classes. And being caught in a position like this gave her an awkward feeling in the pit of her stomach, one that she wasn't willing to have just yet. She pushed Tom away with her pelvis, just in time to make it look as if they were practicing fighting the whole time. Principal Green walked in at that exact moment seeing nothing but Tom fall on his back onto the mats and Kaitlyn land on her feet, wiping the hair from her face.

"Oh, there you two are. Still practicing huh?"

"Yes, sir." Kaitlyn answered as Tom finally realized what had happened to him.

"Well I was thinking that you need time for your studies and such, and with the after school activities going on this season, you can have the use of the gym this week, but then it will only be available every Tuesday and Thursday."

"That sounds great, Principal Green." Kaitlyn smiled as she noticed Tom quickly putting his pants back together.

"Good. So I'll write up the schedule and set it up for you. How did you're class go today?"

"Great."

"That's good to hear. I'll let you two get back to whatever it was you were doing now, just wanted to check in with you about that."

"Okay, Thanks." Kaitlyn smiled. As the two of them watched him leave an awkward silence came over the both of them. Kaitlyn finally turned to look at Tom who was reaching down for his shirt. Part of her wanted to pick up where they left off, but the other part wanted to discuss what they had been doing to figure out what had happened.

"You okay?" She asked to break the silence.

"Yeah, fine."

"I mean I didn't hurt you right?"

"No. I can handle a little shove."

Kaitlyn could tell something was not right but she was also afraid to say anything before figuring out how he really felt.

"You need a ride home?"

"Sure." Kaitlyn knew this was his way of getting back to business.

"Okay, grab your things lets go."

She followed him to his car and sat silently as he started driving out of the parking lot. She remained quiet during most of the drive to her house until Tom pulled up to the back and put it in park. He finally spoke.

"Your father home?"

"No. He works until six-thirty." She answered honestly wondering where this questioning was going. Was he planning more?

"Oh." Tom said.

Kaitlyn wasn't sure what was going on. Did he ask because he wanted to finish what they started or was he just making small talk? And why was he being so abrupt and rude?

"So I'll see you tomorrow at school, I guess," Tom said.

"I guess." Kaitlyn added without thinking; then she realized she wasn't ready for him to leave. She wasn't ready to make love to him either, but they needed to talk, she knew that. "Do you want to come in?"

He avoided her eyes. "No."

She kind of understood his answer and even though disappointed she gave up and opened the car door to leave. She was growing fairly upset by everything that had happened but knew she had to figure this out before addressing the situation. She had to figure out her own emotions first. Just then, Tom reached over and touched her hand with his.

"We shouldn't get involved like this."

Kaitlyn shook her head a second, attempting to stop it from spinning, then stopped and looked back at him.

"Why?"

"We just shouldn't."

"No. I deserve a reason. You were totally into it in the gym, and then when we almost got caught…" She paused thinking about that moment then jumped to the worst possible conclusion. "That's it. You're ashamed to get caught with me like that."

"Kaitlyn, that's not it."

"You don't want to get involved with me because you think it'll send the wrong message to the rest of the school."

"No, that's not it!"

"Then what is it? Why is it okay when no one's around but the idea of getting caught totally turns you off?"

"It doesn't."

"It doesn't?"

"Kaitlyn I was afraid." He remembered his deepest fears that he had pushed back these past few months.

"Afraid of what? Getting caught? We didn't." She knew her emotions were way too high for a calm conversation with him but they were into it and there was no stopping now.

"Well, it's just that, you've obviously had some experience in matters like this and I haven't."

"I've had experience? Ha!"

"But you kiss like you do."

She smiled. "Hey, you weren't so bad yourself, fella."

"So you haven't?" He wondered about her virginity without saying the words.

"Does it matter?"

"No, but…"

"I haven't." Kaitlyn paused before speaking again. "I don't know what got over me. It's just that the two of us… clicked."

"I know."

"It's like the two of us being together was as natural as…" Kaitlyn began to describe it, but Tom interrupted her.

"I just don't think we should become involved that way."

100

"Why?"

"What if something happens?"

"Like what? We fall in love?" She said with anger.

"Why are you getting so angry?" Tom asked.

"Because I *am* in love with you! I have been for some time."

"What do you want me to do? Lay you down right here?"

"No! I don't want you to do anything you don't *want* to do." Kaitlyn hurried out of his car and slammed the door.

"Kaitlyn!" Tom yelled, as the wind from the slamming door smacked his face.

He fought with taking his seat belt off and the door handle to the door and shuffled out of his car. Then he ran around the side of the car and yelled for her again.

"Kaitlyn, don't walk away."

"Don't tell me what to do Tom. You haven't earned that privilege!"

"I don't want to get involved that way. Why can't you understand that?"

"Then why did you kiss me?" Kaitlyn fought back tears. She waited for a response but none came. He stopped dead in his tracks and knew he had messed up.

"Why did you kiss me and hold my hand, and make me fall in love with you? Why did you kiss me like that in the gym this afternoon? Why did you send all of those provocative images to me, and go along with mine so well. Why have you been leading me on all of these months and then when I finally want it, you deny me the opportunity?"

"I'm sorry," he said, looking down feeling ashamed.

"I don't care if you're sorry, I want to know why?" A tear slipped down her cheek. She wiped it away quickly, trying to hide her emotions but unable to stop them from flowing.

Seeing her in pain destroyed him. He walked up to her, pulled her delicately into a hug, and apologized again.

"I'm so sorry. I never meant to hurt you." He stroked her hair trying to calm her down. "I was afraid that if we got too close." He paused again knowing the truth would be too painful. "If we became sexually active, if something happened." He stopped again, completely confused, but then realized the final truth and finished his thought. "I was afraid I'd lose you."

Shocked, she looked up into his eyes.

"What?" She wanted to hear him say it again. He let go of her in the hug to look at her straight on.

"I don't want to lose you."

"How could you lose me?"

Tom kept it simple. "Romance does that to people."

"Not all of the time."

"What if we didn't agree on something or something happened between us?"

"Like what?"

"Anything could come up or be found out and then we'd lose everything we have. Like our telepathic connection; it is so important to me, I feel we have this wonderful connection together and I don't want to let anything come between us. I love you and I guess I just don't know how to show it."

Kaitlyn absorbed his words. "I don't ever want anything to come between us. And so it never will."

Kaitlyn hugged him tightly, and he held her close. The scent of her hair drifted up into his senses, he couldn't help but kiss her on the head. She looked up at him, the tears drying on her face, and her eyes peered into his, warming him. Like magnets, their lips merged, he kissed her delicately, so full of love. Their bodies embraced, lips touching and senses high. Tom couldn't help himself. He held her tighter, pulled her closer to his body and kissed her again. Her warm body embraced his, her touch, the shear fact of her being near him made him feel vulnerable, unable to control his emotions, his actions. He couldn't resist anymore. They were right back where they had left off in the gymnasium but a little more subdued, a little more romantic.

"I do love you," he whispered.

"Oh, Tom."

Tom may not have wanted to risk things changing but he couldn't control his emotions when he was around her. Whether he wanted to risk things or not didn't matter. A telepaths emotions are much more in tune and aware of the emotions around them then that of the normal person. Tom wasn't aware of this fact yet but what he was aware of was he did not want to leave Kaitlyn's arms right now. As they stumbled into her house and then stumbled into her room, kissing, embracing and mentally making love to each other, Kaitlyn closed the door to her room and locked it.

It may not have been planned, it probably shouldn't have happened, but that afternoon they made love to each other. As the afternoon faded into evening and the sun began to set, they fell asleep in each other's arms, exhausted, but happy.

Chapter 10

Tom woke up when someone came in the front door. He was naked in Kaitlyn's bed, and she was still sleeping.

"Kaitlyn." He whispered.

"Pumpkin, I'm home." Her father, Harold, closed the front door behind him.

"Kaitlyn, wake up," Tom whispered again as he jostled Kaitlyn's shoulder with his right hand. His heart pumping wildly at the thought that this 240 pound father would find Tom in bed with his daughter.

"Kaitlyn honey, are you here?"

Kaitlyn was out for the count and Tom knew it. He scrambled out of bed, slid his jeans on, catching his pubic hair with the zipper as he did. He bit his lip to keep from screaming, gathered the rest of his clothes, and threw them in the closet. He threw the covers over Kaitlyn to hide her exposed body. Then, he stepped into the closet and closed the door right as her father entered the room.

"Kaitlyn asleep already?" he asked seeing his daughter in bed. She rolled over in her sleep and her father walked up to her and tucked her into her covers a little better. Then he kissed her forehead and left the room, closing the door behind him.

Tom exhaled deeply, after holding his breath while her father was in the room. He quickly slid his shoes on and his shirt then peeked out the closet door. Once the coast was clear, he walked out and sat down next to Kaitlyn on her bed. He watched her for a few moments before kissing her softly on the lips and then he telepathically told her that he'd see her tomorrow. Then he left through the window.

The next morning Kaitlyn was barely able to remember what had happened. She called out for Tom, but the window was opened a crack and she realized he had left. She showered and got dressed then walked out into the living room where her father was eating breakfast.

"Morning, Honey, how'd you sleep?"

"Hmm? Fine."

"You were out like a light last night. Did you have a hard day?"

"I was? Day? No, good day."

"Good. So I caught you last night."

"Caught me?"

"You went to bed before doing your homework didn't you?"

"Homework? Oh, Homework." She repeated realizing she wasn't in trouble. She began to walk out of the house when her father spoke one thing more.

"No breakfast?"

"No time."

"You should really eat some breakfast."

"I'll grab a granola bar okay?"

Harold stood and followed his daughter into the kitchen. "You've been so busy lately."

"The self defense classes are taking up a lot of time."

"I'd like to spend some time with you tonight."

"That sounds nice daddy."

"There are things that I need to say. Things I need to tell you."

"Okay daddy, I'll see you tonight." Kaitlyn said as she gave him a quick kiss on the lips and skipped out the door. "Love ya!"

"I love you too Kaitlyn." He called out to her as she closed the door behind her.

Kaitlyn ran to school, eager to talk to Tom this morning since she didn't have a chance last night. By the time she arrived, she was ready for a nap though. As she entered the school and walked up to Tom, she imagined falling asleep in his warm arms.

"Hey, there," he said, as she walked towards him. "Sleep well last night?"

"Don't you know?"

"I left shortly after your father came home."

"What?" Kaitlyn panicked immediately thinking about her father's words, we need to talk.

"Don't worry, I hid in the closet until he left your room and then went out the window."

"Thanks." Kaitlyn sighed with relief.

"Hey, I might be a wrestler, but facing a father about his daughter when the daughter is too exhausted to even wake up sounded like suicide."

"You tried to wake me?"

"I tried. Your father tried. I tried again before I left. You were dead to the world."

Kaitlyn had snuggled up on his arm and he noticed she had just gone to sleep again. "Kaitlyn." But she didn't wake up. When the bell rang for class, Tom laughed as he helped Kaitlyn stand.

"Guess I tired you out last night, huh?"

"Don't flatter yourself. I don't know what's wrong with me."

Kaitlyn assumed she would be tired after such activities but after twelve hours of sleep she shouldn't be exhausted. It was like her body wanted to shut down and go to sleep and she just couldn't understand why. As Tom began to walk her to class, Shawn approached, a large bandage covering his nose. Kaitlyn asked him about it.

"Shawn, what happened to your nose?"

"Why don't you ask your psycho boyfriend?" Kaitlyn looked over at Tom who was basically snarling at Shawn.

"Shawn walk away," Tom, spoke low.

"You busted my nose yesterday. I will not walk away."

"You deserved what you got."

"Tom? Why did you hit Shawn?" Kaitlyn inquired innocently unaware.

"It was an accident." Tom quickly informed.

"Like hell it was, you hit me on purpose."

"Tom, is that true?"

"It doesn't matter." Tom tried to walk her away but she stopped walking.

"No. I want to know why you hit him."

"Yeah, Tom, tell her about your short temper."

"The last thing I would think you'd want is for her to know what you think of her." Tom growled at Shawn hoping that the idea of what he said yesterday would get back to her. Unfortunately Shawn saw the scene playing out better than he could have imagined.

"Hey, from the looks of how cozy you two are I may not have been wrong yesterday. Was I right about her?"

Tom tried to punch Shawn again, but Kaitlyn blocked it, stepping in between them.

"What is going on?"

"Apparently, you're a good lay and Tom here took the test drive." Shawn said.

"What?" Kaitlyn scoffed her eyes peering into Tom's who immediately looked guilty and angry.

"It wasn't advice," Tom said. "He's turning everything around. He and his buddies were talking about you…"

"And you set them straight?" Kaitlyn asked with doubt.

"Yeah."

"So what did you say? Did you make something up or just decide to find out for yourself first?"

"What? No! That's not what I meant." Tom spoke.

"I thought we shared something special, Tom. I didn't know you were a locker room gossip!" Kaitlyn growled.

"I'm not and you know it!"

"You can cry on my shoulder, Kaitlyn" Shawn cooed.

Tom began to throw another punch at Shawn but Kaitlyn blocked it again, putting him in his place. She stood in front of Shawn, protecting him from Tom when Shawn spoke up again.

"It's okay, baby, I'll be better than him." He patted her on the butt.

Kaitlyn received a telepathic message from Tom adding exactly what Shawn said yesterday to deserve that punch in the nose and Kaitlyn couldn't help but turn back around and punch Shawn on his already bandaged nose. Shawn fell to the floor again, blood soaking his white bandage as a nearby teacher started their way just in time to hear Shawn scream out loud.

"You can have that bitch. She isn't worth the trouble!"

The female teacher heard this and was astounded. She picked Shawn up off of the ground by his ear and led him to the principal's office.

"You should be ashamed of yourself! Saying such things about that sweet girl!"

Kaitlyn shyly turned to Tom. "I'm sorry I doubted you."

"Me, too."

"But you can understand why I got so upset, right?"

"Yeah, I suppose."

"Okay, you two, have we forgotten that this is school and you are late for class?" Principal Green said, as he walked up to them in the hallway.

"Oh, yes sir. Sorry sir." Tom said, as he and Kaitlyn took off in different directions for their first class.

During class Kaitlyn kept falling asleep again. The near fight earlier had done its job to wake her up but for some reason she couldn't keep her eyes open. It wasn't boredom; she liked this teacher and this class, but she didn't have any energy. The reason had to be what had happened last night with Tom. But that made no sense at all. How could that make her this exhausted? She was beginning to worry but she fell asleep instead.

As the bell rang signaling the end of first class, Kaitlyn stood up to leave yet felt very groggy and dizzy. She sat back down for a moment trying to collect herself when she oddly found herself begin to fall asleep again. She stood up again trying to stay awake, knowing if she moved around some she would be able to stay awake, and then she walked to her next class. Tom was already there when she arrived. He noticed she didn't look well so he went to her.

"Are you okay?"

"I can't seem to stay awake."

"Why not?"

"I'm not sure. I'll be fine though."

As the bell for class sounded Tom took his seat and the teacher began to talk. But shortly into class Tom looked over and saw Kaitlyn start to nod off again. He knew this teacher didn't like sleepers so he kept trying to wake Kaitlyn up telepathically. She'd jump awake when she heard his voice and look over at him. Then he would telepathically tell her to look at the teacher, which she did, and then she realized that the teacher had been watching her.

"Am I boring you, Miss Jones?"

"No, ma'am, I'm just..." Kaitlyn paused, hearing Tom's voice in her mind.

"Get a drink of water."

"...I just need to get a drink of water." Kaitlyn finished her sentence to the teacher.

"Okay, you're excused, but when you return I had better have your undivided attention."

"Yes, ma'am."

As Kaitlyn stood, hiding another yawn behind her hand, she looked over at Tom. She telepathically spoke to him as she walked out the class.

"What? I can't help it."

Kaitlyn stumbled down the hall to the water fountain. As she leaned over to take a sip of the water the symptoms became drastically worse. A hot flash swept over her body, her vision blurred, and then suddenly everything went dark. As her muscles gave out on her, her knees buckled and her body went limp, she fell and hit her head on cold hard cement.

Tom was sitting in class wondered what was taking Kaitlyn so long when curiosity got the better of him. He tried to contact her telepathically but she didn't answer, this worried him. He excused himself from class and went to find her. As he walked out into the hallway he saw Kaitlyn on the floor, and looking closer, he saw a small puddle of blood under her head.

"Kaitlyn!" he yelled, as he ran to her, sliding on his knees next to her. Other classes heard the scream and a few students came out to see what was happening as a teacher walked out to see what was going on Tom cried out.

"Call an ambulance. She's bleeding!"

The teacher sent a student to the nurses' office and then went to Kaitlyn. Tom was frantic. Had Kaitlyn been so tired she fell asleep standing up and then fell to the ground? It couldn't have been from yesterday, could it? It had to be something else. Had he pushed her too hard? Been too rough with her training? Was she really ready to learn all of this? Was he wrong to train her?

He was envisioning the worst. He didn't know what to do when she finally came to. Slowly, her eyes opened. She looked at Tom, his heart sank.

"Kaitlyn, what happened?"

"A dream. My father's in trouble!"

The nurse was running down the hall towards them, and Kaitlyn heard the teacher tell the nurse that she had fallen and hit her head and she was awake but talking nonsense. Kaitlyn decided to keep her mouth shut for the time being.

As she began thinking back to the happenings of the morning, she wondered if her sleepiness was a vehicle to the dream. She prayed it was just a dream, but her pounding heart and partial headache seemed to intensify the situation. Kaitlyn knew if the dream was real she had a very limited amount of time to act upon it.

"Kaitlyn, sit still," the nurse suggested, but Kaitlyn's head itched and she scratched it and panicked when she saw the blood on her fingertips.

"Oh, my god."

Tom took her hand trying to comfort her, but with all these people so close she couldn't handle it all. The room began to spin and she couldn't find anyone in it. Suddenly it became hot in that hallway and sweat began to form on her forehead. Tom tried to talk to her but by now she couldn't hear anything. Before she knew it her eyes rolled back and all went black. Kaitlyn passed out again.

Chapter 11

Kaitlyn woke up in the nurse's office. Two paramedics hovered over her asking questions she couldn't quite make out. Just then Tom came into view and Kaitlyn found the strength to speak.

"Where's my father?"

"They left a message at his work. He wasn't there."

"I have to find him." Kaitlyn tried to sit up but the paramedics pushed her back down onto the table.

"You must remain still for awhile. You had quite a nasty fall, but from what we can tell you'll be fine." Kaitlyn listened to what the paramedic said and then as one turned to get something, she looked at him angrily for making her lay back down if she was supposed to be all right.

"But my dream…" Kaitlyn remembered and turned to tell Tom about it, but before she could explain she was interrupted again.

"Just lay still young lady," the man ordered.

Tom took Kaitlyn's hand into his and looked into her eyes. He then telepathically asked her "What happened in your dream?" Tom's voice resounded in her head much louder than it ever had before and it echoed over and over again like shards of glass piercing the walls of her skull. It made her head pound with a migraine so bad that it scared her.

Freaking. She grabbed her head and cried out. "Stop! The voice hurts!"

The paramedics went to her again and pried her hands away from her head wound, then constrained her to the bed. She fought them, kicking and screaming, pushing them away in a panic, easily over powering them, she pushed them away. Tom suddenly realized she was scared and determined to get to the bottom of her dream. Kaitlyn leaped from the table after knocking the paramedics away and stood up straight. She felt light headed, wobbly, and nearly fell over, but Tom steadied her. She looked at him with tears in her eyes.

"I need out."

He knew what she wanted and so he pushed by the nurse and walked Kaitlyn out of the room. Once outside, the sunlight on the white cement blinded Kaitlyn like a million knives stabbing her eye sockets. She fell to her knees and screamed again.

"Oh, it hurts!"

"Maybe we should go back inside!" Tom suggested.

"No, my dad's in trouble!"

"I'm sure he's fine."

"I'm not!" Kaitlyn yelled, looking into his eyes to assure him she wasn't crazy. "Tom, please help me."

Tom hesitated and then heard the paramedics coming after them. He picked Kaitlyn up into his arms and carried her. She buried her face into his chest, eyes shut tight, and Tom carried her to his car.

"Where are we going?" He asked as he jumped in.

Kaitlyn put her hand up to her pulsing head and forced herself to remember the dream.

"Sharks."

"Sea world?"

"No. Loan Sharks, gangsters."

"Okay, what are they doing?" Kaitlyn thought for a second longer and then spoke.

"Beating him."

"Your father?"

"Stop! Stop it!" Kaitlyn pleaded to the men.

"Tell me where they are."

"The armoire."

"What?"

"The armoire in dad's room."

"They're at your house?"

"They're punching him." Kaitlyn yelled again, her eyes still closed.

Tom wasted no time. He popped the clutch and screamed out of the parking lot towards Kaitlyn's house. He reached over to hold her hand but she jerked away from him. He wasn't sure what was going on, but Kaitlyn had saved his life from a dream many months ago and he wasn't about to let her loose her father because he didn't want to believe her.

As they approached her house, Kaitlyn cried harder. She rocked back and forth in the passenger side seat and pressed harder against her head with both hands.

Tom saw blood drip from her fingers and he knew she was hurting herself, possibly tearing the fresh scab. He reached over with his free hand and tried to pry Kaitlyn's hand away from her head. She unknowingly retaliated by slapping at the air to get him away but accidentally jolted the steering wheel downwards making the car go right. Tom grabbed the wheel with both hands trying to regain control of the car and barely missed a black Chevy Camero with tinted windows speeding towards them, leaving Kaitlyn's house. Tom recognized the car from a previous day at Kaitlyn's house, and he started to worry Kaitlyn could be telling the truth.

As Tom's car skidded to a stop, Kaitlyn's head shot back into the seat and pounded against the headrest. Tom turned to look at the Camero speed by him and he took a look at the license plate. Kaitlyn had other plans and she opened the door and fell out of the car. She crawled a few feet away from the car and then got to her feet looking down the road towards her house. Smoke was rising over the horizon where her house stood, the thought of the house being on fire and her father inside made her determined to save him. She ran, not quite sure what she would do once she got there.

She started out stumbling but each step gave her the strength to keep running and pick up speed. Knowing she wouldn't be able to stop herself once she ran inside, Tom ran after her trying to keep up. What would Kaitlyn do? Did she think she was going to put the fire out by herself?

There was a loud crash as a hand was punched through a glass window upstairs. Startled by the noise Kaitlyn stumbled over her own feet as she looked up to see her father fighting to break through the second story window.

"Daddy!" She screamed, as she saw his hand struggling to loosen the bars constraining him inside the burning building. The oxygen entering the room now had energized the fire and it shot up in front of him blocking his only exit. As Kaitlyn watched him pull his hands back into the house and then get lost in a flash of flame shooting out of the window, she charged towards the house again.

She started through the front door, but Tom, finally catching up to her, held her back.

"What are you doing?" he yelled, pulling her toward him and away from the building.

"I'm going in after him!" She yelled as she struggled in his arms for a moment.

"Kaitlyn it's too dangerous! You're in no condition!"

"Let go of me Tom before I hurt you! I'm going in after him."

Tom released her arm unwillingly and watched powerlessly as she ran inside the burning building. Fear filled him as he saw the roof shake under the pressure of burning pillars collapsing. He grabbed his phone and dialed 911. He knew there wasn't much time and he prayed that Kaitlyn would make it out before the roof came down.

The heat from the fire burned Kaitlyn's skin and the smoke burned her eyes. She climbed the stairs around the flames and began calling for her father.

"Kaitlyn, get out of here," her father choked out, coughing. "Save yourself!"

"Like hell." She kicked down the door and was attacked by the powerful heat of a wall of fire.

Tom got off the phone with 911, unsure of whether he should go in after her, and he almost danced outside with the idea of whether he should go in or not.

"Kaitlyn?" Her father struggled to get to where he had just heard her. His leg was broken and the pain shot through his body crippling his every move. He had at least one if not several ribs broken from the beating he had just received and blood covered his face, blinding him many times as it flooded into his eyes. Though the smoke was thick and the pain was searing he crawled to his feet and treaded on towards the last sound he heard from his daughter. He was just making his way through the upstairs hallway when she found him instead.

"Daddy, the roof is going to cave in!" She threw his left arm over her shoulder and pulled him towards the stairs. When he stumbled and fell to his knees, Kaitlyn reached down, lifted her 240-pound father into her arms, and began carrying him out. Heavier than she expected, she lost her footing frequently but got him to the foot of the stairs right as the roof caved in.

Tom saw the roof begin to come down, tore off his jacket, and ran inside just in time to see Kaitlyn carrying her father to the door. Tom quickly took Harold into his arms and took him out of the house. Kaitlyn followed close behind. Once they were out, Tom put Harold on the ground.

"I'm sorry," Harold said. "I did this to myself. I never should have borrowed that money.

"What money, daddy?"

"When Allison died, all the medical bills were…" He coughed. Kaitlyn couldn't understand why he said her mother's name Allison; he always referred to her as your mother, but he continued. "I borrowed the money from Lenny. I shouldn't have."

"It doesn't matter now, you're safe."

But then things changed, and Harold took her by the collar and pulled her closer.

"I am not your father!"

"What?" Her father ignored her questions and continued.

"In the tool shed... you'll find a file cabinet. Under K ...there's a news article..."

"Daddy, I don't understand." The fire truck arrived with sirens blazing, and Kaitlyn watched as the firefighters tried to put out the flames and three paramedics ran up to help her father. Her father coughed up blood.

"Help him, please!" Kaitlyn screamed. Tom took Kaitlyn into his arms, holding her, embracing her, almost trying to shield her from the inevitable.

The paramedics gave Harold CPR, injections, and oxygen, but he seemed to be fading fast. Kaitlyn watched helplessly as they worked on her father. Finally, they loaded him into the ambulance and Kaitlyn joined them. At the hospital, they took him away from her and rushed him to the emergency room. Kaitlyn was in the waiting room, panicking, pacing back and forth, and trembling with terror when Tom arrived.

"How is he?"

She ran into his arms. "They won't tell me anything yet. I'm so scared."

"It'll be all right."

A half hour later Kaitlyn's grandparents Jim & Kate walked in the door. Her grandfather Jim went straight to the front counter and began speaking to a nurse, Kaitlyn's grandma Kate went straight to Kaitlyn and pulled her into her arms.

"Grandma they won't tell me anything."

"They'll tell your grandfather."

"I am so scared."

"Me too darling. Me too."

Kaitlyn didn't know her grandparents too well. She saw them for a few weeks every summer but they always went out of town for holidays. Her grandmother had once told her that it was just too painful to stay home during the holidays, that the reminder of days with family were too difficult to bear but when Kaitlyn asked her grandmother what that meant, her grandmother would smile and ask "what?" Pretending to not know what she had been saying just a moment before.

Kaitlyn's grandparents were in their late sixties but they looked to be a hundred and twelve. Life hadn't been nice to them, they looked tired all of the time, their white hair had been white for as long as Kaitlyn could remember, their eyes always dark as if they had been crying. But every time Kaitlyn talked to them, every time she asked them a question about their lives, they would change the subject, apparently too shy, scared, or disillusioned to tell Kaitlyn the truth. They would just tell her they loved her and leave it at that.

Now as they sat in the waiting room of the hospital, praying for good news but worried about receiving bad news, Kaitlyn's grandmother spoke to her. Kaitlyn had a hard time hearing her, she spoke so softly, Kaitlyn even had a hard time paying attention, her mind racing, her heart elsewhere, worried about her father but Kaitlyn heard her grandmother's words.

"You are always welcome with us. We are your family and nothing will ever change that."

Almost twenty minutes later a doctor walked into the waiting room and Kaitlyn, her grandparents and Tom all stood and waited with fear for him to deliver his news.

"Jones?"

"Yes?" Kaitlyn said as she took a step towards him, ready to accept the outcome no matter what it was.

"I'm sorry…" He began but Kaitlyn's heart was pumping so fast it made her ears ring.

"Oh God. Oh God. Oh God." She immediately began to ramble.

"Um, I don't know how to put this." The doctor continued.

"Quickly doctor, put it quickly." She had gone almost mad with fear.

"Your father didn't make it. I'm sorry."

Her stomach dropped. "What?" Grandma Kate fell back to her chair, grandpa Jim sat down next to her, his hand on her soft wrinkled hand.

"He was beaten pretty badly. Fragments of the broken bone tore a major blood vessel. The smoke burned his lungs, the fire gave him such serious burns that his heart couldn't keep up with the blood loss and internal bleeding at such a rate he just couldn't...."

Kaitlyn denied what she heard. Throwing her hands over her ears to block out the bad news, she sobbed.

Tom covered his mouth with his hands. He remembered his father's death so well. He went to offer his shoulder for support, and Kaitlyn fell into him, trembling. He kept her from falling, when her legs began to shake below her but he offered her no words. He knew she wouldn't hear them anyway. Slowly though, Kaitlyn turned to the doctor.

"C-can I see him?"

The doctor showed her down the hall; Tom and Kaitlyn's grandparents followed her into the room. Her father looked as peaceful as someone sleeping.

"Daddy?" Kaitlyn whispered fighting back the tears. The doctor walked into the room behind her.

"I truly am sorry. We did everything we could."

"Could you all please... leave me alone?"

Tom placed his hand warmly on her arm for comfort but she didn't want it at the moment.

"Tom, please."

Grandma Kate placed a loving hand on Tom's shoulder and led him out of the room, she knew Kaitlyn needed time. Jim and Kate would grieve when it was their time to grieve, right now though, Kaitlyn had many things to sort out in her head and deal with. Kaitlyn stood next to her father's still body and she exhaled deeply, choking on her own tears as she did.

"Daddy why did you leave me? Why now? I need you in my…" She paused not wanting to say the word, "life." Kaitlyn fell to her knees and sobbed. She felt every muscle in her body spasm as she let loose the floodgate of tears that had been pushing their way out, burning her eyelids as she closed them to keep the tears in.

"What happened daddy? What did I do wrong?" She leaned up against the bed and as she bumped it, her fathers' hand dropped down to her. It was still warm but there was no pulse. She took his burnt hand into hers and held it for a second, not knowing how to deal with this. Her mother, her father, and her home, were gone. She dropped her head to the bed and atop her fathers' hand and cried some more when she had a flash, a dream while still awake.

The scene of her father being beaten by Lenny and his gang. She saw his words, his visions, and those gangster faces. She saw what they did to her father. Torturing him, beating him up, and throwing him into the closet. She heard their words from her fathers' ears, "Torch the place. Let's get back to the warehouse." Kaitlyn heard all of this and then saw her father standing in front of the brightest, whitest light she had ever seen. Smiling. He spoke to her.

"I am so proud of you. You've turned out to be so beautiful, brave, and strong. Your mother and Allison would have been proud of you. I know that this may be tough for you but I know you'll survive. You're going to be okay. I just know it."

Then as quickly as it began, the flash ended. She placed her fathers' limp hand on his chest and kissed his forehead.

"Goodbye dad." Then she turned and opened the door. Tom and the grandparents stood when they saw her emerge from the room and then Tom saw her face. Sad, dirty, tear streaked. Her eyes were dark; she had been through much today and he didn't know how to help her or where to begin. He watched as she walked up to him, took him by the jacket and pulled him into a kiss. He liked the kiss, but it was so forceful and so uncharacteristic of Kaitlyn, especially at this particular moment. It confused him. As she pulled from his lips, he watched her walk away. He was confused but as he watched Kaitlyn walk away he recognized his keys in her palm.

"My keys?" He hadn't given them to her, she just took them. He watched her flip them up in the air, catch them by the automatic keyless entry remote, and then she pressed the button. Tom looked just ahead of Kaitlyn as the lights blinked on in his car and suddenly he realized what Kaitlyn was doing. Knowing well the frame of mind she was in, the fact that she was hurt and that she had never really driven his car he panicked.

"Kaitlyn, no." He started after her but she was already dozens of yards away when he decided finally to run after her. She slid into his car and drove off, right as he arrived to stop her. Confused, he stood in the parking lot as she drove away. No one else had ever driven his car… except his father.

A moment later Kaitlyn's grandfather walked up next to Tom, staring off in the distance with him at the dust trail left by his car, all Kaitlyn's grandfather could offer were three simple words, "She needs time." Tom knew better than to think Kaitlyn would do anything crazy; he knew she needed some time alone and he knew she would be all right. He got a ride home from Kaitlyn's grandparents and they told him what hotel they would be staying in for the week. Then Tom went straight to his room. He didn't know what Kaitlyn was going to do, but he knew at least she would have the shelter of his car and when she returned she would have him and her grandparents to comfort her.

Later that night, or more like early that morning, Tom awoke by the flash of headlights pulling up into his driveway. He leapt out of his bed and rushed to the window to see his car back in its rightful place in his driveway. He rushed to his closet, grabbed the first shirt he could and dashed out of his room. He slid his arms through the white button down shirt he had grabbed but had no time to button up as he ran through the door to catch Kaitlyn. He looked over at the empty car. Kaitlyn was nowhere around it. He began walking to his car, looking past it, to the back of his house, down the sidewalk, then he spotted her sitting alone in the dark on a bench next to the great oak tree in his front yard. He walked over and sat down next to her. She spoke first.

"I'm sorry I took your car."

"It's okay, I understand." He smiled, and then added a bit of humor to help break the ice of the situation. "I didn't see any damage so we're good." Kaitlyn began crying and Tom felt foolish. "I'm sorry. I didn't think."

"I'm so lost. I don't know what to do."

"We'll figure it out together."

"Dad's dead, mom's dead... I don't know what to do anymore or where to go."

"Why don't you come inside? You can have my room, and maybe after a warm shower and a good night's sleep you'll feel better."

"I understand you're trying to help, but I can't sleep. There's too much going on in my head." She looked up at Tom. His eyes were filled with concern and caring, his heart with love. He wanted to help her, to be there for her in any way he could.

"I heard their words."

"Who?"

"I heard them say "Let's torch the place and get back to the warehouse.""

"What warehouse?"

"That's just it. I don't know. I drove all over town. To every warehouse, every abandoned building, every place I could think these evil disgusting men could be hiding out."

"But you didn't find them?"

"No." Kaitlyn quieted. Tom sat there next to her for a moment thinking, silently grateful she didn't find them for fear of her own safety, then he spoke again.

"What would you have done?"

"I don't know. I wanted to kill them."

Tom sat there silently, knowing well her feeling, knowing how he would have tried to kill the man who shot his father, or even knowing if he would have found Jed, the senior who attacked Kaitlyn, he could have killed him also. Kaitlyn leaned forward and kissed Tom, so gently, and then pulled away slowly. He opened his eyes to look at her, and she stared at him, waiting. He kissed her again, pulling her into his arms. He cradled her. His soft cotton knit shirt tickled her arms as the breeze blew past and she smelled his shampoo as she rested her head on his shoulder. She shivered. He slipped his shirt off his body and wrapped it around her shoulders to shield her from the night air.

"Your grandparents are staying in the Distance Hotel, if you want to go there."

"No I don't feel like going there just yet."

"Then come inside."

"I can't."

"Of course, you can."

"I've just got too much on my mind. Too much to do."

"Then let me help you."

"Tom I need to do this on my own, but I promise, when I figure things out, you'll be the first to know." Then she got up and walked away. Tom didn't know where she was going or what she was going to do. He wanted to follow her but knew she didn't want his support right now. He watched her walk away before he went back inside. As he lay on his bed, his eyes wide open staring at the shadows on his ceiling, he couldn't sleep.

Chapter 12

The next day at school, Tom searched for Kaitlyn. He checked her house that morning, and she wasn't there, the house was a shell of what it was. He worried that Kaitlyn left town, or that something happened to her in her vulnerable state, or she had done something to herself. He worried about all of that when he finally saw her walking down the hall towards her first class.

He called out for her. "Kaitlyn, wait up." She kept walking to her class; she must not have heard him. He finally caught up to her when she sat down at her desk. He kneeled next to her, noticing that she was freshly showered and in clean clothes, including wearing his white shirt.

"Kaitlyn, are you all right?"

"I will be."

"I was worried about you last night. Where did you go?"

"I walked around, thought about things."

"Your grandparents, did you see them last night?"

"We talked."

"Do you know what you are going to do?"

"Not really."

"Well I want you to know that if you need a place…"

"I know, Marge called Grandma Kate."

"Oh. Good." Tom said with confusion yet curiosity. Kaitlyn though had too much to deal with. "So how are you doing?"

"Tom, I know you mean well, but I really don't want to talk right now." Kaitlyn snapped at him.

"Kaitlyn it might help…"

"Tom! Just leave me alone!" Kaitlyn said so loudly everyone in class turned to stare. Tom feeling shy all of a sudden and a little embarrassed stood up and straightened his back. He stood there next to Kaitlyn's desk for a moment in silence. Kaitlyn began to feel bad but was incapable of saying so. Finally Tom spoke.

"Okay. I'll be here when you are ready to talk." He turned to leave when Kaitlyn spoke out almost in a whisper, one that Tom did not hear.

"Thanks."

Tom really wanted to help her. Support had helped him when his father died, but Kaitlyn was acting really weird. Yesterday she just took his car. He understood she needed to get away so he wasn't going to press the matter. She had intended on finding the gangsters and revenging her fathers' death, which he knew would have only been suicidal in her current state. He was glad she hadn't found them and that she had come back to him last night, but then she just left again. Then that night she kissed him like it was their last.

They were just beginning their relationship, so he hoped it wasn't that. When he was with her last night she was so cryptic, so mysterious, he couldn't figure her out, how she was feeling. And after all of that, after all she had been through yesterday, here she was at school, dressed and aware but still very much keeping to herself. He worried if she didn't express something, cry, or even yell, it would eat away at her until there was nothing left.

She didn't want his help, his compassion which he reluctantly accepted, but from the conversations around school, Tom also knew that nobody knew about her father yet and when they found out he worried how Kaitlyn would react when facing others wanting to console her. A few people asked Tom about Kaitlyn's fall yesterday, they heard that she hit her head. But her desire to save her father seemed to overwhelm the rest of the issues, and the shock over the loss of her father had made her completely forget about her head wound.

The thing Tom didn't know was that Kaitlyn had learned quite a few new things about her past last night care of her father's ramblings outside the house when the fire truck drove up and the strange dream she had while sitting next to his body in the hospital. He had said he wasn't her father but she had disregarded it as his being panicked and scared. But then when he came to her from the light and tried to comfort her he had said something else, something that she had simply thought she had heard wrong; he said, I, your mother and Alison are very proud of you. She kept thinking back to it and although she truly believed he had said I, and your mother Allison, now she wasn't so sure.

Later that day Tom asked Kaitlyn about her head, but she shrugged as if she didn't care. She acted as if nothing could hurt her anymore because she had dealt with so much pain and agony in one day. He tried to understand her, to be there for her, but she was so solitary, so consumed, he knew she was already in a bad way and he wasn't being any help to her by not forcing her to deal with the situation and grieve. He truly believed if he didn't get her to talk she would become consumed by the situation and it would slowly begin to destroy her.

"I've had a couple people asking me about you," Tom brought up during lunch. He too was worried about her head and how she was feeling.

"What do they want to know?"

"They're just concerned. They want to know how you're doing."

"How do you think I'm doing?" Kaitlyn snapped angrily.

"They don't know about your father yet." Tom realized that they weren't talking about her head but was happy she was talking about her father.

"Well they will tomorrow, Grandpa Jim said the obituary will hit the papers then."

"Oh." Tom said, a little disappointed she wasn't expressing feelings on the matter yet.

"So what are they concerned about then?" Kaitlyn asked sounding a little angry.

"You. You're head. Many of them saw the blood on the floor and that you were wheeled through the school in a stretcher."

"I'm fine. Anything else?"

"They want to know if the self defense classes are still on for today. But I said I wasn't sure if you'd be up to it with all that you've been through."

"Why not? Don't think I can handle it?"

"I know you can handle it, I just didn't know if you wanted to."

"I do. I need something to get my mind off of all of this, and it'll probably be the last class I have where people won't pity me." Kaitlyn grumbled.

"Why would you say that?"

"People pity orphans."

"They'll pity you if you let them. If you show them you're strong and you can handle it, they won't."

"But I can't handle it." Kaitlyn admitted. "Tom, just leave me alone for right now. All you're doing is confusing things." She got up and walked away. Tom didn't know what happened. She seemed sad and angry, confused and determined, and resentful all at once. He knew she was in a bad way and getting worse by the minute from not expressing her true feelings and the way she was acting only made him fear her like a ticking time bomb. If she exploded, he was the only one strong enough to deal with it.

Little did Kaitlyn know but the girls had conspired against her today. They had asked for Tom to be there, saying it was because they were concerned about Kaitlyn's head, but there was an alternate motive. Everyone wanted to see how Kaitlyn and Tom practiced together. They wanted to know if Tom held back, or was it all play. If it was all play then how did Kaitlyn get so good? So as gossip spread and rumors began, everyone grew interested in how exactly they fought. Kaitlyn had said before that her and Tom really got into it. Tom didn't ease up because she was a girl because an attacker wouldn't. And as the girls gathered for the class, Kaitlyn walked out front, Tom entered through the side door, and one of the girls who had initiated this little deception, spoke up.

"So we were all wondering if you two could teach by demonstration."

Kaitlyn was shocked as she listened to the girls' request because she hadn't expected it. As the girl went on to say that a live demonstration from Kaitlyn and Tom, playing the parts of a girl fighting for her life from a male attacker, would be a great learning tool for the class, Tom listened to it, he also visualized something else. If Kaitlyn was angry, which he could tell that she was, this just may help her release some of that anger, thus opening her emotions to the perplexity of the situation she was currently dealing with.

"It's not a bad idea," Tom commented as he walked up to Kaitlyn.

"They want us to fight," she communicated telepathically with him although the look on her face expressed the same thought.

"Maybe it would be good for you." He knew how letting his feelings out about his father had helped him, and he wanted to help her the same way. But Kaitlyn took it the wrong way.

"What's that supposed to mean?"

"Nothing." Tom calmed, seeing the anger already showing itself in her. "Just that it might help you release some of your anger."

"You have no idea how angry I am right now Tom." Kaitlyn growled feeling the entire room was gaining up against her.

"I know you need to release it."

"Trust me, you don't want it."

"Let me be the judge of that."

"Fine. You're on." Kaitlyn said slamming her fist into the palm of her hand. Tom wasn't sure if he was ready for this, but he knew it had to be done. He took a deep breath, tried to collect his own emotions so that he wouldn't over react to her attacks and then pointed to the mats behind Kaitlyn.

"We'll start there."

So they walked to the mats to the left of them and faced each other. As Tom and Kaitlyn prepared themselves by deciding the beginning move, the girls waited with anticipation for the two of them to begin.

Tom grabbed Kaitlyn from behind. He described this as the initial move, the most common grasp for an attacker. Kaitlyn slowly showed what she would do to get out of the grasp by kicking him in the shin. She struck hard though, and when Tom grabbed his leg it was for the real pain. Trying to move on and not let his own emotions control him as they were controlling Kaitlyn, he continued the slow motion demonstration even if Kaitlyn wasn't. He swung at Kaitlyn to knock her over; she sent a high kick towards his head, which he blocked with his arms. Kaitlyn gathered her balance back as Tom reached for her arm, and she allowed him that so she could spin around and flip him over her back.

Kaitlyn and Tom had practiced defense moves and attackers encounter many times in private. Kaitlyn was still allowing the anger to choose her moves, which angered Tom, because in realizing this, he also realized that she could be over taken if a man wanted to and she wouldn't be able to break free. Tom had always told her to avoid confrontation, and if you need to fight, to think. Think not only about what you are doing but what moves you are choosing to take. For in a battle of life and death, choosing the wrong move could be fatal.

She flipped Tom over her shoulder and onto the floor. She missed the mat entirely, and he could tell it was on purpose and the accompanying ooohs from the crowd helped him come to that conclusion. A few moves later she had done it again, knocked him onto his back and added a telepathic insult to follow.

"You suck."

The comment hurt him but not as much as the next kick to his neck which he quickly blocked but realized that he was being way too easy on her. She was fighting. Trying to express her anger the only way she could and he was taking it unknowingly. Kaitlyn was treating him like he was the enemy, trying to egg him on, trying to get him to hit her so she wouldn't feel so guilty for this fight, for her lack of being able to save her father. That is when he decided; he would play the enemy. If she made a wrong move, he would take advantage of it. He was going to need to teach her a lesson the hard way, it seemed this was the only way she wanted it. So as he was down on the floor, flat on his back, he swung his left leg around to the side like a break dancing move and knocked Kaitlyn off of her feet. Knowing this was only the beginning and the pace from here on would be fast and vicious, he gritted his teeth and jumped into the fight.

As Kaitlyn fell backwards, Tom jumped up and grabbed her by the back of the neck. She struggled for a second before striking his side with her fist. He let go but in a push, to knock her away from him, he didn't want to hurt her but he did want to teach her and he knew if she hurt him he wouldn't be teaching her a thing. She leaped back and kicked him again. He blocked her kick with his forearm finding himself angry at the lack of strength behind that kick.

"What a woosie kick," he yelled. She kicked him again with her right leg, putting more strength into it, but he grabbed her foot in mid-kick and pushed her off of her balance. As she fell to the floor, he yelled at her again.

"I could've twisted your foot and broke your leg. Think! Damn it."

She came at him again this time full charge, he stepped to the side, grabbing her and twisting her up into the air, and dropping her to the floor an Aikido move that she had learned just a few short months ago but had apparently forgotten. The impact knocked the breath out of her and as she coughed to force air into her lungs, he bent over to make sure she was all right. She grabbed him and with curled legs pumped him over her head and on to his back again, they were tumbling like acrobats but fighting like cobras. He had grabbed her arms while he was being flipped and now he had her in his grasp. She yanked at her arms to free herself, but he didn't let go. Finally, she yanked him to his feet by his arms, and spun him around kicking him away until his grasp on her arms loosened enough to escape.

As he was pushed away, he yelled at her again, "You're not thinking! If I was trying to kill you I could have in that last move!"

This angered her more and she picked up the pace. With Jackie Chan's speed she sent kicks and punches all of which he blocked easily and he knew her anger was making her choose these moves, these horribly un-thought out moves. With all of the time he spent with her, with all of the afternoons they spent practicing, with all of the times she expressed her need to learn, to be this bad, this uncoordinated and this inept made his blood boil.

He knew Kaitlyn was hiding her fear, he knew she hadn't cried yet for her father, he knew she had been through a lot but if she was going to be angry, if she was going to take her aggressions out on others, if she was going to start fights, he wanted her to be able to win them. Anger made his next decision and as she thrust one last punch towards him, he blocked and sent a retaliatory slap at her so hard across the face that it knocked her back five feet and onto her back. She fell to the mats, feeling her cheek with her hand and looked up at him with more defiance than before. At first he was concerned, but he knew she was angry, knew she was taking it out on him, and knew he was in danger. She charged him, hitting him in the chest like a tackling football player and knocked him to the ground. He hated what was happening but he also hated her smugness, the look of greatness on her face as she waited to see what he would do next so he decided he had to stoop to her level.

With anger searing through his veins, using leverage from his elbows he threw himself at her legs, knocking her onto her butt. She began to rise, but he knocked her feet from under her again, and she landed on her back. She rolled to her stomach to get up through a push up, but he forced her back down again. She struggled under him for a moment until she was able to free herself from him then she punched him in the jaw.

The punch stung his jaw making it throb, which made him send another slap at her. As she fell back to the floor, she looked up just in time to see him stomping up to her to finish the job, ready to strangle her, his back to the audience, Kaitlyn retaliated with every bit of emotion inside her. She threw her arms out to stop him and knocked him ten feet backwards with the sheer force of her telekinetic ability. He flew across the room towards the bleachers where the girls were sitting, and slid to a stop just shy of their feet.

The girls all gasped at the idea that Kaitlyn threw him so far and were all concerned with whether he was all right or not. They leapt to their feet and went immediately to Tom's aide but he was too angry to care about himself. Kaitlyn in noticing that she had just done that to him, had used the telekinetic ability again, snapped out of her anger trance and ran up to him also. She was shocked that it had happened again and suddenly was shocked at herself for taking out all of her pain and anger on him. This telekinetic use was exactly what she needed to snap herself back to reality but unfortunately, she could see anger and disappointment in his eyes; and that stung worse than the slap across her cheek.

"Tom, are you all right?" She asked as she ran to his side, but he grabbed her by the shirt collar and whispered in the deepest and angriest growl she had ever heard.

"Dismiss your class."

Kaitlyn finally looked up at the girls surrounding her. A rock the size of a turkey leg fell to the pit of her stomach and she immediately became nauseous with embarrassment. She hadn't even realized they were there. She had been so out of it, allowing her anger to guide her, she had been unaware. Knowing how badly she screwed up, how horrible she had just acted and how wrong she had just been she took a deep gulp and spoke rather nervously.

"Um, class dismissed."

Tom then pushed her backwards a bit as he thrust his hand from her shirt collar. He then pushed himself to his feet and stood up not taking his eyes off of Kaitlyn once. He could see she was embarrassed. He could see she was sorry. But as he heard the girls gathered around him, next to him, all he could think about was how close they had gotten to exposing Kaitlyn's abilities.

The girls slowly looked around in wonder of what had happened, if they should leave or what would happen if they didn't. As everyone slowly rose some left quietly. Others stopped to see if Tom was all right.

"I'm fine. Thanks for asking. See you all next week." He smiled to show he was all right, but Kaitlyn using her powers in public bothered him immensely.

Kaitlyn didn't know how to explain what happened, as the girls exited the gym, Kaitlyn walked to the opposite side of the room to figure things out, to find silence in a room of madness and a head of confusion. However, sooner than she expected, she got her chance to try to explain herself when she heard Tom walk up and stop directly behind her. She took one shaky breath, then spoke, still not wanting to face him.

"Tom, I am so sorry." A tear streaked down her face and she turned to face him. He looked disappointed and angry at first but then he just frowned and looked at the newly forming bruise on her cheek. He took her chin in his hand and turned her face to the side just slightly to look at it in the light. "Are you okay?"

"Fine."

"What you did just now was bad. I don't even think I know you anymore. I know what you are dealing with but you need to deal with it better."

"Are you finished?" Kaitlyn immediately felt defensive.

"No. If you would have been positioned just a bit differently for the audience to see what you did just now, you'd be spending the rest of your life as a guinea pig in some science lab underground. Your ability can't be taken lightly or used for the wrong thing."

"I know but…"

"Kaitlyn I know what you are going through. I've been there. I know what you are feeling. You're angry that he's gone. Angry that you couldn't do more to help him. You're getting angry with everyone who says they're sorry, or asks you how you are doing. All I want you to know is that I understand and I'm here if you need to talk about it."

"Tom," Kaitlyn began. "How did you get past it?"

"By learning how to release my anger, by learning how to accept it and let it go, by realizing that it wasn't my fault and there was nothing more I could do."

"I'm sorry I must have been acting a little weird." She began, but Tom simply stuck his hand in his pocket, pulled something out, and placed it in Kaitlyn's hand. "What's this?"

"The key to my house. I want you to stay with us until you get back on track."

Kaitlyn looked up at him with a tearful smile on her face; she was about to give him a hug, when she stopped and said,

"I'll talk with my grandparents, but I have a feeling they will be okay with it. Grandma Kate was very grateful to your mother when she called last night and offered that. We discussed that option last night simply for school, if I moved in with them I would have to transfer to a new school, and doing that in the middle of a school year can be pretty tough I hear."

Three days later, after the funeral, Kaitlyn returned back to her house to get away from the people and she looked around at the ruble. Standing there in the pathway to the front door she remembered that horrible day of the fire. She remembered running into the house and pulling her father out. She remembered sitting over him, worried, crying, telling him to hold on, then suddenly she remembered what he had said to her that afternoon. He had been terrified, beaten, he was bleeding to death and Kaitlyn wondered if he was just rambling nonsense, but curiosity got the better of her and she walked out to the shed and checked out the file cabinet he had talked to her about that afternoon. She had to know what it was he had been talking about.

That night as Tom finished his workout and went to his room to change, Kaitlyn walked in on him and closed the door.

"Hey babe, couldn't wait to get me alone huh?" He smiled coolly but Kaitlyn didn't pay attention.

"I have to tell you about what I found."

"What?" He asked as he removed his shirt and threw it into the corner.

"Do you remember what my father said to me that day before the paramedics showed up?"

"Vaguely, what about it?"

"He mentioned a file cabinet."

"Yeah?"

"I found the news article."

"What news article?"

"A news article that at first made absolutely no sense but after I found my journal and studied some of my dreams, and after the dream I had last night… it all makes sense."

"What makes sense?" Tom asked getting confused.

"I was adopted Tom. My father wasn't my father. He told me that day, but I didn't catch it."

"What was the news article?" Tom asked sitting down on his bed.

"Here, read it." She reached into her bag, pulled out a yellowed newspaper article, and handed it to Tom. He looked at it, noticed the date was the day after Kaitlyn's birthday and then he read the title. "Janie McFarell found after eight month kidnapping. Baby's birth her last wish."

Tom's heart sank as he read the article. An article he had read many years ago with his father. Things suddenly became clear. Things he had failed to comprehend, and as he read the first couple of paragraphs he remembered.

"Janie McFarell, a seventeen year old Mustang High cheerleader abducted from her car outside Shepherds Mall February 13th 1979, was found by police early yesterday afternoon. After a gruesome gunfight between the six abductees and the entire police department the outcome was seven dead men and three wounded. Six of those men were the abductors, and it took the police crews close to two hours to find the young McFarell. She was found in a hollowed out room of a basement and from the sight of her she had been forgotten about for some time. When police found her she was naked, nearly bald and pregnant. When found, she was skin and bones and with child. In the operating room there was talk of how to save her and the child but she said to save the baby. One doctor believes the baby was the only thing keeping the young lady alive, and when the baby was taken from her it only took moments for the loss to take its toll on young Miss McFarrell's body. Her last spoken word was a name for the baby, Kaitlyn."

Tom looked up at Kaitlyn who was simply beaming and his curiosity grew even more.

"This is horrible. Why are you smiling?"

"I'm not happy about what happened to my mother, but it explains so much about me."

"Like what?"

"Like, do you remember that day when you said I had the strength of six men?"

"Not really why?" Tom said, knowing what he said that day but trying not to get too emotional over it all.

"Why did you say the strength of six men? Why not five or seven?"

"I don't know it just came out that way."

"How about my telekinetic abilities?"

"What about them?"

"And my telepathic powers?"

"I'm a telepath and my mother wasn't the victim of a…"

"Yes, but yours was acquired by your genetic genes."

"How do you know one of your fathers wasn't a tele…" Tom stopped, realizing his words would get him so deeply involved in something he didn't want to be involved in at the moment. It would be too difficult for Kaitlyn to comprehend if she hadn't already.

"Okay, so you don't believe me about that but how about this?" She pulled out a partially charred journal and handed it to Tom.

"What's this?"

"My dream journal. I wrote down every dream I could remember in it since I was like eight. There weren't that many but five were dreams that actually were future happenings, one of which saved your life, and seventeen were dreams of my mother talking to me."

"What?" Tom asked, believing he had just heard her wrong.

"Okay, this is hard to believe and you'll probably think I'm nuts, but hear me out first."

"Okay."

"All of my life I've heard a voice in my dreams. A very friendly, young female voice. Until now, I didn't know the voice but it just seemed familiar. After reading that news article something occurred to me but I had to test it first. So I went through the remains of my house and found my journal between two charred mattresses. I found every single entry that seemed to not be a real dream and tore them out. Then I sat and played with them like putting together a puzzle. And do you know what I discovered?"

"No. What?" Tom asked carefully.

"When put together in a particular way they make a complete thought, a complete prayer."

"A prayer?"

"Yeah, look here." Kaitlyn took back the journal, opened it, and pulled out the torn pieces of paper. She read them in the order she put them in the night before.

"*I pray you will be strong. As strong as six men, those six men.*" Kaitlyn looked up at Tom and continued reading "*I pray you will use that strength to help others in need, other women in this sort of predicament."*

She stopped to ask a question.

"What predicament Tom? Huh?" She continued.

"I pray you will have every ability to do this, and so I give you all of my abilities. Take my sight from me, the sight that has grown so accustomed to the dark that I can now see no matter how dark it gets, no matter how black it is. Take my agility, the gymnastics that I learned as a child, I can not use it now."

Kaitlyn expressed this part saying it more clearly for Tom to hear. *"Take my dreams, I give them to you. My fantasies of being able to see this before it happened, so I would never have gotten into this. Use my dreams to help others, see them before they get hurt and help them. Take my mind, the mind that I use to talk to you with and share it with someone special."* Kaitlyn paused letting Tom think about that, and then continued again.

"Oh if only I could will the door to open. If only I could make those men fly off of me with the power of my mind. I may not have the ability to do so, but maybe my prayers will give it to you. The ability to move objects with your mind." Kaitlyn stopped for a moment allowing for dramatic effect then she explained something.

"The dates range between May of 1986 and Present day." Then Kaitlyn knew she had to tell Tom the next part. "Tom I had another dream last night. A dream that allowed me to realize that everything I had written before was actually said maybe not out loud but by telepathic link between a mother and her unborn child. I heard her voice one more time, I heard the entire prayer from beginning to end, and the rest of it goes like this.

"I know you will be a girl, I can feel you growing inside of me and I feel your strength and promise. You will be everything I want you to be, I just know it."

Kaitlyn waited when she stopped speaking. Tom thought for a few moments then spoke.

"How do you know that dream wasn't brought on by reading that news article?"

"What about the previous dreams? Look at the dates, Tom. I'm not making this up. My mother had been communicating with me telepathically while I was in the womb and it was that connection and her strength that gave me this gift. Don't you see? Everything I am, I owe to my mother."

Tom thought about that for a second then he looked at Kaitlyn. With one last thought on the subject he pressed it down into his subconscious and moved on with the future.

"You may not have been bit by a radioactive spider, or fallen into a mutant gene pool, but I think our little town has its own little Super gal. I guess what we need to do is figure out what abilities you do have and work on them. I mean, after all, it was your mothers wish."

Kaitlyn smiled because Tom believed her and she gave him a hug. As he hugged her back, he wondered what her future had in store for her. Would she be safe or always in danger. From that moment on he decided he would work towards matching her strength and telepathic abilities so he could always be there for her no matter what happened.

Chapter 13

It had been a couple of months since Kaitlyn's father's funeral. Kaitlyn now lived with Tom and his mother. Marge had been very kind and compassionate to Kaitlyn buying her clothing and taking care of her needs. Kaitlyn's grandparents helped out financially, however all of this made Kaitlyn miss her own mother quite a bit. The longing for her own mother made her think of her adoptive father's murder, and it brought back all of the memories every time; memories she was unwilling to deal with.

Kaitlyn had spent quite a bit of her free time at the police station, telling them everything she could, but all she ever got from them was they would take her information and see what they could do. "We'll be in touch." Was all they would say which the first few times kept Kaitlyn hopeful, the next ten, not so much. Kaitlyn wasn't sure anything would come from all of this. She also didn't believe they were actually working on the case and this angered her deep inside, more so than she realized.

Kaitlyn knew it wasn't Marge's fault that all of this happened, so she never took her frustrations out on her. She was always very kind and Kaitlyn appreciated how understanding she could be. But the memories, the loss, it seemed to keep Kaitlyn in a funk. Tom, being so close to Kaitlyn, seemed to be the easiest output for that emotional turmoil, and whether he realized it or not, he was her friendly punching bag.

Kaitlyn had taken up the game room, using a very nice Papason Chair for her bed. She shared Tom's bathroom, and they created a very ingenious schedule for it. Every so often one couldn't follow the schedule and they ended up walking in on one another but although awkward, they just went on unfazed. They had decided before Kaitlyn moved in that they would remain platonic, despite already sleeping together. Tom had decided that the idea of them living together in his mother's house and having sex wouldn't be proper. Tom thought it would be best for them to go back to just being friends so nothing would come between them or make Kaitlyn's living arrangements uncomfortable.

The plan seemed sound, and fairly agreeable although even as he said it, Kaitlyn gave him a look like, "We'll see about that."

The sexual tension was high though. Kaitlyn thought it'd be fun to stay with Tom even in a platonic way, but it had proven to be more difficult than she imagined. At night, on the couch together watching a movie, the moon shining in on them through a nearby window, during a time when they seemed to be getting along so well, it was just too much temptation for a person too handle and they broke their own rules more than once.

Other times, as Kaitlyn was just getting out of the shower, Tom would accidentally walk in on her. He would apologize and cover his eyes but she was so beautiful he couldn't help but look. Kaitlyn would playfully try to push him back out the door, but when her wet body touched his, he couldn't help but scoop her into his arms and ravish her.

Those were the good times. The times Kaitlyn cherished. Times when the day had just started and there wasn't a thought in her head about her father. Or times at the end of a busy day when she had successfully made it through a day without thinking of her father; usually a weekend. Weekends were the easiest. There were chores yes, but there was off time. Time to play, go out, explore, hike, just be with Tom where she could be herself; the self she wanted to be and escape. Not deal with the realities of her life.

Sunday's was church, getting dressed up, socializing, lunch after, those were good days as well. Marge always fixed a wonderful dinner that evening, the weekends were relaxing. Unlike the weekdays.

Weekdays were school. Friends and social clicks, gossip and stares. Everyone who knew Kaitlyn before her father's murder knew her after. Watched her arrive at school the days preceding the funeral and stared waiting to see her cry. Some, whether truly concerned or truly spiteful would ask her how she was holding up, how she was doing.

"Fine." She would give them but then try to walk away. Sometimes it was enough, but other times, they would force their way into her emotions. They would say are you sure? Do you want to talk about it? They would bring up memories they had of her father. They would mention driving by the rubble that had been her house. Whatever the topic, they would push further into it.

Maybe they didn't know the pain she was in. Maybe they really were concerned and cared. But the fact of the matter was, at least in Kaitlyn's case, it pained her more than words could express to think about what happened. Remember her father, think about her mother, relive that day in the fire, hearing her fathers' final words, actually deal with these emotions.

"No I don't want to talk about it? What are you sadistic?" Kaitlyn would bite the persons head off.

"I just thought you'd want…"

"That's the problem, you didn't think! If you would have been thinking you would have realized that this topic is painful and avoid it. But no! You have to bring it up. You have to remind me; in front of all of these people."

To Tom, it seemed she wouldn't even try. She refused to deal with these emotions. She refused to accept what happened and let it mold her, strengthen her. "What doesn't kill you…" he'd begin, but the end of that phrase would always fall on deaf ears.

The first few weeks he coddled her, he went to her, he held her while she cried. He stepped back when she pushed away. He accepted that she didn't want to talk about it and he avoided the subject carefully. But as the weeks turned to months and Kaitlyn would watch a father daughter commercial and sigh heavily or leave the room, he realized she needed to deal with it; it was time.

This was when the tales turned. Tom at first tried kindly to encourage her to talk about it, maybe with him, maybe with a counselor, but talk about it.

"Why? It happened, he's dead."

"But you haven't dealt with those emotions."

"Dealt with them? I've been to the police station a dozen times adding more details to the case, checking in on their progress."

"You're looking for resolution and you may never get it. You need to find another way to deal with it."

"May never get it? You mean I'll go the rest of my life knowing that my father's murder is still loose on the streets? I think not!"

"I'm just saying these emotions, this anger... you need to find another way to release it."

"Like punching on someone? I can do that. Step up."

"Kaitlyn..."

"Come on Tom. You afraid?"

That was when it began. Kaitlyn had subconsciously turned Tom into the bad guy, the punching bag, the second jar for her spillover. They fought that afternoon, and when she was exhausted she fell to her knees in his arms crying, which made him feel she had made progress, but the next day was a repeat occurrence. The third day another repeat. She was expressing her anger, releasing her tension, but she had stopped crying at the end. She was walking away from a battered Tom smug. He knew now, he had to fight back.

The problem was, when he did, it made her fight harder. She fought as if she was trying to survive. The fight or flight response kicked in without the flight. She grew angrier, this wasn't helping and it was devastating their relationship; tearing it into painful shards of glass. He put a stop to it, the fighting, but to Kaitlyn, it felt like he had given up.

"I'm not going to fight you." Tom began the next day.

"Why not? It was your idea."

"Well I'm putting a stop to it."

"What happened to deal with it, let it out?"

"Find another way."

"Like what? Maybe I can teach Sam the bully a few lessons." Kaitlyn would smirk.

"So you will become the bully? Is that why I taught you to fight?

"No. But…"

"Why don't you go back to teaching your self-defense class?"

"They would ask me about it…" Kaitlyn would begin referring to the day of her father's murder.

"Then tell them."

"Tell them what? I had a dream that led me there?"

"Then don't tell them."

"Oh you're helpful."

"All I am suggesting is try to do something that makes you happy."

"Happy? How can I be happy?"

"And that's the problem, you are refusing to let go and move on. You're pushing people away."

"You would know. You did the same thing."

"Yes, but I got back to my wrestling, and that helped."

"Well I'm not you. And it won't help."

Tom couldn't even suggest that it might, he couldn't get through to her. She would just walk away so she wouldn't have to continue the conversation or deal with it, or admit he might have a point. This caused a lot of friction between them; and while Tom wanted to help, he also wanted it to end.

They couldn't stop arguing. They went from lovers to fighters without even trying. Tom, in an attempt to skirt the true problem would focus his attention on other things that was upsetting him about Kaitlyn. He'd complain that she wasn't eating right, not exercising enough, and getting too much sleep. Kaitlyn grew intolerant of the griping. The more she told him so, the more she expressed her anger, the more he took it as selfishness and got after her even more.

Kaitlyn couldn't express her feelings without yelling or crying. Tom tired of it quickly, so the more he yelled back at her, the angrier she got. Everything seemed to be going wrong and soon she took it out on anyone in her way.

"What do you mean too much sleep?" Kaitlyn yelled at Tom.

"You sleep thirteen plus hours a day. You're school work is slacking off."

"Thanks for noticing, daddy." She would say to Tom with spite and angry sarcasm.

"You're skipping classes, won't restart your after school lessons; everyone is worried about you."

"I'm dealing with a very strong case of depression. Everyone at school seems to realize it except for you."

"They feel sorry for you and you're soaking it up like a sponge. I thought you didn't want that but it seems to me that you do."

"Why shouldn't they feel sorry for me? I lost both parents, my house my belongings! Found out I was adopted in the first place…I feel like I don't have a single friend in the world and all I get from you is complaints."

Tom shook his head. "You do have friends, if you'd just stop blaming them and let them help."

"I don't blame them."

"Then why do you take it out on them?"

"I don't!" Kaitlyn yelled, almost crying now.

"You do. Admit it."

"I don't blame them. I blame you!"

"Me?"

"You've been like this authority figure for me which I know is just because you care but you never asked if I wanted it. You get after me all of the time. I don't eat right I don't sleep right I'm not studying hard enough. And then there's the other stuff. I'm not trying as hard on my training, I don't practice enough with the mind control, and God forbid if I try to even discuss the telekinetic ability with you, which is starting to tear me apart from the inside out. It's beginning to seem that you are more jealous of me, than worried about me."

"That's a crock of shit and you know it."

"You think I haven't seen the way you act when I mention it? You get all nervous and twitchy. I don't doubt that you worry and I'm not saying I know what's going on in your mind, but actions mean a lot and you're beginning to not *mean* that much to me."

"So, what? You want to break up? This isn't working out for you?"

"Break up? I didn't even know we were going together. You keep everything about us a secret. I don't know what's going on between us most of the time. Don't let anyone find out the truth about our powers, and lets make sure no one finds out about our relationship either."

Tom tried to calm her. "I thought we were taking it slow."

"Why wasn't I involved in that decision?"

"I thought that's what you'd want, to be left alone while you discovered yourself."

"I have discovered myself! I am a homeless orphan who's boyfriend doesn't even like to touch her unless their fighting or he's horny!"

"That is so not true."

"Then touch me."

"You're behavior has been erratic ever since your father died."

"Touch me!"

"Why so you can push me away? That's all you've been doing."

"All I've wanted from you is a little compassion!"

"No, all you've wanted is to just give up and I'm not going to let that happen."

"You're not helping me." She finished. "You sit there in judgment over me like you're better than I but you have no idea what I'm going through!"

Tom's face reddened. "I lost my father too! I know exactly what you're feeling."

Kaitlyn turned to leave when Tom continued to yell at her.

"Don't walk away from me when we're talking."

"Don't tell me what to do!"

"You're anger is only going to get you killed. I thought you were past that."

"You don't know do you?" Kaitlyn asked, gritting her teeth." I am so angry with you I could take your head off with a single thought but I'm controlling my anger the best I can and it is so hard. It's so hard to keep under control and still get yelled at by you." She turned from him to hide her tears and continued. "I needed you to be understanding, to help me through this with friendship, with kindness. I needed someone to be there for me, to love me, to be nice to me because they cared not because they pitied me. But you couldn't do that could you Tom? You can't involve yourself into an emotional relationship can you? You have to be in control or else you're not going to allow yourself to be involved." She turned to him so he could see her pain. "You are the only one who has made this hard on me. Yes I do blame you."

Kaitlyn stormed out of the house and past Marge who was just coming in from work. Marge said hello as Kaitlyn walked past. Kaitlyn forced a smile. "Hi Marge."

Marge noticed the tears and grew concerned. "Kaitlyn?" Marge asked, before turning her attention to Tom. "Tom? What was that all about?"

"Nothing, mom."

"You know when you're father died, you were angry at the whole world. You blamed everyone that tried to help you."

"Mom, this is different."

"Is it? You wouldn't leave your room. You wouldn't eat; you wouldn't go outside and play with your friends. I was worried sick about you. I sent you to camp since it was summer break. I sent you to camp to help you get past this, to move on with your life and you were so angry with me. You swore I was trying to get rid of you. You swore I didn't want you around, but do you remember what you said when you got back from camp?"

"No."

"You thanked me. You said that what I did for you was the best thing I could have ever done."

Tom thought about that for a second then smiled.

"Thanks mom." He gave her a hug, and then he went after Kaitlyn.

He now knew what he had to do to help her. He drove to her old house and saw her standing near the ruins. She stared at the rubble, and when he got out of his car he saw the real reason she was here. She stood there for a second longer then lifted her right hand and shot it forward to the house making a piece of burnt wood fly off the rubble into the air and fall back down again. It was amazing to see, even if it didn't fly that high, and didn't shoot that fast. She didn't have great control over the objects, but he knew immediately what she was up to and he also knew she shouldn't be doing this out in plain sight.

"Kaitlyn?"

Kaitlyn had just lifted a piece of a copper metal pipe into the air, trying to control it, when her concentration had been distracted by Tom's word. As she turned to face him, the pipe flew directly towards Tom like a large arrow just released from a bow. She wanted to stop it but didn't know how too. She hadn't practiced stopping the items, just throwing them. She panicked.

"Tom, look out!"

Tom dove to the ground to avoid the projectile pipe, and turned to see the metal pipe hit a tree like an arrow hitting the target. He looked up at Kaitlyn with true anger in his eyes. He could tell Kaitlyn didn't mean to hurt him and she was sorry but that didn't help things. He got to his feet and walked up to her. She began to apologize but he wouldn't let her. He spoke to her defiantly and angrily. Barking his words in a way that demanded respect and attention. Kaitlyn knew he meant business.

"You go around complaining that you're upset and no one cares. You say you have no way to let loose your anger but you do; you just refuse to see it. And now I catch you using your telekinetic powers in public!"

"No one's around here. I needed to let some of it out before I…"

"Don't back talk me, Kaitlyn. You *are* different, whether you want to believe it or not, and you have no right to act this way. You have no right to use your powers in anger and you have no right to apologize. You have been moping around here taking your aggression out on the entire town."

"Tom, you don't unders…"

"I warned you not to use your telekinetic powers, that they were dangerous but you just wouldn't listen would you?"

"They are a part of me!"

"I'm tired of being afraid around you!"

"Afraid?" Kaitlyn stepped back in shock.

"I'm tired of others being afraid. And I know now what I need to do. You will leave, Kaitlyn."

"Leave?" She took one step back away from him.

"You will leave this town! You will leave my home and not return until you've fully been able to learn how to control your emotions."

"I'm not a Vulcan! I can't just turn them off!"

"You are a woman who's been given many wonderful abilities to help others, whether you like it or not. You have all of the abilities and powers of a small time super hero and with it comes certain responsibilities. People need to look up to you, not be afraid to come to you for help. There's good and then there's evil. You need to learn that."

"I can learn that here."

"Not where the entire town pities you. Not where your friends are being pushed away and fear you. You need to start off fresh in a new town and a new school. You will learn to control your emotions and powers or you will reap the consequences. Only then will you be able to move past this problem."

"Why are you doing this to me?"

"To help you," he said, then he paused and spoke with true caring. "Kaitlyn, I can't teach you how to control this because I'm not dealing with it. No one else can help you either because you are the only one like this. I'm giving you the only help I can possibly offer."

"Tom, I'm sorry I nearly hit you with the pipe." She hoped he'd accept her apology and forget this whole idea.

"I know you are, but this is for the best. You have three months until the end of school. You can transfer to the school in your grandparents' town, and have three months to get yourself back on track. If you can do it, and I have enormous faith in you that you can, you can come back for summer break and start senior year back here in the fall."

"I guess you've done a lot of thinking about this?" Kaitlyn said, completely shocked and mortified.

"It's for the best."

"I don't want to leave."

"There's one other reason I'm doing this."

"And what's that?"

"Where your grandparents live is the same town your mother was kidnapped. There will be families living there that know the truth, and know more of the story that you need to hear so that way you can move past this and on with your life."

"Sounds nice."

"Trust me it's not. The school is one of the worst ranked schools on the continent. It's going to be dangerous and hard to live there."

"Good to know you don't mind sending me to dangerous places so I can get killed."

"You're almost stronger than I am."

"So what do I do? Go to school, find out about my mother's past and send telepathic reports back to you daily?"

"Pretty much, yes."

"You are unbelievable! Why not put a collar and leash on me and walk me off of a short pier while you're at it?"

"You may not think I care and you may think I'm doing this to be mean…

"And you don't read minds," Kaitlyn interrupted.

"…But I'm doing this because I care."

"Pffft." Kaitlyn huffed as she rolled her bright green eyes and shook her head.

"You need to grow up. You need to take charge of your life and your abilities. You need to act responsibly and you need to do this without my help. You've been handed the solution to life's problems on a silver platter and that's going to change.

Life won't stop revolving because you can't handle your emotions and it's time you learn that. And since you couldn't do it here in a town you know, around people who care, then you're going to do it in front of strangers who don't care. And if you don't like it, tough, I'm tired of your abusive nature. You will change or you will never see me again."

"Oh, I'm shaking."

"That attitude is going to get you killed in the new town. Think about that before speaking next time."

"This is ridiculous."

"No, what you've been doing the past few months is ridiculous. People are afraid of you." He paused seeing she was beginning to get it. "I love you, and although you don't believe it now, it's true. And I hope that one day you'll forgive me."

"Tom I never meant to behave so…"

"I know, but this will help you. You can learn how to control your emotions, and you can learn more about your family at the same time. It's my gift to you."

"I would have accepted flowers," Kaitlyn joked.

Tom smiled and pulled her into his arms and hugged her. As they hugged he spoke again. "You'll leave on tonight's bus. Pack light and don't forget to keep me in the loop. I will worry about you every minute your gone."

He kissed her on the lips and she kissed back, her one last attempt to get him to forget but he didn't. As he walked away, past the metal pipe sticking straight out of the tree trunk, she realized in a small way that he was right. She did need help and maybe her grandparents were just the people to provide it.

So that night Kaitlyn and Tom said goodbye. Tom hurt inside as he watched Kaitlyn drive away towards her grandparents but he knew if he stopped her, if he pulled her into his arms and held her tight, something he desperately wanted to do, had wanted to do for so long, it would not help her in the long run. Whether she would ever forgive him, was entirely up to her. He prayed she would but wouldn't hold his breath. She had been through quite a bit this year and sending her away didn't seem like the nicest thing to do, but he knew it would help.

He promised to keep in touch with her, but she said she would call him if she wanted to. That was her way of staying strong. As she rode off, a single tear slid down her cheek but she quickly wiped it away. Tom had warned her that the city was nothing like this town and she would have to be strong. So she would be strong from the beginning, and no crying for the past.

Chapter 14

Kaitlyn had two things to do once she arrived in town. Secure a job, and enroll in Mustang High School. She had the entire weekend to get settled in with her grandparents and prepare herself, which she was sure she didn't need, but did so anyways. She found her room small but livable, her grandparents hadn't changed much from when Allison, her adoptive mother lived there as a teen. But Kaitlyn didn't care, thanks to the fire she lost just about everything, everything she owned fit neatly in a medium size suitcase now and that was a real eye opener.

Then, first thing Saturday morning Kaitlyn went out and started her search for work. Her grandparents told her she didn't need to work but Kaitlyn realized they lived on a fixed income and if she saw something she wanted she would have to buy it herself. Kaitlyn was pleased to find a hand written help wanted sign in a diner window just down the block. Her luck was starting to come back and as she was accepted for the job, she even felt like calling Tom to tell him. She chose not to call him so soon though.

She started work that night. She looked forward to trying something new and was excited about doing something for herself but as she walked into the diner crowded with people of all races and colors, she began to feel a little uneasy. She wasn't sure why. These were people just like her; this job would be just like her summer job at the Mac two years ago. The crowd of high school students was wilder than a bunch of zoo animals on a full moon.

Kaitlyn was a waitress now, wearing a polyester uniform, paper hat and degrading nametag. The rap was blaring, food was being thrown around the room, and the floor that she had to mop tonight after they closed at one in the morning was getting messier than the bottom of a birdcage. As many guys would smack her butt as she passed by their tables, and whistling and cat calling persisted, Kaitlyn simply envisioned herself pummeling them and it helped her move on without doing so. She knew this was a test. She had to stay calm or lose her job. She knew if she lost her job she'd lose her freedom to buy things and that she didn't want.

The impact of everything was coming to a head. She was forced to hold her tongue and take it all with a grain of salt. She would have to forget she was stronger than all of those people put together. She would have to be a normal person. One who can't throw things with her mind; one who can't throw someone across the room with a simple shove. The entire situation would make a sane person nuts and she was going there as someone already angry at the entire world.

As she made it through the weekend and prepared for school the next day, she felt it would get easier. School was a nice place. One of order and many possible friends she could make. It was the start of something that would be simple, and Kaitlyn looked forward to it. As she entered school Monday morning, her outlook changed drastically. Littered with graffiti, the hall smelled of urine while the students ran like wild coyotes in the middle of hunting season. Music blared. If you could call rap, music, Kaitlyn thought, and every corner in the place was occupied as a virtual sex outlet. Girls were all over the guys; guys were all over the girls and the nerds were the butt of every joke and push.

This place was noisy and crowded, and smelly and scary. Even for Kaitlyn, a master of every fighting form, was afraid of this place. Her heart pounded as she squirmed through the hall. The others seemed to hear it, like predators after prey. Like wolves, they broke into packs and stared at her like dinner. She tried not to make eye contact but that seemed to encourage their behavior. As she shyly passed one group, a girl knocked the books from Kaitlyn's hands. As she bent to pick them up, she held her tongue, determined to not lose her temper on her first day. This was just another Sam the bully and it didn't take much to get her started. As Kaitlyn was gathering her books another guy spoke out.

"Mmmm, Mmmm, Mmmm. Fine ass!"

Kaitlyn spun her head with murder in her eyes, which only tempted them more.

"Ah, I think you upset her." They laughed at him. Kaitlyn quickly swallowed the anger, looked away from them, got back up with her books, and walked away. She had to meet with the Principal first thing this morning and she didn't want to go in there with fire in her eyes. What kind of message would that send the guy?

"Jones, Kaitlyn. Small town, good grades, until your father died. Sad. You live with your grandparents now?"

"Yes."

The Principal continued to read her file. "Said here you left because you were angry and needed a new start?" the Principal said with a question.

"It's a long story." Kaitlyn admitted.

"Long story, huh? Is this long story going to be taking any of its anger out in the halls of my school?"

"Principal Johnston, I came here to learn how to control my anger."

"Not the best place to calm down."

"I don't need to calm down; I need control. I need to be able to control myself in the toughest situations."

"Brave girl." He continued to scan Kaitlyn's school records. "Says here you were teaching a self defense class?"

"Yes, sir."

"You qualified for such a task?"

"I did kind of. I was taught by a friend, then the girls of the school wanted to learn as well, so the principal set up part of the gym for our afternoon classes."

"Interesting, we could use something like that here."

"I'm not here about a job. I just want to finish my junior year."

Later that day Kaitlyn again became the butt of aggression from the other students of the school. They bullied her, tempted her, teased her, and took advantage of the situation because she refused to fight back. Kaitlyn had to be strong; she had to avoid her urge to fight. But each time she eluded confrontation, it all seemed to get worse.

Two very dark-skinned girls, twins, were the most aggressive towards Kaitlyn. They seemed to be the head of all of this anarchy, and not even the school officials could control them. They were the ones who sought the attention, thought of the jokes and were head of the bully gang. They chose who was in and who was out, and for the new girl, Kaitlyn, a white girl who dressed like she was better than they were; she was not only out, but the main ring circus for attacks.

As Kaitlyn walked down the hall to her locker that day, the two girls blocked her way. As Kaitlyn politely asked them to move away from her locker she was shocked that they did. That's when she saw her locker had been ripped from the wall. It just wasn't there anymore. Kaitlyn wanted to fight, but she knew if she said something negative, there would be confrontation. Kaitlyn was trying to keep negative confrontations down for her sake as well as theirs.

Kaitlyn decided that maybe she could get past all this. Maybe if she showed some spunk, some coolness, they would stop harassing her and finally accept her. She smiled.

"Funny, I thought I left my locker here. I guess it got just as tired of school as we do."

"You trying to be funny, new girl?" one of the twins spoke, obviously not impressed.

"I suppose."

"Don't try to be funny. You're not."

"Why won't you give me a chance?"

"Why should we?"

"I haven't done anything to any of you to deserve such a rotten welcome."

"You're weak, and the weak don't survive."

"And what makes you think I'm weak?" Kaitlyn said, feeling her strength growing inside of her.

"Step outside and we'll just see who's the weakest."

Kaitlyn really wanted to put these two girls in their places but she knew better. If she fought them, she would suffer the consequences, both from the administration and from the students and the girls themselves. A fight would solve nothing, because no matter how strong someone is, they can't fight constantly with hundreds of people without rest and that is what it would happen. Kaitlyn remembered Tom's words that she is special, and excused herself from the confrontation.

"Where are you going new girl?"

"To class."

"What about finishing this?"

"It doesn't need to be finished today, or that way."

As she walked away she felt proud of herself; she had avoided confrontation just like Tom would have wanted. She was walking away feeling really good about the situation when someone threw a small paperback book at her. It hit her between the shoulder blades. She stopped in her tracks. She wanted to turn and face them, fight them, she wanted to get even, to teach them a lesson and she wanted to let out some aggression. However, she took a deep breath and continued to walk away.

As the cat calling, mean names and insults continued, she kept walking and forced herself to block them from her mind.

She wanted to do something, even scream, and the more she held back, the more she wanted to cry. She wondered how something so dumb could get her so riled up but it was her duty to keep in control.

Later that night as Kaitlyn worked at the diner that same group of kids and the twins walked inside. Kaitlyn knew there would be trouble but she needed this job. She walked up swallowing her pride as she did, and asked them as politely as she could.

"What can I get for you today?"

"Cheese burger, fries, coke."

"Yeah, same for me."

Kaitlyn was shocked; they were polite and didn't pull anything. Maybe tonight will go smooth, she thought. When she brought the food later, they turned mean.

"Hey, I ordered a hamburger."

"No, you said cheese."

"Customer's always right. I ordered a hamburger!"

"Yeah, me, too!" came the response from the other twin. Kaitlyn knew they were getting back at her. She bit her tongue and took the burgers back. As she brought two new burgers, they spoke again.

"What took you so long, huh? You mess up our order and then take your time at getting our food out to us? Is this a prejudice thing?"

"No, I'm just busy tonight." Kaitlyn explained; knowing it wouldn't help.

"What? You back talking me girl?"

"No."

"I don't want this. I don't like your attitude girl."

"You'll have to pay for that. You did order it."

"I ain't paying for shit girl. You pay for it." The overweight twin bellowed as she threw her burger on the floor. Kaitlyn was about to explode when the manager came out.

"What seems to be the trouble here?"

Twin number one spoke up first. "This girl here gets our order wrong the first time, complains as she takes it back, and then takes her time getting it out to us. It was cold when she brought it to us."

"That is a lie!" Kaitlyn screeched.

"How did it end up on the floor?" the manager asked.

"You accusing us of somethin'?" the other twin asked. He stared at the girls patiently but with a frown. "We ain't payin' for nonedible food!" the same girl added.

"Then don't pay," the manager almost yelled. "But please leave this restaurant before you disturb my other paying customers."

"You kickin' us out?"

The manager was almost rude." You're not eating, and you're not paying, so you're leaving."

As they got up and marched out, they splattered their drinks on the floor, making both Kaitlyn and the manager step back. As the two girls walked out the door, Kaitlyn turned to thank the manager for his help. However, once the girls were gone, he turned and yelled at Kaitlyn in front of everyone.

"If you ever mistreat one of my customers like that again, you'll be fired! Now go home and cool off!"

"But my shifts not over."

"It's over!"

Kaitlyn walked solemnly out the back of the diner, so furious she could barely see straight. She was so angry she could punch down a brick wall with her bare hands and then cry herself a river. Her emotions were on a rampage; she was ready to give up when she saw her saving grace through a window. To her extreme left, Kaitlyn saw a large punching bag hanging in a corner of a dingy old gym. She knew if she could take her aggressions out on that bag she'd feel a lot better and not have to worry about destroying other people's property. She walked inside the gym.

"We're closed!" a grumbling voice said from a separate room.

"I'm sorry. I wanted to ask you a question?"

An old white haired man wearing a 1950's brown suit walked out from his office along with a middle -aged buff man wearing a tight black tank top and jeans.

"This isn't a very safe neighborhood for a girl like you." The old man began once noticing Kaitlyn.

"I'm fine."

"I can see that," the younger man said as he checked out the small-framed brunette standing in front of him.

"Whatcha want to talk to me about?" The owner asked.

"That punching bag." Kaitlyn said, as she pointed to the dusty bag hanging from the ceiling in the corner.

"What about it?" the younger man asked.

"I'd like to use it from time to time."

"Membership is two hundred dollars a month." The old man added quickly.

"Kind of pricey don't you think?"

The younger man walked up to her looking her up and down. "We can come up with another arrangement if you'd like." He circled Kaitlyn like a hungry vulture.

"Like what?" She asked curiously yet knowing exactly what was spinning through his pea-sized brain. He slid his finger down her arm.

"Whatcha got?"

"Please, don't do that." Kaitlyn said, as she rotated her shoulder away from him and twisted to look at him.

"What? This?" he said, rubbing her arm again.

"I asked nicely. I won't ask again."

"Oh, boss, looks like we got a real dangerous girlie on our hands." He circled around behind Kaitlyn.

Kaitlyn stood her ground just waiting for him to do it again so she could teach this punk guy a lesson when she got her chance. He grabbed her from behind, and it was exactly what she needed. She grabbed his arm, flipped him over her shoulder, twisted him around, took his head in her hands and smashed his face against her knee then threw him backwards against a wall. As he slid to the floor looking like a whipped bag of Jell-o, Kaitlyn wiped her hands and spoke to him.

"I told you to leave me alone. Maybe next time you hear someone say that, you'll do what you're told."

She then walked up to the older man and when he took a step backwards she stopped.

"I'm not here to hurt you. I actually need your help." She said quickly.

"My help?" He laughed. "What could you need me for?"

"I've been trying to learn to control my anger."

"I can tell." He smiled; she smiled also and continued.

"I'm having a very hard time here. I go to Mustang High. I work at Mike's dinner, and I've got this group of kids out to bully me…"

"So take care of them. It sure looks like you can."

"Can we sit down for a second?" Kaitlyn asked knowing that it wouldn't be a quick conversation after all.

"Sure." He pointed to his office chair. Kaitlyn followed him in to his office and began to tell him as much as she could without exposing her true abilities or reason for being here. Not that he would really believe her; most people wouldn't, nor would they know what to think if they ever saw her real powers.

"I came here to learn how to control my temper. I can defend myself easily, I can handle myself if something comes up but it takes a stronger person to avoid confrontation, at least, that's what I've been told. The thing is, I'm losing this battle. I

164

want to kill these kids and I can't risk it. I'm sure this town wouldn't miss them…" She started but stopped in mid thought. "I need some place to let out my anger where it doesn't hurt anyone, you know?"

"I get it. What do you want me to do?"

"All I want is to come in every once in a while and punch on your punching bag."

"No problem."

"Actually there is a problem. You're technically closed now, right?"

"Yup."

"I'm sorry for keeping you here so late."

"It's okay, I was working late anyway. What's the problem?"

"I work. Every night until one thirty."

"And then you go to school?"

"I don't need much sleep."

"So you want to come in after work is that right?"

"I wouldn't dream of asking you to stay late just for me." Kaitlyn admitted.

"Tell you what. I've been looking to replace Frank."

"Frank?"

"The guy you pummeled earlier."

"Oh," Kaitlyn said, slightly ashamed of herself.

"You can take his place."

"I couldn't Mr.…"

"Call me John. Frank's a jerk. He deserved what he got. And you deserve to have a better job more equipped to your abilities."

"What did Frank do?"

"Security, from four to midnight. Then you can close the store and have the place to yourself to work out as long as you need to."

"That is really generous."

"I need the help, and I think I can trust you a bit more than Frank."

"Thank you, sir."

"Don't thank me, let's see what you can do on that bag!"

The two of them then walked over to the punching bag and John held it steady ready for Kaitlyn to hit it.

"I don't think you should hold it."

"You think you're that tough, huh?"

"Please, just stand back." Kaitlyn asked, and he did.

Kaitlyn laid into the bag. Punch after punch until the three hundred-pound pillow shimmied, shook, and nearly pulled the roof down but Kaitlyn tired out before the steel beam that held the bag up.

"Impressive."

"I had time to calm down."

"So it can be done without aggression."

"I did lay into Frank."

"Granted. Here." John said as he threw a set of keys to Kaitlyn. She caught them with her left hand and looked at him.

"See you tomorrow after school."

"Thanks, John, I appreciate it."

Chapter 15

The next day at school it seemed the twins were on a rampage. They pushed Kaitlyn around in the halls, pushed her books out of her hands, purposely tried to get her in trouble during class, and even tried to jump her after school. To avoid the confrontation, Kaitlyn ran the other way escaping the issue for only a few hours. Kaitlyn didn't know what to do. If she avoided them the aggravation would persist, if she stood up to them but held back her true abilities, they'd continue to bother her. If she showed what she really could do, she'd easily kill them.

She escaped to her new job at the gym and laid into the punching bag. How was she going to make it through three months of this if she couldn't make it through the first two days? She was almost beside herself with exasperation when her new boss John walked up to her.

"Bad day?"

"The worst."

"Want to talk about it?"

"Not really."

"It might help."

"All I want to know is; how can I just go to school, go to class, and leave school without being harassed, bullied and teased?"

"That doesn't sound like the girl I met last night."

"That's because I'm trying to get by without fighting. I shouldn't have to prove myself to be left alone by them."

"How did it start?"

"I walked through the door."

"You didn't do anything to temp them? To egg them on?"

"If I had I wouldn't be so upset."

"Well, I can tell you are a smart girl. You'll work through it.

"Thanks, at least you believe in me."

Wednesday, only halfway through the first week, proved to be the hardest. Kaitlyn was hoping, maybe, it'll calm down eventually; and suddenly it looked like it would. Kaitlyn was walking down the hall, the twins waited for her, and as they began their assault upon Kaitlyn, a nice looking guy walked up and put a stop to it.

"Come on, leave her alone. Haven't you put her through enough?"

The twins eyed Kaitlyn, and then looked at the guy. "All right Brad, she's all yours."

As the group disbursed Brad walked up to Kaitlyn and began a conversation. "You all right?"

"Fine... thank you."

"New here, huh?"

"Is it that obvious?" Kaitlyn half smiled.

"I'm Brad." He offered his hand.

"Kaitlyn."

He shook her hand then bent over and kissed it. Kaitlyn was baffled and a little surprised, but at least she felt things were going to get better. He was a good-looking guy, relatively pale looking with greased back jet-black hair. He dressed down, wearing baggy jeans and a black leather jacket and his personality was laid back. Kaitlyn hadn't seen him up until now; however after really looking at him, she assumed she wouldn't have noticed him either way.

He slid his hand through his hair, then started a conversation with Kaitlyn. "So where are you heading?"

"Class, I don't have a locker anymore. See it used to be there, but it decided to leave."

"We'll just have to have that fixed." Brad smiled wickedly.

"You can do that?"

"I can do a lot for you." He smiled with a twinkle from his eye. Kaitlyn was perplexed and yet curious. She found herself completely enamored by his charm, especially in such a horrible place. Maybe it was due to the fact that she hadn't experienced any charm in this school or that those with it were too afraid to show it, but she was relieved to finally feel she could breathe.

Kaitlyn wasn't quite sure about his intentions, but he seemed nice enough and she was grateful to have someone to talk to. After school he found her outside of her class and asked her into dinner. She didn't want to ask for time off of her new job so soon, but Brad said he'd wait. He joked about a late desert instead to which Kaitlyn found endearing. So after locking up at the gym that night, Kaitlyn met Brad at a late night diner and they sat down for a snack.

"I really want to thank you for your help today." Kaitlyn began.

"My pleasure. Your parents don't mind you being out so late?"

"My parents are, uh, dead." Kaitlyn spoke a little shy.

"Oh, I'm sorry."

"I'm getting over it." She tried to be cool, but her esteem faltered. "Slowly."

"So what brings you to this town? Our school?"

"The challenge."

"Looks like you were failing." Brad laughed.

"Actually, I was succeeding."

"At what being a loner?"

"No. That just came easy I suppose."

"You're funny."

"Thanks, I guess." Kaitlyn wasn't trying to be funny, in fact she was feeling uneasy about the conversation and emotions that went with it.

"No. I mean it. It's not very often around here I meet someone with... intelligence."

"Thank you, Brad." Kaitlyn smiled at him. Was it what he said or the way he said it, or was she finding ways to move on? She wasn't sure when he spoke again.

"Hey, you wanna go for a walk?"

"Sure."

As they walked, they talked and somehow, Kaitlyn followed Brad back up to his place. His father was out of town on business, his mother had skipped town years ago; according to Brad. Brad's apartment wasn't much to look at, but then, neither was the neighborhood. He offered her a drink, she graciously accepted a soda, and then he turned on the radio. Brad sat down next to Kaitlyn on the couch, his hand on top of hers and before she knew it, he leaned in and kissed her.

She didn't quite mind the kiss. He wasn't half-bad, but something kept irking at her about the speed this all was going. But then again, she and Tom weren't even considered a couple when they made love for the first time. "I'm sorry, am I going too fast?" Brad asked as he pulled away. Kaitlyn appreciated that. He cared about her feelings, he was giving her the opportunity to stop it, she hadn't expected that. It endeared her to him.

"It's fine." She mused as she watched him lean in to kiss her again. It was nice feeling the warmth of someone else caress her. Maybe she allowed it to continue for the wrong reasons, maybe they were the right reasons for her at the time, but against Kaitlyn's better judgment and for all the reasons that made her just want to be held, to be loved, and to be accepted, she ended the night with Brad and woke up early the next morning to go home.

Brad had said he loved her; he said all the right things, and Kaitlyn felt good about the way things trailed off that morning. She was smiling as she recalled the actions of that night when she entered the halls of the school that morning. She felt something very different about the morning, about the people, about the situation. People stared, but did not poke fun, throw things or knock her books out of her hands. The twins left her alone, and her locker, with a bad spray paint job and pretty bent up, was back in its place. She wasn't going to use it, but it seemed things were getting better at least. She looked forward to the day, to experiencing how it was going to unfold, but then it happened.

Kaitlyn headed down the hall to her class when she began to wonder why everyone seemed to be staring at her. Kaitlyn sensed something was really wrong here and an icky feeling began to build inside of her. Not knowing why she felt this way or why it made her uneasy as to everyone's supposed staring, she saw him. Brad was standing in the middle of the hall surrounded by guys, a girl on each arm. While she hadn't expected much from him in regards to the locker room gossip, she had not expected the girls.

Kaitlyn knew immediately by the goggled eyes and bump with his pelvis into the air what he was talking about; and it took only a moment before she was able to hear what he was saying, and what he said; hurt.

"Best lay yet. She was so willing to give it to me I barely had to try." The guys began to laugh which made Kaitlyn miss the next thing he said but when they stopped laughing she heard the last thing he said before noticing she was standing there. "Yeah, I bought her for a scoop of ice cream, cheapest date ever guys!"

So much for school today, Kaitlyn thought as she stood there in shock. She wasn't sure if she wanted to beat him to a pulp, scream out loud, or just cry and run away. Everyone waited for her reaction, hoping it'd be to see her cry, so she didn't give them that. Her eyes creased into a glare though, her hands tightened into strong fists, and she kept her mouth closed. She turned on one heel and walked to the door. As she neared it she slammed it open with the sheer force of her hate and walked

171

through not even sure if coming back to this disgusting horrible place was worth it. As the door began to close, she heard laughter erupt behind her and she knew she had been conned.

Kaitlyn walked straight to the gym. She dropped her books on the bench beside the punching bag and then laid into the bag. Oblivious of anything around her, which wasn't much, she beat the bag, cried, and screamed in her head to Tom that she just couldn't take it any longer. Tom was currently in history class when he heard Kaitlyn's cries and he silently and telepathically began trying to calm her down.

"Kaitlyn, what's wrong?"

"I can't take it here any longer! I can't go back to that horrible place. I can't face those horrible people again."

"Tell me what happened." Tom asked, as Kaitlyn continued to beat on the bag.

She cried silently to Tom in her head. "They're worse than the devil's minions themselves."

"It can't be that bad," Tom suggested.

"You have no idea what I've been going through! Trying desperately to hold my tongue and my fists."

"Are you behaving?"

"Did you just hear me say I'm having a hard time controlling my fists? It means I'm controlling them." Kaitlyn hollered as loud as she could through telepathy.

"Okay, fine. What did they do to you? You know you can talk to me."

"Can I really tell you the truth and not get the third degree?"

"What happened?"

"Everything!" Kaitlyn exhaled with exasperation, feeling the world was about to end.

Kaitlyn told Tom about the twins, what they've done, what they've said. She told all about the school and her job at the dinner and then finally getting the job at the gym.

"So you got a better job. Things are looking up. What happened at school today to get you so upset?"

Kaitlyn didn't answer at first; she didn't know how to say she was weak enough to allow herself to get used like that.

"Kaitlyn, you've been doing fine. What was it that made you want to contact me; today?" Tom asked again.

"I can't tell you." The last thing she wanted to do was hurt Tom and she knew if she told him, he'd be hurt. Curious why she didn't think about this before, why she just immediately contacted him without thinking about his feelings, she continued to hesitate knowing well he wouldn't give up.

"Kaitlyn, you know you can talk to me."

"I'm sorry Tom. I shouldn't have contacted you."

"Come on Kaitlyn, you called me for a reason, just tell me."

"I don't think I can."

"Then show me." Tom suggested and suddenly Kaitlyn understood. He wanted to see it rather than hear it and it seemed easier than telling him Kaitlyn quickly considered. As she thought about the happenings of the afternoon and evening she willed them to escape her and travel to him. She sent him images of the twins harassing her, and Brad helping her, then Brad talking to her, saying all the right words. She skipped over the graphic details but went straight to the hallway scene then stopped short of her leaving the school. She waited for a moment for Tom to respond but he didn't. She waited even longer, wondering if he was upset or angry. She wasn't sure if she should ask him about it, or send the images again. She began to worry.

Tom had been sitting in class, the teacher constantly asking him to tune back into her class, but the images Kaitlyn was sending him, held him hostage. When the images stopped,

Tom was still in a trance, still in shock, oblivious to the teacher calling his name. Too consumed with his own feelings on the matter to understand Kaitlyn's need to be held, to be understood. He excused himself from class without the teacher's permission and walked all of the way outside before taking a breath to calm down. But he couldn't calm down. He felt Kaitlyn's worry, her fear, her guilt but then he saw what happened. He saw how vulnerable she had left herself and allowed herself to become and it hurt him to see it. When he finally spoke to her again with his telepathic powers; he was so angry and full of rage regarding the situation, he couldn't fathom her reason for sharing. His words came to her like a gunshot: loud and painfully, and he did not hold back.

"What do you want me to say to you, Kaitlyn?" He began rather calmly Kaitlyn thought.

"Anything" she said which was not exactly what she meant but it was only one word and it seemed easy to say.

"That was a pretty stupid thing you did." He began still rather calm, however gradually getting angrier as he continued. "I don't need to tell you how ignorant that was to sleep with a man you know nothing about. It was cruel to do that act and then tell me about it knowing how much I care about you. The sheer fact that you obviously can't take a little bullying disturbs me since I was the one who taught you fight. I find myself completely disappointed in myself for not seeing this before. I'm beginning to underestimate my own beliefs in you as well as my own judgment. I doubt you have any idea how absolutely furious I am right now, and I truly wonder if you will ever have what it takes to be someone I can ever love again! You are pathetic Kaitlyn! You have no idea who you are or what you are capable of and instead of finding yourself you go and throw yourself into anyone who will give you attention."

Kaitlyn wanted to block him out, to stop hearing his attack; she had heard enough already but she couldn't make it stop. She couldn't control the telepathic power as well as Tom could. She was crying out loud now, grabbing hold of her head like it was about to burst.

"You did this on your own accord. You were the one who put yourself in this mess, and you will be the one to get yourself out. You're on your own, Kaitlyn! You hear me? On your own!"

"Tom, please..." Kaitlyn began, but Tom cut off the connection with her. She knew when he got it into his head he could keep her pleas out of it, but she had nothing more to say to him, anyway. He didn't understand her, and Kaitlyn didn't want to listen to his yelling anymore either. She fell into the corner behind the punching bag. Holding her head from the pounding and ringing, she cried out loud and hard into her knees until she finally fell asleep, a large headache pummeled her into unconsciousness.

While she was asleep she dreamed she was walking through the gym, uneasy about her surroundings. The place was dark and quiet except for bursts of voices coming from John's office. Kaitlyn slowly walked into John's office and saw a man holding a gun; he was yelling something at John who was begging for his life, his hands high into the air. Just then the gunman pulled the trigger and John fell backwards against the wall.

Kaitlyn jumped awake from her dream and knew immediately the dream was more than a dream; it was a premonition. Kaitlyn ran to John's office where a conversation was already in progress.

"Where is it?"

"I don't have it," John pleaded.

"Wrong answer." The gunman said as he began to pull the trigger back. Kaitlyn ran into the room that very second and with one quick reaction kicked the gun from the gunman's hand. The gun fired.

"Who the hell?" the gunman yelled, but Kaitlyn was still in fight mode. She quickly landed two punches onto the guy's chest knocking him backwards and kicked him on the diaphragm, throwing him into the wall. There he slid to the floor and passed out. Kaitlyn looked up at John who was still trembling and without breaking rhythm she asked him one question.

"What was that about?"

"Kaitlyn, don't get yourself involved."

She looked at the man on the floor; his smoking gun in the corner and the fresh bullet hole in the wall beside John's head.

"John, I am involved."

Kaitlyn listened as John told her what was going on. He told about this particular gang trying to scare him out so they could take over the building. That the gang ran the town, scared all of the business owners out of their goods, threatened the authorities families to stay out of jail, and vandalized everyone's possessions. Kaitlyn knew she had to get involved and she had to stop this gang. It was her duty, her unwritten destiny, and her life. Suddenly a fire lit up inside of her and she felt she had a reason to stay here, to be here and to fight back. She had to fight for the townspeople and she had to win.

After Kaitlyn had heard enough she sent John home and locked up the gym. She pulled the gunman out into the alley, and then she waited for him to wake from his slumber. As he stirred she kneeled down next to him and with her most innocent sounding voice she spoke.

"Have a nice nap, Mike?"

At first, he freaked out and quickly checked his pocket for his missing gun.

"I already mailed it to the police station with a note to check the bullets against any recent local murders. I also sent your ID with it. Hope you don't mind." Kaitlyn sang.

"You little bit..." he began but Kaitlyn quickly grabbed his throat and yanked him to his feet.

"I sure do hope you don't plan on using any negative language in front of a lady." She then threw him against the building wall. "Because I just wanted to let you know there's a new game in town and this game won't stand for it. You get what I'm saying?"

"Who the hell do you think you are?"

"The names Kaitlyn Jones. Pass that along to your boss. I'll be waiting for his response."

"You're a dead girl!"

"That's what you think!" She walked around the corner to the front of the building. The guy gathered his balance and ran after her but when he got to the corner where she had just turned a moment ago, he saw nothing. No one was on the sidewalk in either direction. No one. It was like she had just disappeared.

That night Kaitlyn checked around town and found out everyone was being threatened by this gang. She figured she had seen plenty of the gang members at school but still had no idea who the leader was exactly. She was just leaving Shepherds Mall as it was closing; the parking lot was almost empty and dark. She had gone to see if the gang hung out here as well. They did usually but not tonight she found out. She was growing curious about it all when something unusual happened to her.

A powerful rush of exhaustion swept over Kaitlyn's body and she suddenly felt the need to go to sleep. Aware that the last time this happened was when she fell backwards, busted her head open and dreamed about her father's demise, she realized this was a dream and she forced herself to stay awake. Like a flash of hot air hitting her face she began to see something happening. She realized it was something of the past, the area looked the same and yet it looked different. All of the cars were models no later than the late seventies, the parking lot seemed new, no potholes and very clean. It was very empty, barely any cars in the lot and even though there were large streetlights shining upon the few cars remaining, the area was very dark.

Kaitlyn looked ahead in her dream and saw a young lady walking towards her car. Her arms were filled with shopping bags, which made her stumble and jostle with the car keys. As she stood at her car trying to unlock it a green van drove up next to her and skid to a stop. As the young lady turned to look at them, four scruffy men leapt out from the side door and attacked the woman. It was only a fraction of a second before they had the screaming woman in their arms and they shoved her into the van and sped off. As Kaitlyn came out of the dream she suddenly realized, she had just seen her mothers kidnapping.

After a moment of thought about the dream she realized that it had only taken up a second of her time, it had been a flash. And as she regained her whereabouts she looked on ahead and saw almost the same exact scene being played out directly in front of her. Immediately realizing that this was not a flash but real life, the car was a nineties model Ford mustang, the girl was an Asian teenager and the black minivan pulling up next to the Asian teen was screaming trouble. Kaitlyn reacted immediately. She ran towards the scene as fast as she could, leapt over the Asian girls' car and kicked one man down as two others grabbed the girl.

The girl screamed. She tried to fight back but she had no strength. Lucky for her Kaitlyn was there, because Kaitlyn took down the other two men as the fourth man in the drivers seat sped away from the scene. As Kaitlyn collected the three men and checked to see if the girl was all right, mall security drove up and arrested the three men. They thanked Kaitlyn for her help but the real thank you of the night came from the Asian girl, who hugged Kaitlyn and kept crying her thanks.

Kaitlyn was pretty proud of herself that night, so much so she nearly forgot about the flash of her mother until much later that night. As everything settled down and she got back home and was finally alone in her room, she remembered that dream and began thinking about it. She had always had dreams of what was going to happen, premonitions of the future, but she had never dreamed of the past. She felt for a moment like her mother was trying to tell her something, but what she focused on more was the fact that this gang had to be stopped.

She got some rest that night as she thought things through and decided now was not the time to be evasive or shy. If people were going to take her seriously, if people were going to confide in her and tell her the truth of what was happening, they would need to trust her as well as have faith in her for being able to do something about it. She wanted to give something to this town, freedom. Sure the town hadn't been kind to or accepting of her, but this had been her mothers' town, and her mother wouldn't have wanted to see it like this.

As Kaitlyn entered the school building Thursday morning she had all but forgotten about the problem with the twins and the issue with Brad. As she entered she heard laughs from the many students that had gathered to see her reactions to Brad. On the other side of the hall there was a crowd of students who had heard about what she had done to save the Asian girl, in the center of the crowd that Asian girl stood smiling. At first, Kaitlyn didn't know what to think of it, her mind was too filled with the problem at hand with the gang. But as Brad stepped into her path she had to deal with the task at hand whether she wanted to or not.

"I can explain about yesterday," he began, trying to get her going again.

"What about it?"

"The talk, the other girls…"

"Is that what you want to talk about? Look, Brat,"

"Brad."

"Whatever. Look I've got more important things to do than assure you that I wasn't lying when I said you were good. You aren't worth it. Now if you'll excuse me." Kaitlyn pushed past him.

By now all of the kids in the hall were ooh-ing and listening intently to see what the new girl had to say about her treatment. Brad however was not ready to let this girl, Kaitlyn, put him down in front of his friends.

"Look, tramp, you may not want to break the connections you got with me or things around here will get worse for ya."

"Whatever. I'll deal with you later."

Kaitlyn waved as she walked by him and directly into the Principal's office. All the students were sure Kaitlyn went to go tattle, and they waited to see what the nearly nonexistent Principal would have to say about it. They all knew this guy was too scared to get involved and that he'd send her back out in the hall to fight her own battles.

"Miss Jones, I've been meaning to call you." The Principal started right up when he saw Kaitlyn walk through his door. "You haven't seemed to be able to make it to classes the past couple of days."

"I know and I promise to work harder on that, but right now there are more pressing tasks to deal with, Mr. Johnston. The gang, what do they call themselves, the scallops?"

"The Scorpions."

"Right, they sting you now and you die later, what a crock." Kaitlyn laughed.

"Kaitlyn, if I were you I wouldn't get involved."

"So is that why this school is in such bad shape? Because you didn't get involved?"

"You've seen those kids, the twins, they do what they want, they're not afraid of authority I don't know why I'm upset; the school is the worst in the country."

"Why is it the worst?" Kaitlyn asked sitting back in her seat.

"Most of the good teachers have left. They were too afraid to stay. Can you blame them? The cops are even too afraid to get involved with the gang activity, the bad kids have taken over... should I continue?"

"I checked the local library. This was a very good school a couple years ago. Not one of the best but it was doing well. What changed?"

"The students, I guess. They began to fight with the teachers, scared them away. They fought with the police, it became easier to let them continue rather than try to stop them and risk our lives."

"So your motto is let them be anarchists and let the gang take over. Why?"

"Why are you so interested? You think you can stop it?"

"You may not want to believe it, but I can."

"You talk the big talk, Kaitlyn, but I've seen you in the halls, avoiding confrontation, running from fights, letting them bully you."

"I told you before, I'm learning control."

"That's not what it looks like from this side of the door."

"Do you want this to happen?" Kaitlyn asked changing the subject.

"I can't stop it."

"Do you want it to happen?"

"I've been a Principal here for twenty years. I suppose its time for a change."

"Do you want it to happen?" Kaitlyn asked louder, demanding an answer.

"No. "

"Have you been threatened by the gang?"

"You don't think what's standing around in the halls is threatening?"

"I'm going to help this town."

"Okay, two questions. What makes you think you can help, and two, why would you?"

Kaitlyn knew she couldn't tell the absolute truth, about her abilities. He wouldn't understand or believe her. But she needed this man to have faith in her. She needed him to trust that she would be able to help and that she was more than capable.

"Those are difficult questions to answer but I can tell you this. I'm stronger than I look. A lot stronger. I came here to learn to control my emotions, but I'm not the kind of person to sit idly by while good people get hurt. Your town has been terrorized by some bad people and I'm going to stop them."

"Okay, but I'd still like to know what you think you can do about it."

Kaitlyn sat on the chair opposite his desk and slid it up to the desk.

"Okay," She spoke with a smile as she took the position, placing her elbow on the desk and opening her hand to accept his. "Let's arm wrestle."

"Arm wrestle? Are you kidding me?"

"No. I'm not."

The one-hundred and eighty pound man shook his head and chuckled a little as he set his elbow on the desk and stretched his hand flexing his boulder-like arm muscle. "I can bench press two-fifty. Can you?"

"I've never been sure about that."

"Why's that?" he asked, as Kaitlyn gripped his hand and they began.

"The machines don't hold enough weight."

Kaitlyn looked deep within his eyes until he turned his attention to his hand. "You can start whenever you're ready."

She smiled as she knew he was pushing as hard as he could already.

"What do you mean start?" Sweat started to form on his brow.

"You can use both hands if you want." Kaitlyn said, feeling no tension on her muscles.

"Preposterous, you're supposed to arm wrestle with one hand." He scoffed but ended with a grunt as it seemed he was losing ground.

"Okay. Whatever you want." Kaitlyn said, as she looked at her other hand like she was checking her nails. Principal Johnston looked at her as if he was annoyed she wasn't giving this her whole attention but then realized if she was, what would happen. He grew agitated and threw his left hand into the mix and began to try to pull Kaitlyn's hand down. He pulled with all of his might but she held her own.

"You ready to finish this?" Kaitlyn asked as she looked up at the man trembling with exasperation as he tried with all of his might to sway Kaitlyn's arm.

"Finish it?"

In one swoop, like he hadn't even been trying, Kaitlyn slammed his hand down on the desk. At first he was shocked, then angry, then pleased.

"How did you do that?"

"You can't see my muscles but they're there."

"What are you going to do?" The Principal asked as his mind raced with questions.

"Send a few trouble makers to detention." She smiled. The principal smiled back and then told Kaitlyn everything he could think of, starting with the twins' arrival.

Chapter 16

As Kaitlyn walked out of the Principal's office, Brad, the twins, and all of their followers stared at Kaitlyn. One of the twins spoke up.

"So you gonna leave again crying?"

Kaitlyn held her tongue for a moment. "Brat, you got a second?"

"The name's Brad!"

"Nah, I don't think so. Anyways, Brat…"

"You have some nerve!" He growled as he gritted his teeth and clenched his fists.

"I do, don't I? What are you going to do about it?" Kaitlyn egged on.

Some people laughed, but Brad was stunned. He didn't know what to think, and as the others laughed at him he got angry. He went to slap Kaitlyn for making him look stupid in front of his friends, but she expected that maneuver from him. As his hand neared her face, she blocked it with the left arm and grabbed it with her right hand. , She then spun him around, pinning his hand behind his back and knocked him to the floor.

"Brad, I know you can't be so shallow that you would attempt to hit a girl because she out smarted you. Are you?"

"I am!"

"You're shallow? I never would have guessed." Everyone began to laugh except one of the twins who stomped up to Kaitlyn ready to throw down.

"You can't just start mouthin' off in this school."

"Why not? You do."

"Who the hell do you think you are?"

"The name's Kaitlyn Jones. Learn it. You'll need to know it later."

"You can't just walk in here and run the place!"

"Why not? You did. Now I'm repossessing your leadership. Stand down before I take you down."

"We're not afraid of you. This is our school and we're kicking you out."

"I don't think so." Kaitlyn said, as both twins lunged for her throat. Kaitlyn knew these girls were the brunt of the schools problems. She also found out thanks to the principal that these girls had shown up in school just before the place went downhill, just before the gang showed up. She knew the two girls had acquired a team of followers, scared the teachers and police from getting involved, and helped the gang take over. In fact Kaitlyn was positive that these girls were very much main players of this gang and they would have to be the first to go.

As the twins attacked, Kaitlyn blocked. She was amazed at how unprepared the twins were for this fight. They walked around school like they were the best and yet all they seemed to be was talk and excess weight used for pushing people around. Kaitlyn knocked them both to the floor and waited for them to get back up again. One did. She began to stand, getting ready to throw a punch, when Kaitlyn crouched down and with a slide of her left leg, knocked the girl's legs from under her, making her fall down to the floor again. As the students laughed at what could have been a comedy skit, the twins stood carefully back up again and yelled.

"This isn't over yet!"

"I'm sure it isn't." Kaitlyn watched the two girls disappear around a corner.

Then Kaitlyn turned and walked away, heading to her first class. The students were shocked. She had defeated Brad and the twins without breaking a sweat. The rest of the bad students weren't sure if they should try to find out Kaitlyn's story or just jump her before she jumped them. The good students began to feel like things were going to get better. But everyone standing there did have one thing on their mind, curiosity as to why Kaitlyn let the twins and Brad push her around those first few days if she could have taken them down so fast.

After class it was as if it had been intermission at the theater and once everyone was back in the hallway, the show picked up right where it left off. The students' curiosity was peaked. The twins and a few others led the way towards Kaitlyn to teach her a lesson. But it wasn't going to be a fair fight, Kaitlyn could tell because a few men from the actual gang had shown up to help. Kaitlyn looked over and saw the Asian girl rooting her on with her friends but Kaitlyn knew that other than moral support she would be by herself in this and so she made a decision. She needed more room and so she led them all outside.

Once outside the crowd seemed to take its places. Spectators gathered in the outer circle, attackers gathered in the inner circle and Kaitlyn stood alone in the middle. She had no time to be afraid but she did feel her adrenaline pump through her body faster than it ever had before. Kaitlyn looked around at the half dozen people ready to teach her a lesson. She recognized the twins and Brad from the school but the other three were a little too old for high school, two she had never seen before, one she recognized.

"How's the nose Mike?" She asked as she looked over at Mike who had just touched his nose as if it was throbbing at the thought of being hit again. Mike then leaned over and whispered to his boss.

"That's the girl that did this to me." Mike said remembering that evening at the gym.

"You were beaten down by a girl? That girl?" His boss laughed out loud.

"She's a lot stronger than she looks." Mike offered but was ignored.

Kaitlyn knew this was the grand finale and she only prayed that things wouldn't get too gruesome.

"We're going to have to ask you to leave." The leader of the gang began as he pulled out a switchblade and pointed it at Kaitlyn. The others did the same and suddenly Kaitlyn felt that this fight might not be fair at all. She knew the twins were slow, she knew Brad was weak; she knew Mike would be protecting his nose and she was fairly certain the boss was all talk. The fact everyone but her had weapons was a little discerning but Kaitlyn knew she was all the weapon she'd need.

"Really? What makes you think I'm going to?" Kaitlyn countered buying herself some time to come up with a plan.

"Because if you don't there's going to be trouble."

"I like trouble, do you Mike?" Kaitlyn asked looking at his bandaged nose as if she were planning on hitting it first. Just then Mike reacted to block and protect his nose and his sudden maneuver signaled the beginning of the fight.

Kaitlyn shot a straight kick directly at Mike's groin, throwing him backwards a few feet, then sent a hard turned punch towards the second unknown guy, knocking him back. She had just slipped his knife from his hand and had grabbed the leader, shoving the tip of the knife into his neck when Brad spoke.

"Hold steady."

Kaitlyn had just apprehended the leader and held him like a human shield. "Put your knives down or your boss gets a hole in his neck."

"She's bluffing guys, take hostages!" The leader yelled. The twins grabbed a couple of the closest students near them. They screamed as it happened, but the following scream from the boss made everyone stop and look. Kaitlyn had just thrown the knife into his right foot and had taken the boss's spare switchblade and had it back at his neck ready to go.

"I'm warning you let them go," Kaitlyn hollered. The boss was near tears, he wanted to reach for his foot, to look down and see if it was still attached but Kaitlyn had a tight grip around his neck and was quickly cutting off his air supply. Still angry enough to retaliate, he gave a look down at Mike telling him to attack her. Mike was just about to when Kaitlyn hit the boss on the back of his head knocking him unconscious and sent a powerful kick at Mike knocking him backwards again.

The sudden action confused the twins and the hostages ran for their lives, and while Kaitlyn looked over at them, the third guy lunged for her throat. The attack reminded Kaitlyn of her training, her favorite Aikido move and she just took one step aside and used the rush of the attackers' momentum to retrieve his knife and send him falling face first into the grass.

The students had swarmed the twins and were beating them down so they wouldn't get back up, but the last guy, Brad, was all Kaitlyn's. Once he noticed he was next he turned to run. She ran towards him, leaped with both feet forward, and knocked him into the wall. He turned and grabbed Kaitlyn by the neck and attempted to twist it off when Kaitlyn used the leverage on his left leg to spin him around the opposite way until he lost footing. As he began to fall, Kaitlyn hit her hands to the ground and as a horse kicking backwards at a foe; she knocked him backwards onto his butt.

Kaitlyn was just standing up ready to assess the situation when one of the twins tried to make a run for it. Kaitlyn chased her down across the field, nearly catching her, but as she hit the parking lot, the police had just shown up and apprehended her before she could go anywhere.

Two policemen showed up and took over cuffing the other twin the students had taken down, and two other cops went over to check on Brad and Mike who were laying unconscious in their own drool. Kaitlyn then went back to check on the boss who was just now waking up. She pulled him to his feet by his hair and handed him, arms constrained behind his back, over to another police officer.

The officer read his Miranda rights as Kaitlyn walked over to check on her broken nosed buddy Mike. "Mike Lynx, you are under arrest for the murder of Angela Smithson and Jeremiah Jackson. You have the right to remain silent, anything you say can and will be used against you…"

Kaitlyn suddenly felt very good.

With the gang either arrested or leaving town, Kaitlyn felt fairly secure in her position. With the situation looking up, she decided that she finally had time to focus on some of her own issues. Friday night Kaitlyn went to the local law enforcement office and asked them for a favor, for her to see the file of her mother, Miss Janie McFarell. At first they didn't assist her, but then they acknowledged her request and asked a nearby deputy to take Kaitlyn down to the old file room and help her find Janie McFarell's file. Kaitlyn thanked them and then followed the deputy.

Once he had located the file he showed Kaitlyn to a desk, turned on the lamp, and told her to take all the time she needed then return the file in its proper place before leaving. Kaitlyn shook her head then sat down at the desk. As she looked at the unopened file her stomach felt queasy. This was the first moment of the rest of her life. This was going to answer so many questions, and lead her to the right people to help her understand. As she slowly opened the file the first thing that grabbed her attention was a picture of her mother before the kidnapping. It hit Kaitlyn hard as she looked at the woman and saw a lot of herself in her. Her mother was beautiful.

She turned the page and what she saw shocked her. A picture of her mother, the day she was found. Kaitlyn looked at it and watched it grow blurry as her eyes swelled up with tears. She couldn't breathe and it felt as if a powerful gush of heat had hit her face. She turned the page and continued into the file. To her surprise it seemed the file was missing a lot of pertinent information. There was no contacts listed, no parents listed. It was a brief report of the scene of the crime the day she was found, and the pictures.

Kaitlyn felt such disappointment, such frustration. Of all of this time, what she wanted to find out, the information she had been searching for wasn't in here. After reading the report a third time, knowing nothing more would show up, knowing that there was nothing truly useful in this file except the address of the kidnappers house, Kaitlyn replaced the file in its original location, turned off the lights and left.

It was Saturday morning when Grandma Kate walked in and woke Kaitlyn up.

"You have a visitor."

Kaitlyn quickly got up, dressed, and walked out into the living room where her visitor stood. It was Tom. Kaitlyn didn't know if she wanted to talk to him or not. She waited for him to make the first move, to break the ice.

"How are you doing?" Tom asked.

"Fine," she answered, not willing to give him more. He shook his head.

"Looks like things have gotten better around here?"

"They have."

"I heard what you did yesterday, pretty impressive."

"Thanks." She spoke and waded through the awkward silence.

"Can we go somewhere to talk?" Tom asked trying to push forward with his intentions for being there.

"I don't know." Kaitlyn looked at her grandparents in hopes they would say no. They didn't.

"It won't take long." Tom added as he walked Kaitlyn out of the house.

Kaitlyn walked outside onto the front porch and leaned on the railing. She stayed silent waiting for Tom to speak first.

"I thought about what you said to me the other day." Tom spoke low. "I understand why you did it."

"I'm glad someone does."

Tom realized and felt the guilt and shame she felt so he skipped to the next subject. "I had to send you away, you wouldn't have discovered this about yourself otherwise."

"You didn't have to do anything." Kaitlyn embellished the 'have' feeling he was trying to make excuses for something else. "You just didn't want to deal with me and my problems." Kaitlyn started in already angry.

"That is not true."

"You turned me away, Tom. You didn't want to deal with me.""

"No. I knew I couldn't help you but you were strong enough to help yourself."

Unwilling to hear him, she spoke again. "Why couldn't you help me? All I wanted was someone to comfort me. To tell me they loved me. Is that so hard to ask?"

"No." Tom admitted, then sighed. "I'm sorry."

Kaitlyn looked down. Tom continued.

"I'm sorry I turned you away when you needed me most. I'm sorry I couldn't help you get past your father's death."

"Is that what you came here for? To apologize?" Kaitlyn asked not willing to accept his apology.

"I'm sorry I wasn't the friend you needed when you contacted me."

"No, you weren't. Were you?"

"I'm sorry I didn't listen to your cries."

"You should be."

He looked at her fighting her emotions, trying so desperately to stay in control while so completely falling apart on the inside. Suddenly he felt everything that she had been going through. He wasn't sure if she was sending him these feelings, or if she even knew how to. Their connection had grown. Whether she realized it or not all of a sudden he felt everything, every feeling she had and his heart ached for her.

"Kaitlyn, I couldn't be the friend you needed and that was my fault. I feel such pain for what I put you through. I never meant to hurt you. And I'm sorry I sent you away, but… when my father died, my mother sent me to camp for the summer…"

"So because you didn't *get* the compassion you needed you don't know how to *give* it?"

"Sending me to camp was the best thing my mother could have done for me, because it forced me to stop blaming the world. It forced me to open my eyes and see that the world doesn't just stop when I do."

"So I was being selfish when I wanted you to slow down, to stop pushing me back into my life?"

Tom sighed. "You are making this much harder than it needs to be."

"Good. It's about time you deal with something a little difficult. Maybe now you'll understand what I've been going through. When I got here, these kids were the worst bunch of jerks that I had ever met."

"And it helped you."

"No Tom. It hurt me. I had breakdown after breakdown beating my knuckles into blood on a punching bag that never seemed to do the job. I was suicidal. I kept trying because of you, and when I finally contacted you for help you turned me away."

"You slept with someone else!"

"So your jealousy and spitefulness nearly killed me. You don't love me; you don't care if I live or die, but you want me to come back to you. Forget you, Tom. Go to hell!"

"Don't talk to me like that."

"Does it hurt your feelings? Oh, I forgot you don't have any!"

"All I was doing was trying to make you a better person."

"God you just don't get it do you?" Kaitlyn yelled yanking at her hair. "I am what you see and this is what you get! I can't change myself for you because then I would cease to be me. I'm tired of trying to be a better person for you when I feel I'm already great.

According to you I'm constantly wrong, constantly childish, constantly insane with everything I think, say or do and I'm tired of this harassment. I need to be me. I need to make mistakes, learn my own lessons, run my own life in the way that I see fit and it seems to me that you don't want to let me do that."

"I just want to help you through it."

"No, you are trying to manage the situation. Trying to keep it under control."

"I thought I was helping."

"That is the problem. I didn't want help, I wanted support."

"How could I support you when you were bringing yourself down and those around you?"

"I wasn't trying to. I was just trying to be me."

"You couldn't see what you were doing. You refused to."

"Just like you couldn't see what I needed."

"You needed direction, coaxing and consistency…"

"Maybe that's what you needed, but I am not you. It seems you've got my life planned out for me already and if I don't like it, then too bad. Maybe I am not what you expected, maybe I am not what you wanted, but maybe that is because we weren't meant to do this. Either you let me lead my own life or I'll lead it without you in it."

She knew what she wanted and it shocked him because she had never really been this clear before. For a second he knew he wanted to say something back to her but he didn't know what to say. He wondered if she would ever love him as much as he loved her this very moment.

"Kaitlyn why don't you just come home, get back to your normal life..."

"Tom, I'm not going to come home because I have no home to come back to, and I don't think I ever want to return back to that town again anyway."

"But you've got so much there.""

"I have nothing there! No family, no home, no friends."

"You have me."

"Not anymore."

"Kaitlyn...."

"You were right Tom. This did help me get past my father, but it was in the worst way possible. I do thank you for sending me away, because I was never able to see myself anywhere but stuck in that town. That I survived here proves that I can survive anywhere."

"Kaitlyn, don't do this." Tom didn't like where the conversation was going.

"Tom, I love you. I always have and always will, but I can't be with you any longer. I've moved past you. I've moved past the childish need for you."

"Childish?"

"I wanted somebody to love me. You wouldn't do that. The only person in the world that I wanted didn't want me, and pushed me away to grow up and I did."

"Kaitlyn I didn't mean it to go like that."

"Now I know that I don't need you anyone. I don't need someone telling me they want me because I'm stronger than that."

"Are you?"

"Am I what?"

"Stronger than that?"

"Yes."

"So you have one good day and it makes up for three months worth of moping around?"

"It's not like that and you know it! I was mourning."

"You were soaking it up."

"You pushed me away."

"I did it to help you."

"I've found out who I am now and I don't need you to help me express that."

"You can't just turn your back on us."

"Watch me." She turned to walk inside the house. Tom followed.

"Kaitlyn, don't walk away." She continued to walk towards her room. He followed her and watched her pick up her purse. "Kaitlyn, where are you going?"

"Away."

"Where?"

"That's none of your business any longer!" Then she walked right past him out the front door.

As he watched her leave, he didn't know what went wrong and he didn't know what to do about it. He stood there confused for the longest time trying to figure things out. Kaitlyn however didn't really know where she was going, but she wasn't going to stop until she was far enough away to feel better. She also wasn't sure if she'd ever feel better. She found herself minutes later at a bus station, minutes after that, on a bus heading out of town, and the scary part about it was she wasn't sure she was ready to take this step. The unknown was to Kaitlyn, something to fear but she refused to let those emotions stop her. In fact, she refused to let weak emotions dictate anything to her any longer.

Tom knew she was upset, and he also knew she had every right to be. He decided he would give her some time. He prayed she would have a change of heart. He hoped that maybe she would come around on her own. He confessed to himself that if he didn't chicken out again he would find a way to share his true feelings with her and prove his intentions.

Chapter 17

It seemed like multiple days later when the bus came to a stop by a barren field, but it had only been about eight hours. Kaitlyn had been deep in thought, going over everything, every last detail, of her life, of her dreams, of her actions, of her conversation with Tom and of her mother's police report. Kaitlyn knew this was her stop so she grabbed her bag and started off of the bus. The bus driver spoke to her before she stepped off.

"You sure this is where you want to go?"

"Yes, thank you."

"But there's nothing around here. No one lives out here, and you'll never get another bus out here."

"I'll be fine." She turned and stepped off the bus and watched it drive off. Then she looked over the vast barren field and felt the magnitude of the isolation surround her. It would be a long walk, she acknowledged, but she was ready for it. She had been ready all of her life without even realizing it.

As she walked up to her destination, she stopped to take in the sight. A rickety old shack; looked like it hadn't been taken care of or even looked at for years. Kaitlyn knew for a fact that it had been abandoned for at least seventeen years, and as she looked at it she remembered the article. Kaitlyn knew the last seven people in this house all died, and she knew that one of them had been her mother.

She noticed bullet holes in the crumbling walls. As Kaitlyn walked through the door, she felt a surge of uneasiness go through her. The damp cold air inside was frightening and as suddenly as that had swept over her an idea of the first day came to her.

A young, duct tape bound woman, struggling for her life was brought into this room. She was carried like a heavy rolled up rug by three men, then tossed onto the floor. Sliding into the corner only to look up at the six smiling faces of her captors, not quite realizing what was about to happen to her. They drank in front of her, throwing beer cans and bottles at her and laughed aloud, singing old drunken songs.

The young girl trembled, fearful of her life, but she had been ignored for so long she started to wonder if they had forgotten about her. Before she knew what was happening though, they stood up, grabbed her by the hair, yanked her to her feet and shoved her towards three other men, one of which was opening an old cellar door. As they pushed her down into the darkened room, following her down as they did, they shut the door behind them and the rest went to black.

Tom had driven back home after Kaitlyn left. It had been a number of hours when he decided to go out and get something to eat. As he sat there in the restaurant, something weird began to happen to him. The past half an hour he had been experienced weird mood shifts that weren't his own. He had been excited, scared, lonely and then frightened again. Then suddenly the feelings had stopped. He wasn't sure what was happening to him, but he had one idea, Kaitlyn.

Kaitlyn knew she had to keep going. She hadn't traveled all the way here to stop in the doorway and chicken out. As she walked towards the back of the shack she spotted the rickety door leading to the cellar. She hesitated then lifted the hatch, opened the door, and stared down into the blackness. She knew she had to go down there; her life started there. She knew it would help her understand, and maybe even allow her to see with her flashes what actually happened. So before she could chicken out again, she took one step onto the cellar stairs and continued down until finally making it to the cellar floor.

There were spider webs all over the place, and sounds of small critters rustling around. Kaitlyn wanted to leave, but gathered up her courage to explore. When her eyes adjusted to the faint light, she finally saw the room where her mother spent her last eight months of life.

As Kaitlyn looked around she couldn't help but feel the pain and agony. Her mother's soul was still here in a small way. She saw the spot on the floor that had been rubbed clean where her mother had sat for eight months. She saw the footsteps on the dirt, unmoved from the day her mother was rescued. She took in more of her mother's memories.

There was a noise behind Kaitlyn, and as she turned towards the door she saw the ghost of one of the men. He slowly came down the stairs, moved right past her, through her, and went over to her mother. The flash quickly faded leaving Kaitlyn's imagination to help it along. Kaitlyn sat in her mother's spot and wondered to herself how sick she was for being here. She wanted to learn more about her mother but was sitting in this spot, the spot she was most likely conceived in, normal?

A storm had begun brewing outside. Kaitlyn was unaware of it though, feeling this whole trip may have been a mistake, but as her foot touched the first step of the staircase, the cellar door slammed shut. The loud thud of the wooden door rang in her ears and the shock startled her right off of her feet. That was the first time she heard the wind rustle around and through the house, screaming through the cracks.

Kaitlyn gathered her footing and ran up the stairs to the door, and then tried to push it open but when it fell the latch slid into place, trapping her. She pounded on the door, trying to break it free, but the hard wood was as tough as stone.

Tom had been sitting at the table writing down every feeling when the most horrible sense of fear overwhelmed him.

A helplessness he had never felt before helped him realize Kaitlyn was in trouble.

There wasn't a cloud in the sky, but suddenly he started wondering about the weather. Like a shot in the dark he had an epiphany of what was happening. He ran home and did a quick search on the Internet pulling up the current weather. A flashing icon showed a terrible storm and tornado watch was currently in effect in a town he only recognized from memory. What did this have to do with Kaitlyn? Why would she be there? He wondered. Then it occurred to him. He grabbed his old journal, found the old copy of the newspaper article describing Kaitlyn's mother's death and found the town. That's when Tom knew exactly where Kaitlyn had gone and what she was up to. Tom wondered to himself if that storm had trapped Kaitlyn in the middle of an abandoned field with nothing for miles around. He tried to contact Kaitlyn telepathically.

"Kaitlyn, can you hear me?"

He tried quite a few times but realized he must not be reaching her over such a great distance; either that or her abilities hadn't grown enough to receive a message so far away. Then how could he sense her emotions but not be able to reach her through their telepathic link? He would worry about that later. Right now, he had the sudden urge to get to Kaitlyn as quickly as possible. As he jumped in his car, he knew he was going on a long shot, but so had Kaitlyn the day of his wreck. Something in the depths of his soul told him she needed help so he was going to help her, no matter the fact that it was nearly a days' drive away.

Kaitlyn had nearly wrenched her shoulder out trying to break through that cellar door. She couldn't budge it, and she was absolutely positive she had just been through a tornado. Moments earlier the wind just picked up out of nowhere, debris smashed through the house walls, tearing them down around her. The train-like sound passed directly over her head and seemed to deafen her. She felt the suction of the funnel, sucking everything around her up towards the cellar door.

She scrambled to the back corner of the cellar, trying to get as far away from the door as possible in case it got torn off the hinges and was pulled into the tornado. But the commotion ended abruptly. As if it couldn't get any scarier, the sound of the entire house falling onto the cellar door erupted, shaking the ground and Kaitlyn with it. She was sure she was stuck. Trapped down there like her mother had been, with no way of escaping.

Her only hope was if the bus driver had enough wits about him to let someone know he had dropped a girl off in that area earlier that day. She wondered if her telepathic ability would be able to reach Tom, but then she realized she'd only be doing what she didn't want to do; depending on a man. She decided not to contact him. She would find a way out of here herself, come hell or high water.

Depressed at not finding anything and worried about the weather, she settled down on the floor and prepared for a long night. She knew she was in for a long haul especially if that bus driver didn't think about her or remember about her being out here. As she sat there wondering, worried, she slowly began to fall asleep. But she didn't stay that way for long; every sound woke her from her subconscious.

That night, an odd thing happened. As dusk filled the room, it went cave black. Kaitlyn dreamed of her mother, sitting in the same corner as she had been, huddled up, trembling, crying. And Kaitlyn knew her mother had been there for a few weeks. She could tell by the torn clothes, dirty face, and stringy hair, and oddly enough Kaitlyn seemed to also feel her mother's hunger.

As she sat there, she remembered her mother holding onto a gold heart locket that had been around her neck, but she quickly took it off and hid it so it wouldn't be taken away from her. She remembered crying as she held it, and she leaned over and shoved it into the dirt wall behind her, covering it with loose dirt, to keep it hidden.

As Kaitlyn woke from the dream and opened her eyes, she realized it did her no good. It was so completely dark in there that she couldn't see her hand directly in front of her face. She sat up, looked around the room, and suddenly remembered the prayer from her mother.

Take my sight from me; the sight that has grown so accustomed to the dark that I can now see no matter how dark it gets, no matter how black it is.

Like a sudden miracle, Kaitlyn was able to see. She wasn't sure if the clouds outside had dissipated allowing light from the stars through the debris or if a miracle had actually happened, but Kaitlyn was able to see her hand. It wasn't the best sight, it was still incredibly dark, she could only see about a foot in front of her and it was a dark charcoal gray at best, but it gave her hope.

She began looking around the room for that wall, trying to find that locket. She dug her fingers into the rock hard dirt and began clawing into it, breaking loose only a small bit of dirt. She did this for close to an hour before giving up and sitting back down to rest. She was certain her dream was trying to tell her to look for the locket, but she failed and couldn't find it.

"Maybe the locket had been found long ago and it was gone."

She had given up and was trying to go back to sleep again, when a large earthworm poked out from the dirt and tunneled back into it a quarter inch from the spot he had tunneled out from. Kaitlyn leaned back against the wall, crossed her arms in front of her chest and blinked her eyes a few times, feeling them grow heavy. She was about to fall back asleep again when something from inside that earthworms tunnel picked up a bit of light and twinkled once. Kaitlyn blinked to make sure she wasn't hallucinating and noticed the twinkle again.

She jumped up, ran to the wall, shoving her fingers into the hole, and pulled out fresh dirt. She had found the locket. It was tarnished, covered in dirt and dust; she looked at it and nearly cried. This old trinket had once belonged to her mother. She wondered what pictures if any were inside, if it had her family picture or an old boyfriend. She wondered if her mother somehow knew her daughter would one day come along and find it.

Kaitlyn struggled with the clasp; it had been welded shut by the years of decay in the dirt. She didn't want to give up, but finally after six broken finger nails and a sore tooth from biting at it, she gave up. She would have to take it to a jewelry store and have a professional open it for her. As she lay back down and tried to get some more sleep she felt as if she had been successful in her trip up here. She had found something of her mother's that she prayed would answer a few of her questions.

When Kaitlyn woke, assuming it was the next morning, she stood and looked around. No sunlight. No light of any kind came in through the cellar door, and she knew that was because the house had fallen down on top of it. She tried the door again, but she didn't have the strength for it. Not even six men could push this thing open. Only someone on the other side, could pull the pieces of wood and debris off of this pile and save her. Kaitlyn thought about contacting Tom again. He would know where to find her to help but she thought about her decision and decided silently that the bus driver would come through for her. She would only call Tom as a last resort.

As the morning progressed and the sun lifted high into the sky, the basement got hot. The basement seemed to become a furnace and the heat began to get to her. As she sat there sweating, her mind played tricks on her. She was sure she heard noises outside, but when she called up to them, she heard nothing.

The longer she sat there, the more vulnerable to her weakened state she became. The heat was making her hallucinate. More memories of her mother began to flood into her head, and they were very disturbing. Her mother had sat here on this floor, in the dark and heat, just waiting. Listening to every noise outside in fear, hearing the talking of the men who were sure to come back down later and hurt her again. Kaitlyn felt the pang of hunger hit her and suddenly she started to feel her mother's hunger, as if she hadn't eaten in days, weeks, even months. She wondered how it must have felt, being pregnant, scared, hungry and hot all at the same time.

Before long the lack of food, fresh air, and heat started to take its toll on Kaitlyn. She became ill, sick to her stomach, nauseous and dizzy. Her head felt like it had swollen and the blood vessels began to pound at her skull. She lay back down on the floor, feeling the gritty grimy texture of dust, rodent droppings and whatever else was under her body. She was grateful she couldn't see much because she was sure things were crawling on her. It seemed every muscle in her body trembled; she shivered as if she were cold, but it was all in her mind. As she felt herself begin to pass out, all of it being too much on her to take, she came in and out of consciousness and had ongoing dreams, rather past premonitions of her mother.

As she was lying on the floor praying for freedom, she saw the door to the cellar open. She saw the six men start down the cellar to her, and as they surrounded her she screamed. The scream woke her and she realized it was a dream, but as the day progressed Kaitlyn found it incredibly hard to determine the difference between her dreams and reality. Her body, mind and soul played tricks on her and she knew if she didn't get out of there soon she would either die or go completely nuts.

Later that day, closer to evening, the door to the cellar opened again. Kaitlyn had seen it open so many times that day in her dreams that she was sure it was just another dream. She saw light; the same light she had seen before, that blinded her as the men came down the stairs and surrounded her. She screamed again, trying to wake herself from this nightmare.

"Go away. Leave me alone!" She screamed nearly in tears, her words mumbled since her mouth had all but swollen shut from the dirt and lack of water. As the silhouette of a man started down the stairs she reacted as her mother would have, crawling to a corner, screaming the best she could and throwing harmless punches.

As the darkened shadow of a man approached her and leaned over her, Kaitlyn knew she wasn't waking from this nightmare so she tried to fight back, she knocked the flashlight from the mans hands and began trying to beat him off of her. He grabbed her upper arms, trying to keep her from hitting him, and he easily over powered her. She struggled, shifting back and forth on the floor trying to break free. Hardly able to see a thing, it seemed as if she were struggling with herself. It was so dark the shadow of the man seemed to disappear in the darkness and she had no idea if her mind was still playing tricks with her.

As she squirmed, she realized he was too heavy and she couldn't get away. She began to scream again, frantic and fearful, and as she screamed so did he, but she didn't hear anything from him. She could sense he was trying to say something but all she could hear was the frantic beat of her own heart. She couldn't hear him if she wanted to. Finally, as the fight was almost out of her and she felt the end drawing near, he sent one hard blow of a fist to her face and knocked her into unconsciousness, her limp body lost all tension. He had won this fight.

Chapter 18

Beep. Beep. Beep. Beep.

Kaitlyn heard the faint sound of a heart monitor rouse her. She wondered if she were still hearing things, but the sound grew louder. She forced her eyes open. The blinding white light stung her pupils like a thousand needles. She closed her eyes again. On the third try, she opened them all of the way, blinking twice at the light until she was able to see a room where Tom sat watching her. She stared.

"How are you feeling?" He asked.

"Tired." She admitted weakly.

"You should get more rest."

But she was ready to talk now. Still in her weakened state, she began asking questions.

"Where am I?"

"The hospital. I brought you here."

"How did you find me?"

"I heard your cries for help."

"I never called you." Kaitlyn admitted without thinking.

Tom worried she was about to find out about his ability to tap into her emotions and he didn't think this was the time for it. He decided to back peddle just a bit playing on her drowsiness.

"Don't you remember?"

"I chose not to call you." Kaitlyn spoke sure.

"I got a distress call." Tom said, with so much sureness to him that Kaitlyn couldn't disagree.

Kaitlyn knew she wasn't very good at controlling her telepathic abilities, maybe she had called unwittingly? Since she was still very tired, she just let it pass. Tom felt fortunate at times to have this emotional connection with Kaitlyn. It led him to her when she needed him, but he knew she wouldn't see it that way. He didn't know how to explain he felt her emotions

205

from a hundred miles away, or if he even wanted to tell her about that. Now was not the time to worry about that though. Kaitlyn had fallen back asleep so he took this opportunity to call the nurse back into the room to check on Kaitlyn's vitals.

"She's starting to wake up." He explained, as the woman walked into the room.

The nurse checked Kaitlyn's over then spoke to Tom. "It looks as if she's going to be just fine."

"Okay, thanks." He spoke quietly as the nurse walked out of the room, Marge and Kaitlyn's grandparents walked in.

"Tom? How is she?"

"She's starting to wake up, she'll be just fine."

Kaitlyn's grandparents hugged each other. Everyone had had a scare today. Marge walked over to Tom and held his hand.

"She is very lucky she has you as a friend." Finally Grandpa Jim spoke.

"How did you find her again son?"

"I knew where she was going yesterday and when I didn't hear from her last night I went to find her."

"Yes, but when she left she was pretty angry at you. Why would she have told you where she was going?"

"Oh Jim," Kaitlyn's grandmother spoke up. "At least Kaitlyn is safe now, that's all that matters."

Kaitlyn opened her eyes and looked at the room full of people.

"You gave us all quite a scare." Marge spoke up.

"I'm sorry."

"I'm just glad you're okay," she said with a caring smile. Grandma Kate kissed Kaitlyn's forehead and Grandpa Jim sat down on the foot of the bed and immediately began with the questions.

"So tell us what happened."

"She just woke up, give her a chance to get her bearings." Grandma Kate griped at her husband. Jim held his tongue but Kaitlyn could tell he wanted answers. So she gave them the best she could offer.

"I went to the house my mother had been in."

"Allison?" Her grandmother asked.

"No. Janie McFarrel." Kaitlyn corrected. An awkward exchange in glances happened between Kaitlyn's grandparents and then suddenly Kaitlyn's grandfather changed his tune.

"That's all right sweetheart. You should get your rest now. He kissed her forehead and walked his wife out of the room. Kaitlyn was very curious about that but was distracted when Marge spoke.

"They're right child. You should get your rest now." And she too left the room. Tom was just about to get up and leave but Kaitlyn stopped him.

"Look inside my pants pocket."

Tom stood and reached over to the shelf where Kaitlyn's clothes sat folded and reached into her pants pocket. As he pulled out the tarnished locket his eyes opened wide, focusing in on it.

"What is it?"

"My mother's locket. She buried it in the dirt walls when she was thrown down there."

Tom was confused. How could she possibly know this unless?

"I saw her place it there in a dream," Kaitlyn added, answering Tom's question before he had a chance to ask it. Tom tried to open it, but failed.

"We'll take it to a jeweler tomorrow."

"I was planning on it," Kaitlyn said, as she sat up in bed, starting to feel better and more awake.

Tom sat down next to her on the bed. "What do you think is inside?"

207

"Not sure, but I can't wait to find out."

"What if it is empty?"

"I'll be disappointed. But I don't think she would have hidden it unless if it had true meaning to her. She went through a lot to keep that a secret."

"I know. Maybe you should get some more rest tonight. I'll check up on you in the morning." Tom stood to leave but Kaitlyn stopped him.

"Tom." He paused then turned to face her, her eyes showed the caring curiosity she had always had before.

"Thank you."

"For what?"

"For finding me, and for taking that black eye from me."

Tom stopped and turned towards a mirror and noticed for the first time why his eye was hurting. He then smiled and looked back at her.

"Any time, babe."

The next morning Tom saw her sitting in a chair, staring out the window. As he walked up he noticed she didn't stir. He was sure she had heard him open the door, but she didn't turn around and greet him.

"Kaitlyn? What's wrong?"

Kaitlyn lifted her hand to his and dropped the locket inside. He looked at it, and saw that she had cleaned it, and that she had opened it. He peered into the locket and saw two faces, very unrecognizable faces but before he could say so Kaitlyn spoke.

"Grandpa Jim and Grandma Kate, my adoptive mother's mom and dad."

Tom was shocked for a moment, what did this mean? How could Kaitlyn's real mother have pictures of her adoptive mother's parents in it, and hide it almost twenty years ago? He was completely confused, leaving the thought of the answer deep in the back of his mind, refusing to believe it. Kaitlyn once again answered his questions before he asked them.

"My adoptive parents would take me to visit my grandparents during the summer. They were always so happy to see me. They'd hold me and cry, and when my grandpa Jim was done, he'd pull Grandma Kate away and they'd change their faces and attitudes, like they had over reacted and from then on it was just like any other visit."

Tom still didn't see the connection, he had an idea, but it was so farfetched he wasn't sure he'd believe it. Kaitlyn seemed to be able to tell he was not quite following. She reached into her bag and pulled out a picture in a frame and a folded up piece of old newspaper. Tom took them and looked at them. The picture was of Kaitlyn and her mom and dad; Kaitlyn was about ten. The newspaper was the missing girl ad for Janie McFarell, her real mother, when she had been kidnapped. Tom all of a sudden saw the resemblance. Kaitlyn looked almost exactly like her mother did back then. As Tom put two and two together, Kaitlyn verified his suspicions.

"My grandparents Jim and Kate would see me walk up and believe they were seeing their long lost daughter, Janie."

"Janie?"

"They were so relieved and so pleased to see her that they temporarily forgot she had died and they were looking at her daughter, their real granddaughter. Then when they realized I wasn't Janie they changed their tune. It was all a charade."

"What do you mean by charade?"

"They never told me about my real mom. My mother never told me, or should I say my aunt. That picture in that locket is a picture of my grandparents when they were young enough to have a sixteen-year-old girl. After her death I suppose they put away all of her pictures. They didn't know what to do with me, so they let my mother's younger sister take me in. They decided it would be too difficult to talk about so they never did, and they all lead me to believe that my adoptive parents were my real parents. The grandparents I've gotten to know have been lying to me all of these years."

Tom jumped in to try to console. "They were probably just protecting you."

"From what? The truth? Tom, what am I supposed to think?"

"I'm sure it was hard on all of them. Your father only told you the truth on his death bed."

"I'm not sure what to believe."

"I think you need to ask your grandparents about it."

"What? Ask the ones who planned on never telling me the truth in the first place?"

"You were too young to tell before. They're the only two people alive who can answer some of these questions for you. They're the only ones who can help put this all together for you. You have to go to them."

"How do you start out a conversation like that? So grandma and grandpa, tell me about Janie the daughter you chose to forget about."

"I think with a little more tact that is a very good start."

He placed his hand on her shoulder to comfort her, but she didn't seem to need it. She stood, allowing his hand to slip away and faced him.

"I know you're right."

"How can I help?"

"You can't. I need to do this alone."

"Well let me know if you need anything."

"Tom," Kaitlyn sighed. "I believe I made my feelings clear before. I need to find myself on my own, and until I do there is no room for you in my life."

"But our connection…"

"Our connection is strong enough to maybe last until the end of time, but I can't waste what time I have now on a possibility and neither should you.

"I really think you're wrong about that."

"And that's why I need to do this alone, to find out for myself, to make my own mistakes."

Tom knew she wouldn't change her mind. "Okay, Kaitlyn. Contact me if you need anything." As he walked out the door, Kaitlyn felt bad again about treating him so badly, but she couldn't lean on a man to solve her problems. As she heard Tom walk out of the door she almost wanted to take it all back, but before she could reconsider he was gone, and she knew it was for the best.

The drive back to her grandparents' house was quiet. They didn't talk and she didn't want to start in with the questions yet. She wondered what had been going through their minds all of these years? Were they even ashamed of their actions in turning their backs on her, a defenseless baby, away for fear of what the other townsfolk would say?

After a nice dinner, but still very silent, Kaitlyn realized the only thing left to do to break the silence was to come right out and ask her questions. She had a feeling they knew what she was going to ask but they were too ashamed or too afraid to say anything on their own. Kaitlyn pulled the locket from around her neck and under her shirt and handed it to her grandmother without saying a word. As her grandmother took it into her hand and recognized it she began to cry. Kaitlyn's grandfather had another emotion.

"Where did you get that?"

"I found it in the basement Janie was held captive in. I know everything."

"You think you know everything." He said somewhat angrily.

"I just need to verify it," Kaitlyn assured. Her grandmother decided to sit quiet as her husband took over the conversation.

"Let's see what you might be thinking." Grandpa Jim spoke up. "Your real mother Janie was kidnapped, and later died after giving birth to you. We didn't want you so Allison adopted you. Am I on the mark?"

"That's what I've come to believe. Yes."

"Well, you're wrong."

"About what?" Kaitlyn asked with too much shock.

"We wanted to take you in but the county hospital had to hold you because you were a preemie. As they were trying to nurse you back to health complications came up. Your brain had swelled and was pressing against your underdeveloped skull. They had to operate to release the pressure but they couldn't do it there. So they flew you to Houston where the best children's doctors were, and we would have flown down with you except your grandmother began having heart problems." He paused and placed his hand on his wife's hand, then continued.

"I stayed with your grandmother and sent Allison who was then only sixteen to her aunt in Minnesota. We didn't see her for half a year and by the time all was calm here the hospital had transferred you three times and had lost you."

Kaitlyn was stunned. "Lost me?"

"We signed tons of papers agreeing to whatever treatment was necessary. Agencies of all sorts kind of took over your case. Your papers were transferred so many times from one agency to the next…"

Kaitlyn watched as her grandma Kate dropped her head into her hands. Jim continued.

"I got on the phone with everyone who would listen but by then the old game Telephone had taken place. You know the one where you say one thing to someone and they repeat it down the line but at the end it's something completely different?

Well, that's what happened, somehow you went from Kaitlyn to being named Linda and had been placed in an orphanage and later put in a foster family.

We figured you were with a nice family, we didn't want to give you up but we also didn't know what we could do for you. It seemed easier for you to believe you were born of a loving family rather than the situation you were in.

A year later after Allison graduated she married Harold and went out in search for you. By the time she found you, your foster family had moved and the orphanage had lost touch with them. She kept searching for eight months until she found you and then went to the courts to take you into her possession. And at the age of 28 months you were finally adopted and renamed your original name, Kaitlyn, taking the last name of Jones."

Kaitlyn sat there in complete astonishment. Not only had she been wrong but she had doubted the love of her own grandparents. Ashamed, she apologized for jumping to conclusions, and they all had a group hug. Later, her grandmother pulled out an old dusty box from the attic and placed it in front of Kaitlyn. As she opened it she noticed a picture of her mother as a baby. Then she noticed another picture of her mother as a young girl. The entire box was filled with every picture ever taken of her mother, even if it was a family portrait or had other people in it. Kaitlyn looked up from the box with even more questions than before but she began and ended them all with one word.

"Why?"

"Allison decided after your adoption that she didn't want you to know about the ghastly outcome of your real mother. She said it would be a terrible thing for any young girl to hear happened to her own mother. The way she explained it made perfect sense. All she had to do was explain the emotions that she had gone through, during the whole ordeal and then say, imagine now that this was your own daughter. So we agreed, and put away everything that would remind us, or rather you, of Janie, and swore to never mention her again. It was the hardest thing any of us have ever had to do. I was forced to never speak of my first born child ever again."

"That's horrible!"

"It became very difficult to deal with as you grew up. You looked so much like your mother, but we couldn't ever say so. After Allison died we wanted to tell you, but knew you had been through enough already. And later we thought about telling you but Harold thought it would be wrong. To find out that we all had been lying to you all of your life. So we waited, not sure if we could ever tell you the truth."

Kaitlyn stood and began to pace, thoughts forming into her mind way too slowly.

"I've heard quite a bit today. Would you mind if I rested?"

"Not at all." Her grandmother spoke soft, "Can I do anything?"

"May I take these photos with me?"

"Of course, darling. Anything you want."

That night Kaitlyn rested for a few hours but woke up in the wee morning hours and started going through the pictures. Pictures of the life of a woman who was supposed to mean so much to her but only seemed to be a distant stranger. As she flipped the pages of the photo albums, she stopped at a picture of her mother and a boy of the same age. They were about sixteen and at a high school dance.

As she looked at the face of the boy standing next to her mother she seemed to recognize him, but oddly it was no one she had ever met before. Finally, she turned the picture over and read the back.

"To my Dearest Janie,
May that night and every other be
as special as you are to me.

Love,
Dave"

"Okay, now I have a name." Kaitlyn thought, but the only Dave she knew was a sixteen-year old nerd in last years Algebra class. She put that picture aside and kept going through the box finally coming across an old yearbook. She opened it and started flipping through the first few pages. It wasn't signed from any of her friends in school the way any teenage girls yearbook would be. Kaitlyn then closed the book, looked at the date on the front cover, and realized that it was the same year her mother was kidnapped; she never had it signed because she never made it to the end of the school year.

Kaitlyn started flipping through the pages looking for a picture of her mother. After a few moments she came across it and noticed a printed wreath around it; they did this as a memorial for her. As she flipped to the back of the book, she stopped on a page dedicated to Janie. It had a collage of pictures of her and her friends and nice words written about her. Kaitlyn looked over the pictures and noticed the same picture of her mother and that familiar guy. Kaitlyn looked for that guy in the yearbook. She found the picture of him under the M's. As she slowly looked over to the names next to the row of pictures her mouth dropped. The name of the guy was. David J. McKinney, Tom's father.

As the reality hit home, many weird questions, actions, and outbursts began to make sense. Suddenly she realized what might have been going through Tom's mind for so long and she realized something even more upsetting. If this was all true, then Tom knew the truth about her and her family long before she did, and he never said a word.

"Tom?" Kaitlyn called to him telepathically to see if she could find him. A few moments later he answered.

"Kaitlyn?"

"We need to talk."

Tom knew right then what she wanted to talk about but he stayed calm. He knew if he tried to cover his fear she would sense it now. He needed to do this in person and he wanted her to go into it calmly.

"What about?"

"I think we need to talk in person."

"I can meet you tomorrow afternoon."

"Fine. Meet me in the museum at two."

"I'll be there."

The conversation ended. Tom did not look forward to tomorrow. If Kaitlyn had found what he thought she had found, tomorrow was going to be the most difficult day of his life.

<u>Chapter 19</u>

The next day Tom drove up to meet Kaitlyn at the designated meeting spot, arriving forty-five minutes early. Kaitlyn seemed so different when she arrived. The talk with her grandparents must have been difficult, but it seemed to help her as well. She stopped in front of him and didn't say a word.

"Kaitlyn, are you okay?" She removed a picture from a bag she carried and handed it to him. He looked at it, and his worst fears had come true. He stared at it for a moment not quite sure what to say when Kaitlyn spoke.

"Good picture huh? That's my mother."

"She's very pretty."

"And do you recognize that guy?"

"Um, well it looks like…" He paused trying to look like he was trying to figure it out. She answered for him.

"Your father?"

"Yeah." He said carefully.

"It is your father isn't it?" Kaitlyn questioned impatiently wondering why he was stalling.

Tom realized it was time to come clean so he admitted what he knew. "Yes. It is."

"Were they a couple?"

"Yes."

"How long."

"Quite a while."

"Serious?"

"Very much so."

"How serious?"

"Engaged."

"You knew about this all along didn't you?"

"I did. Ever since that afternoon after I took you home."

"How did you know? How did you figure it out?"

"The picture of your mother, um Allison, she seemed familiar to me so I researched why and found this."

Tom pulled a picture from his pocket and handed it to Kaitlyn. It was a picture of Janie and Tom's father and Allison and her boyfriend at the time, Harold. Their names were on the back. Tom explained.

"They had the same last names. I realized they were sisters and in this picture they were double dating. When I realized they were sisters it all came together. My father had told me once about the love of his life, Janie McFarell, your mother. He told me how she had been kidnapped and not found until eight months later. Then he showed me the newspaper article. The day you showed me that news article wasn't the first time I had ever seen it."

"Why didn't you tell me?"

"Tell you what? That your aunt adopted you because your mother died at birth? If they didn't want to tell you, then why should I? They must have had their reasons."

"I know, but…" Kaitlyn drifted off, knowing he was right. "But why didn't you tell me what you knew that day when I showed you the article?"

"What could I say that you didn't already know?"

"I didn't know your father and my mother were an item. You could have told me about that."

"Right. And maybe then I should have added in there my growing fear that you could be my sister. I couldn't ask my father if the two of them were sexually active before she was kidnapped because he was dead."

"And what makes you think they were… that the two of them were…"

"That would explain the gene of telepathic ability wouldn't it?"

"How do you know my mother wasn't a telepath?"

"Because I know my father was and if she could have called to him then he would have found her eight months before she was finally found."

Good answer, Kaitlyn thought. She hadn't even taken that into consideration. Then she thought of something else.

"So you're control always wanting to keep our relationship platonic was from fear that we could have been related?"

"Wouldn't that stop you?"

"No. Well, yes, but if my feelings were that strong I would discuss things and find out all I could to determine if it was truth before ruling out the option of love all together."

"Do you know me? Do you know what goes through my mind?"

"No. Not really." Kaitlyn spoke angrily, feeling she knew him less and less each day.

"What went through my mind was if I told you the truth, would you believe me? Or would you say I was crazy and never speak to me again. And then when you found out the truth, if it ever happened, would you ever come back to me and apologize? Would you even care about me after all of that? Kaitlyn I never wanted anything to come between us, you know that. I never wanted to take any risks at loosing you, and when you found out about your being adopted I could have told you that day but you weren't ready to listen. And the more I watched you, the more I got to know you. That's when I realized you had to do this yourself. I knew in my heart then, when you asked me about it, I would not lie because that would throw away any future we could have ever had. And I hope you forgive me for keeping the secret but I had my reasons and now you know them, too."

After a few minutes of comprehending his words Kaitlyn spoke. "You were right." Tom stood there knowing better than to gloat. She continued. "You knew me much better than I knew myself." She paused feeling the fear she had felt before when he came to her in New York. "How did you do that Tom? How do you know me better than I know myself? How can you sense what I'm feeling and know when to let go?"

Tom knew she was nearly hitting on his biggest secret of all and he feared her finding out about that more than anything in the world. He knew in his heart she would feel it was an intrusion into her privacy, whether he wanted it or not, and she would never trust him again. This was one thing he could never get past no matter how long he worried or tried to explain. He had a connection to Kaitlyn that not even he could explain. He could feel her emotions.

"Tom, I know that you care about me, and I love you for it. But like that, I have to find myself. I can't truly be the person I need to be if I can't even figure out what's going on in me before you do."

"I understand what you're saying, but this is something we can work on together."

"No, Tom. It's not. I am not angry with you, not at all, and so this is not a punishment, but…"

Tom wasn't ready to give up on her, though. He sat her down on a nearby bench, kneeled down in front of her, and took her hands into his.

"If I told you that my pushing you away was the hardest thing I have ever had to do, would you ever forgive me?"

"Tom, don't do this…"

"If I told you that you are the only one for me, would you deny me that opportunity?"

"Tom." Kaitlyn tried again to stop him not ready for this talk now.

"If I told you that I would go anywhere, do anything, to prove my love for you, would you still withhold your love from me? Would you lie to yourself, to your heart?"

"It's not a lie." Kaitlyn said, trying to believe it herself. Then something occurred to her. "What changed?"

"What do you mean?"

"When did you go from worry of genealogy to following your heart?"

"The night you shared your dream with me."

"Oh." Kaitlyn realized he finally had taken her seriously; something she felt hadn't happened.

"Can you honestly tell me that a life without true love is still worth living?" Tom began speaking bringing Kaitlyn's attention back to him. "We were made for each other; heart and soul, and to deny that love would be unforgivable. I want to spend the rest of my life with you. I want to be everything you need, everything you want in a man, and I promise I will never, ever, push you away again."

Kaitlyn was taken aback. She had wanted that, she felt it in her heart that she had desired hearing those words... but something was off about it. Kaitlyn looked deep within his eyes, his soulful, loving eyes and as her heart warmed, the ice surrounding it cracked. "Tom I was hoping you'd understand where I was coming from. You're certain as to what you're going to do with your life and I'm not. I would be standing in your way and you would be forcing me to make a decision that I'm obviously not ready to make."

"Kaitlyn," Tom tried to protest but Kaitlyn continued. "For now, I think it best if we continue to stay apart. At least until I figure things out."

Tom sighed, feeling she was right, feeling what her heart's desire truly was, but understanding what her brain was telling her. "How long?"

"I'm not sure."

"Then I'll wait." Tom spoke brightly.

"I know you will, but I don't want you to."

"What?" Tom questioned not believing what he heard.

"Don't wait for me, Tom."

"You don't mean that."

"I don't want you to move on with your life, but that's me being selfish and you don't deserve that. If the right person comes along for you then I don't expect you to throw that away hoping I'll come through.'

"Kaitlyn, you *are* the right person."

"You don't know that. Life is so uncertain."

Tom bowed his head as she continued talking, and he knew there was only one more thing to say. "Okay."

He kissed her on the forehead and embraced her. He didn't want to let her go but he knew it was the right thing to do. As she got up to leave, he didn't call after her. He did, however, send a telepathic message to her. "But I *will* wait for you."

Kaitlyn finished out the school year and watched it transform back into the school it should have been before the gangs took over. Yes, there was still plenty of work to do to clean up the streets but the developers had received the message loud and clear and focused their attention and muscles elsewhere.

The following months were a whirlwind with work and extracurricular activities. Kaitlyn kept herself secluded for the most part, allowing her grandparents the peace of mind of not having to worry about her. She didn't send cards or make phone calls, send emails or anything that may allow for any reminders of her past life. She drifted away from that life farther each day, forgetting about what it had meant to her and allowing herself to focus on the now.

All she wanted to do was move on with her life; with no parents to tell her what to do, no Tom to look over her shoulder, and no so-called friends asking her to do things for them. She chose to be alone, at least for now, and she liked it that way. At least that's what she thought she wanted.

Over time, she became a bad influence on herself. Her mood collapsed as she continued running the gym's security, pushing her toughness on a nightly basis. The idea of becoming part of the "in" crowd, becoming cool, she didn't want anymore. She already had respect, and she was being left alone because of it; it was ideal to her situation. Having no friends seemed fine but she became quiet, didn't have a reason to speak, didn't have a need to socialize, and this was not a good thing. It took her down emotionally. Unaware of what it was doing to her, it isolated her. It allowed her emotional status to fester

She had blown off Tom, the love of her life and she wanted desperately to rewind time and take it all back, but she stuck with her guns, acquiring her late father's stubbornness to give into others. He had asked her as close to a proposal as one could get without actually saying the words, and she chose instead to find herself without him. He had promised to wait for her but she truly believed a guy as great as Tom, one so loving and handsome wouldn't be alone for long. With that one thought, she knew she must move on with her life and forget about him. He would simply be a wonderful, heartbreaking past memory.

Kaitlyn hadn't done much that summer, just kept to herself and did a lot of thinking. Thinking about herself, who she was and what she wanted to be. School was just about to start again when something occurred to Kaitlyn. This school oddly enough seemed to be just like the one she left with Tom. There were cheerleaders, perky little women who believed there was no one better than them. There were the jocks, the guys who knew they would get the cheerleaders and spoke all about it in the locker room. There were head-bangers in their heavy metal, death-rock black jeans and black shirts, the kickers in their traditional Wrangler jeans, boots, belt with big buckle and hat, and the normal people who didn't wear any of the style of the others and still didn't fit in anywhere in the school. Then there were the nerds, the smart kids with glasses, who stayed to themselves and only longed secretly to get a pat on the back for a job well done rather than a punch in the stomach. There were the bullies; which Kaitlyn knew of well but feared no more; and ironically, it seemed they feared her more than she ever feared them. In fact, as Kaitlyn considered the population, she realized that they gave her space, stepped away as she passed through, quieted their conversations as they watched her walk by, it was quite an empowering feeling.

Kaitlyn's wardrobe had also changed with her mood. She wore dark clothes, leather, tight jeans and daring tops. To avoid eye contact and yet keep an eye on things (as she did at the gym) she wore sunglasses. She walked with a strong upheld stance and she enjoyed seeing the stares and wrenched necks from the guys as she walked by them. She had wanted to be different, to be herself, and then she realized; she had wanted to be new; and now she was.

"A new person," Kaitlyn said, as she stood in front of the mirror in her bedroom. She started thinking about what this new personality personified. "Strong and tough. Someone who demands respect. Someone who scares people but not like a bully, more like a champion who doesn't have to prove herself."

She walked into her closet and looked at her new clothes. Clothes that she had acquired during her off time; wasting time at the mall either before work or after. Getting in the mood for security, for power, for keeping tough guys in check... red leather, black leather, tight black tank tops, stripes and solids, silver chains, silver Goth bracelets with spikes; she had reinvented herself through her wardrobe without even realizing it.

As she walked through school she found she enjoyed liked the attention... and the fear. Looks of awe, looks of mystification, looks from guys who wanted to get to know this girl with every ounce of lust they had inside of them. She even enjoyed receiving the looks from the cheerleaders, all thinking the same thing. "Who is she?"

Still sensitive to rules and not wanting to offend any teachers she removed her sunglasses for class yet left her jacket on, not wanting to draw negative attention to herself because of her shirt. But she still tested her new view out and when she dropped her pencil on the floor, three guys dove for it. The winner, the one who got it and returned it to Kaitlyn, looked smug in front of his friends. Kaitlyn smiled wickedly at the thought of her new found power and decided this was exactly what she wanted. Now for the next step.

Kaitlyn knew she didn't want the traditional boyfriend; it was too phony but she did have cravings. She didn't like it, having a need that wasn't being fulfilled. She reminisced of many times with Tom and how whole it made her feel but she wasn't going to go back to him and she wasn't going to fall into the trap of relationships. She didn't want that feeling of vulnerability. She didn't want to spend all of that time working on a connection… she just wanted something quick, something casual. So her next step was to find a guy. Not a need to be loved, not a lifelong commitment, just a temporary fix, but she needed to manage the situation. She couldn't have it get around that she was easy. She couldn't deal with sharing and she didn't want to be a thief. She wanted someone unattached, but easy on the eyes with stamina. One with whom she could have power over, someone to believe; to fear, losing this opportunity, and someone who can keep their mouth shut.

She found Randy in the cafeteria. He was a five-foot-eight, black hair, brown eyed, well-dressed and smart young man. He was cool enough to be second leader in charge of his group of guys but not talkative enough to blurt out their little scheme. She initiated phase two.

As she walked up to his table the guys all stopped talking and turned to look at her. She looked down at a guy sitting next to Randy and raised her eyebrow. He quickly got up and offered her his seat. She sat down next to Randy and looked around at the other guys, just double checking to make sure she picked the best guy and when she was sure she had, she turned to Randy and placed her hand high up on his thigh and squeezed it enough to really get his attention. He enjoyed her touching him, enjoyed looking at her, and as he smiled back so innocently yet with the slightest bit of curiosity and excitement she spoke to him.

"Join me."

He followed her out of the cafeteria and as they left, him following close behind, Kaitlyn heard the conversations pick up.

"What do you think that's all about?"

"She is so hot."

"Why didn't she pick me?"

"Randy is so lucky!"

Kaitlyn half smiled at that but said nothing nor turned to look at him until they were out of the cafeteria down the hall to the elevator. There was an elevator that had been built into the school a few years ago for students in wheelchairs but it was hardly ever used, so it was the perfect place to finalize phase two.

As the doors opened, Kaitlyn took Randy's hand and led him into the elevator, as the doors closed she pushed the stop button and the elevator stood still, unmoving and unopening. They were alone; with no distractions. She pushed Randy against the wall, rubbed her body down his torso and then back up again, sliding her hands up his arms and stopping around the back of his neck, and then she kissed him, only for a moment, leaving him with a longing for her. Then she spoke right into his lips, locking eyes.

"I have a proposition for you."

He looked at her curiously at first but as she explained what she wanted he grew more than accepting to her terms and more than eager to begin.

"Now you understand the terms?" She finished.

"Yes, definitely."

"I catch you talking about this, bragging to your friends…"

"I understand but…"

Kaitlyn already knew his next question and finished the thought. "But what about today? What did we talk about? What did we do?"

"Yeah."

"None of their business. The guys can talk all they want, but you will not deny or confirm their suspicions. If you do, this will be over before it starts."

"I understand completely."

"Good. How about you get back to lunch before you're missed."

"What about you?"

"I'll call you."

As Randy exited the elevator he stood up straight, his head held high, a cool smirk attempted to be concealed. Everyone saw the difference.

The following months everything went as planned. Kaitlyn would call Randy when she needed him. He never called her, never spoke to her in school unless she spoke to him first, and he never talked about their relationship. The other guys tried to find out the juicy details, but he still gave a non-detailed answer. His smile was enough though. They knew something was definitely different about him. They were dying to know his secret.

"So Randy, stop keeping secrets, what's going on between you and Kaitlyn?" They'd ask.

He'd smile and shake his head. "We're just friends."

"You all don't act like friends…"

"There's nothing to say guys." He'd smile.

"Oooh, he *is* seeing her. You can see it in his face," the leader of this rebellion would say. "What do you two do huh? Is she good?"

"You have no idea what you're talking about." He smiled, as he turned to leave. One of his buddies reached over and grabbed a pager from his belt.

"What's this Randy? Does she page you and you come running? Are you her little lap dog?"

Chris grabbed it and looked at it. "What is your story Randy?"

"Hand it over now and I won't break your nose." Randy said calmly.

"Ooooh," the other guys chimed expecting a fight.

"What'll happen if you don't have this Randy? Will she spank you?"

"You don't want to go there, Chris, I'm warning you." Randy was determined to not lose this thing he had with Kaitlyn.

"I think maybe I'll just ask her about it." Chris laughed.

"I think you're about to get at least one black eye." Randy punched his fist into his hand showing Chris he was ready to defend his turf.

But Chris and the guys had other plans. Without missing a beat Chris ran out of the locker room and down the hall to Kaitlyn's locker. She was just walking towards it when he ran up to her; the other guys following close behind. Randy was being blocked by a couple other guys who were laughing and eager to watch this play out. Chris ran a circle around Kaitlyn, stopping her as the other guys surrounded her.

Chris laughed and threw the pager around, trying to see if Randy would try to fight him for it, or try to grab it from his hands. He didn't. Randy looked angrily at Chris and then shrugged at Kaitlyn. Kaitlyn could tell he had continued to uphold his end of the bargain and this was just childish funning from his pals. She smiled wickedly and let Chris continue to set himself up as a fool.

"So Kaitlyn," he began not looking at her yet but still trying to catch his breath while egging Randy on. "Maybe you could settle a dispute for us."

"Chris, I'm warning you." Randy said, but Chris interrupted him, not paying attention to Randy's idle threats. Two guys held Randy's arms to hold him back.

"The guys and I here believe something's going on between you and Randy." Chris began.

Kaitlyn listened and then played along for a bit. "Do you?"

"Yeah, and rumor is…" Chris began again.

"Chris!" Randy said, failing to free himself.

Chris was enjoying this power and just to twist it enough to make Kaitlyn just as angry he said the only thing he could think to really upset her. "Rumor is you're Randy's lap dog." She listened to Chris dig himself deep into this hole. "This pager is like your calling card isn't it?"

"Oh, you can do better than that, Chris," Kaitlyn said with a sneer. "Think about it, darling. Randy carries the pager, not me."

"So you call him?" He asked curiously allowing the reality wash over him like a flood.

"That would make a little more sense wouldn't it?"

"I suppose." Chris paused thinking and then spoke his thoughts. "You call Randy and he comes running?" He asked wanting to confirm it, certain she wouldn't.

"Wouldn't you?" She asked as she pressed up to his body and left her lips just inches away from his. She was luring Chris into a sense of unknown danger.

"Yeah," he said, looking up into her eyes. She turned. Grabbed his ear with her fingernails and tilted his head back. He fell to his knees, his head cocked in a direction to look up at her towering over him.

"You got a problem with that?"

"No! No," he screamed, nearly begging her with his answers to let him go.

She looked around at the other guys standing there completely dumbfounded and spoke, "Any of you got a problem with it?"

"No." Came their reply. Then Kaitlyn took the pager from Chris's hand, tossed it back over to Randy, who by now had been released by the guys, and then she let her grip go of Chris. He fell onto his knees on the floor.

"Good." She turned and walked away, leaving all of the guys awestruck.

A few seconds later Randy walked up to Chris who was still on the floor rubbing his ear and spoke. "You just had to be stupid, didn't you?" Then he walked away. The rest of the guys had a newfound respect for Randy and laughed at Chris for being leveled by a woman.

Rumor and talk of Kaitlyn and Randy's situation spread like wildflowers in bloom, everyone was talking about it. At first, Kaitlyn wasn't concerned. The guys all gave her this look like, I can be better. Or pick me instead. The stares from the guys were priceless; the stares from the girls, however, were horrible. Kaitlyn heard the words whore and slut quite often as she passed by groups of girls, and it was starting to bother her but she didn't know what she should do about it.

If the students wanted to turn evil, if they wanted to make judgments and name call, let them. She wouldn't let it bother her anymore, but what she would do is tell it like it is. Show them what she was about so there weren't any lies. So when she saw Randy in the hallway that afternoon, she made a move on him. She threw him to the wall, grabbed him by the shirt collar and pulled his lips onto hers forcefully.

He loved it. Forgetting he was at school, he fell right into his roll. He grabbed her butt with his hands making her jump up and wrap her legs around his hips and then he spun her around so her back was to the wall. She ripped his shirt half open and as much as it excited him, it also gave him a sense of control. He took her hands into his and lifted them above her head, pinning them against the wall, which was like foreplay to her, making her even more ravenous. She was straddling his pelvis and gyrating her hips enough to completely turn him on. He let loose his grip on her hands to hold her up there and she clawed his back right before she raised her head opening her mouth and moaned with a sigh of airy breath as if she had just had an orgasm.

It was as if he knew that was all she wanted, and as he moved back an inch so she could drop to her feet, he looked at her and suddenly remembering again where they were; he panicked. His eyes grew wide as if he were afraid to turn around, afraid to see who had been watching.

"Thanks, babe." She winked and walked away. Dropped jaws was enough for Kaitlyn. All she knew was now it wasn't going to be as much fun to talk about since the rumor had been confirmed.

Chapter 20

The day before spring break and the school was as close to anarchy as you could get. The rumors had all but ended and things seemed about normal, for Kaitlyn's taste but as she headed to her last class before lunch she bumped into someone just coming around the corner.

"Sorry," she said to the girl picking up her books but wouldn't kneel down and help her. Kaitlyn was looking for Randy to clear up his schedule.

"Kaitlyn Jones?" The girl said, as if she knew Kaitlyn. The girl stood up and faced Kaitlyn who at the time wasn't paying much attention to her until she heard her full name. "It's Susan."

Kaitlyn suddenly recognized the girl. "Susan?" She smiled not realizing how much she had missed seeing old friends. "How have you been?"

"I've been good. My mom just got a promotion so we packed up and moved here for her new job."

"Well, that's good I guess."

"It's okay. I really wasn't looking forward to moving away from my friends especially during my senior year of high school muchless during the middle of it, but I'll get over it."

"Good," Kaitlyn said, ready to move on now.

"So what have you been up to? We have so much to catch up on? Like what's life like here in the city. How are your handling life with no parents and are you still teaching Self Defense classes?"

Kaitlyn hadn't thought about any of that; she had just been absorbed into herself. She wasn't ready to answer questions about herself or her life and she didn't like being asked and put on the spot. It made her very nervous and irritated. She was just about to say so when Susan hit her with a tough one.

"Tom's not doing so well."

Kaitlyn hadn't thought about Tom in months; she hadn't even considered calling him. She had been so final last time they talked and so sure he would move on that she didn't want to call and disrupt him. And here, from out of nowhere, she finds out he isn't doing so well. Was he sick? Was it something serious? No, this news is coming from a cheerleader; it could be something simple like he lost a wrestling match. Curiosity got the better of her though and she asked. "What do you mean he's not doing well?"

"After you left he just changed. He stopped talking to people, stopped joking around; it was as if his father had died all over again. This entire season he hasn't dated anyone. It's as if the entire school just became sad. It's a shame you had to leave."

"Well, I did." Kaitlyn said, somehow feeling she had to defend herself. It was Tom's choice to push her away… of course it was her choice to stay away but she didn't have to defend herself! Kaitlyn became agitated.

"Anyways," Susan continued rambling on like anyone with half a brain would. "We must sit together during lunch, catch up on things. Hey, have you become a cheerleader yet?"

"What?" Kaitlyn scoffed.

"You would have been such a good cheerleader. With your strength and agility, and your self-defense classes were great. I just don't know why you never tried out for the team at home."

"I did, Susan. You didn't want me."

"Well, that's ridiculous. Tell you what, I'm trying out for the team here, you can join me. Wouldn't it be great? You and I as a team?"

Kaitlyn politely excused herself and walked off. Susan smiled and waved goodbye like any blonde cheerleader would do, jumping up and down.

Kaitlyn was thinking about Tom, wondering if what Susan said was true, completely lost in thought when Randy walked up to her. He saw her but she didn't see him so he decided to surprise her. He pulled her into his arms and kissed her so passionately Kaitlyn couldn't resist. Still thinking about Tom, she closed her eyes imagining Tom was kissing her, and as she kissed him back, believing it was Tom, she got lost in him. When the kiss was over Kaitlyn waited, eyes closed and longing for more.

"Oh, Tom."

Randy didn't know what to think of it, but he suddenly laughed. "Are we playing character games now? Because I can think of some killer characters for you to be."

Kaitlyn opened her eyes and looked at Randy. First disbelief and then disorientation came to her because she believed in her soul it had been Tom kissing her just now and it wasn't. She felt sadness and then finally rage. "What do you think you're doing?"

"What? I kissed you." Randy said with bewilderment.

"The deal was I initiate contact. Not you! What is your problem?"

"My problem? What's your problem?"

"My problem is this deal with us. I initiated it so there would be no attachment and now after you kissed me I feel like you think we're attached. I don't want any attachments. I can't have strings!"

"Whatever, psycho, I was just being nice and here you are biting my head off!"

"Don't be nice! You are my toy and nothing more! If you can't handle it then leave!"

"Fine!"

"Fine!"

As Randy retreated, Kaitlyn stormed off, but suddenly she felt eyes boring in on her and she felt dirty.

Ring. "Hello?"

"Tom?"

"Kaitlyn?" Tom inquired curiously, "How are you doing?" He sounded happy. Kaitlyn didn't know how to react, she expected him to be sad, depressed.

"Fine."

"So what's up?" Tom questioned.

"Up?"

"Why are you calling?"

"I can't call?"

"Of course you can call."

"Good." She barked quickly then paused for a moment before Tom spoke again.

"Are you all right?"

"Yeah. Why shouldn't I be?" Kaitlyn still felt like she was on the defensive.

"No reason, just curious."

"Don't think I can handle myself without you?" Kaitlyn snapped.

"I never said that." Tom sighed heavily. Attempting to keep the conversation going he asked again, "So why are you calling?"

"Do I have to have a reason?"

"With an attitude like that you do!" Tom grew annoyed. Kaitlyn now had no idea why she called but knew she was angry with him but didn't know why.

"Then fine, I'll hang up!"

"Kaitlyn, don't hang up." Tom backpedaled.

"Back to telling me what to do already, huh?"

"Why are you so angry?"

"You just bring out the best of me."

"I hope that's not true. I'm trying to be nice here." Tom calmed, hoping she would follow suit. "Can't we have a civil conversation?"

"I suppose so."

"Okay. So how's school going?"

"Fine."

"Making any friends yet?"

"I guess."

"Good."

"Don't treat me like a child."

"How am I treating you like a child?"

"The only thing you haven't done yet is ask if I've finished my homework and tell me to brush my teeth and go to bed."

"Okay," He sighed, "what do you want to talk about?"

"I don't know."

"There's got to be a reason you called? Anything new or different happen today?"

"Susan is now going to my school."

"Oh, good! She left here last week and everyone's going to miss her. Anything else?"

"No, not really."

"Oh." Tom said, sounding just the wee bit disappointed. He had gotten her to say something and now, nothing.

"I missed you," Kaitlyn admitted quietly.

"I missed you, too." He sounded as if he heard the most wonderful news ever. "I really miss you. Do you want to get together? To talk? To catch up?"

"No," Kaitlyn said, after a long hesitation. Suddenly she wasn't too proud of herself and what she had been doing. Suddenly she felt extremely guilty about Randy.

"I understand." Tom assured. "You want to do this alone, on your own. I'm proud of you for your decision."

"Thanks." Kaitlyn said, not meaning it.

"Are you sure you're all right? You don't sound happy."

"Well I am," Kaitlyn snapped, but then added quietly. "I think."

Tom knew how she felt. He didn't know how he felt her emotions; he attributed it to just being connected to her, but he also knew it was wrong. He felt her emotions and sometimes he didn't know if her emotions were hers or his. He had once been feeling angry for hours, and when one of his friends tapped him on the shoulder to ask him a question he turned and snapped at him, completely biting the guys head off with one word. "What?" It was Kaitlyn's emotions, so he quickly apologized, but knew something was wrong.

Tom knew he had to control this bizarre gift. Feeling Kaitlyn's emotions were starting to kill him. He felt when she was happy, when she was angry or scared; he felt when she felt foolish and then her feelings when she got even. He felt her spitefulness and aggression; each time she had an emotion no matter how little or precise he felt it. He could almost see what she was doing or going through because of this connection via the emotions. He knew she was sleeping with someone else, that she was using him, and this hurt Tom. And this afternoon, before she called, he sensed her thinking of him, feeling him around her, longing for him. He felt the love she held so deep within her heart for him. It gave him hope, but he knew not to put too much anticipation into it.

He had tried many times to block the emotions, but he just wasn't strong enough. Over the months he had been taking mediation classes, trying to control these emotions, trying to learn how to block them out, so they wouldn't consume him, but he knew that time was the only thing that would cure him of this plague. He didn't know if he'd ever be strong enough to block all of her emotions, even the ones so strong they consumed him entirely. He hoped he wouldn't have to and he also knew he couldn't continue life this way. He couldn't let Kaitlyn turn him into herself.

"I hope you find happiness, Kaitlyn. I hope with all my heart that you find yourself out there, and I hope once you do all of this, that you call me back and let me know when you are happy."

"Thank you, Tom," she smiled fighting back tears.

"I love you, Kaitlyn Marie Jones. Don't you ever forget that!" And with that he hung up the phone, knowing well, that she was crying and that there was nothing else he could say to comfort her.

Spring break was slow for Kaitlyn. She hated going back to school. She didn't look forward to seeing Susan and being blocked in the hall listening all about her break. She didn't look forward to seeing Randy after how badly she had treated him and she didn't look forward to seeing anyone at that school, knowing well what kind of person she had become.

She was ashamed of herself. She had attempted to be a new person, to find herself. All she found was how to make a mockery of yourself and loose the respect of the entire school. She thought she had been doing so well, and now after a week off to think about her actions, she couldn't stand to look at herself in the mirror. She hadn't made any friends. She had successfully become a loner and screwed up what could have been a good thing with a guy. She would never admit out loud, but a guy she really liked. Of course, she loved Tom with all of her heart, and he was still waiting, but she did like Randy and now he would never speak to her again. Not that he should. What she did to him was absolutely…

"Absolutely wonderful," Susan exclaimed in front of her new friends at school that day. Kaitlyn was surprised at how quickly some people can make it to the top; she kept walking down the hall until she heard something from Susan's conversation that intrigued her. "We met right after school before the break and hit it off almost immediately. He is a great guy with so much to say."

"So who is he?" One of the girls asked and Susan paused with a smile before answering.

"He's coming through the door right now."

Everyone turned to see this wonderful guy they didn't know of in their school, excited for Susan, curious about her new boyfriend, but as they turned they knew they didn't look through the right door because the only person they saw was Randy.

Kaitlyn realized what was going on, and as Susan ran up to Randy Kaitlyn felt sick to her stomach. Oh, how the tables of life can turn so viciously when you don't treat them with love. She had come to apologize to Randy, but now he was with someone else. Someone she had despised for over two long years.

Susan ran up to him and they kissed. He wasn't forceful or demanding; he held her lovingly and with caring, and didn't throw her against the wall and maul her. She didn't rip his shirt open showing off his abs, showing her catch off to others. She didn't have to make a deal with him, didn't have to be mean or rude, and Kaitlyn was certain by how oddly they kissed that they hadn't slept together yet either.

Susan turned; holding hands with Randy, to her crowd of friends and spoke as happily as anyone in love could. "Everyone, this is Randy."

The blank stares and dropped mouths said it all, at least to Randy who knew what everyone was thinking. Susan thought no one heard her. "Hello? This is Randy."

Suddenly everyone spoke in unison but no one could finish his or her sentences.

"But Randy is…"

"He can't be…"

"How can he…"

Then like an odd exorcism exercise, everyone turned to look at the shell shocked Kaitlyn standing just down the hall from them, also in a state of shock. Everyone including Randy who hadn't noticed her standing there until now didn't know how to act. Kaitlyn felt the eyes boring in on her and suddenly didn't know how to react. Without thinking she turned to walk away, ready to leave this awkwardness and get to class when Randy ran up to her.

"Kaitlyn, I'm sorry."

"For what?" She turned to face him, wanting to kiss him but also wanting to slap him, and then realized she should slap herself. "It was me who didn't want strings remember?"

"I know, but…"

"You moved on pretty quickly, though."

"There wasn't much to move on from." He admitted quietly.

"You're right." All they had together was sex, and she was the one in charge.

"I wish there would have been more."

"Me, too." Kaitlyn said, admitting every vulnerable feeling. "But there wasn't, was there?" She asked, trying to find out for sure.

"No, I guess there wasn't."

"You guess?"

Kaitlyn knew by the way he kissed her that last day that something better could have happened. But there was no more time for talking. Kaitlyn heard Susan's voice echo through the hallway and knew things were about to get bad.

"What's going on here?"

"Susan," one of the girls spoke carefully. "Randy is Kaitlyn's boy toy."

"Boy toy? You don't call them boyfriends here?" Susan seemed confused.

"Oh, we call them that when their boyfriends, but Kaitlyn made sure Randy was just her toy."

Susan was completely confused. "What about Tom?" She looked at Kaitlyn curiously, waiting for a reply when Randy spoke up.

"Who's Tom?"

"He's like her fiancé or something back home."

"He's not my fian..." Kaitlyn began, but the damage had already been done.

"Now I know who Tom is. You were thinking about him that day. That's sick. Had you been thinking about him all of those nights as well?" Randy attacked her verbally.

"What nights? Susan asked, wanting to know just whom it was she had been kissing on the past two weeks.

"I can't believe you used me like that when you were already engaged. I have half a mind to tell this Tom guy just who he's marrying."

"We're not engaged. I turned him down." Kaitlyn said, trying to clear things up. But Susan made them worse.

"You turned him down? Then why has he refused to date anyone in half a year? He acts like he's waiting for you, like you're coming back or something. He tells every girl interested that he's taken."

"He does?" Kaitlyn spoke, with pure shock. She was truly disgusted with herself now and angry with Tom for waiting for her when she told him not to.

"I can't believe you, Kaitlyn," Susan said. "You are so two faced."

"I'm two faced? Look who was all happy to see me and excited to be here only to turn when she finds out the gossip."

"I was happy and I had hoped you had changed."

"Changed?" Kaitlyn snapped.

"Yeah, Miss bitch walking around campus demanding pity because her daddy died," Susan said, frowning.

"He was killed!" Kaitlyn yelled, as she stormed up to Susan ready to slap that smug look off of her face. Kaitlyn was just about to hit Susan, her arm was flying, the back of her palm ready to strike, when Susan stepped forward stomping her foot down for leverage and lifted her left arm up to block Kaitlyn's strike. Kaitlyn's arm hit hard against Susan's but she didn't flounder and as the two girls caught each other's eyes, they froze and stared each other down. They stood there still in fight mode, still holding their last move as if one of them moved the slap would proceed from stopped position. Susan spoke through gritted teeth.

"I may not be able to beat you in a fight, but I *can* defend myself."

Suddenly Kaitlyn's eyes began to burn and they began to whelp up. Tears formed too quickly to stop and, although, she refused to blink, refused to let her stare go for even a second, tears suddenly streamed down her face. Susan was shocked; she didn't know what to do. Kaitlyn had never taught her what to do in a fight if an opponent broke down crying, so she asked.

"Kaitlyn?"

"I was such a fool." Kaitlyn whispered so quietly she couldn't breathe. Susan took her into her arms and gave her a hug.

"It's okay," she whispered confused and confounded.

Kaitlyn fell to her knees and Susan followed, and all the while Kaitlyn was crying and saying, "I am such a fool. I am so sorry."

That day during lunch one of the girls walked up to Susan. "Hey how did you learn how to do that this morning?"

"What block a punch?"

"Yeah? Did you take a defense class?"

"Actually, yeah I did." Susan smiled.

"Do you think you can teach me some of those moves?"

"Actually, I couldn't teach you as much as someone else I know."

"Oh, really? Who?"

"Kaitlyn."

"I have a proposition for you." Susan began as she walked up to Kaitlyn in the hallway that afternoon.

"And what's that?" Kaitlyn asked, as she closed her locker shut.

"You pick up the defense classes and I won't tell Tom about Randy."

"That's blackmail."

"Call it what you will, but I have thirteen girls already signed up if you'll do it."

"Do what?"

"Continue the self defense classes."

"I can't do that anymore."

"Why not? Did you forget how to?"

"No, of course not, I just..."

"Don't want to be reminded of Tom?"

"You always knew how to get on my nerves, Susan."

"I'm right." She smiled. "I knew it."

"I don't even know if the school will let us." Kaitlyn tried to make excuses.

"I've already talked to them, and they will."

"You've covered your bases haven't you?"

"Well, not all of my bases, I still don't know what to do about Randy."

"Me, neither."

They laughed.

As Kaitlyn stood in front of her new class, a class for the first time since she threw Tom across the room almost a year ago, an odd sense of finality swarmed over her. Oh, how the tables turn, she thought as she finished saying that well prepared speech to her new class. The speech that said to the effect, don't waste my time and I'll teach you everything I can. Don't expect this to be a gabfest or slumber party, because I don't do that. Everyone sat silently as she spoke, and then she looked over at Susan who had heard the speech before and was smiling. And then Kaitlyn remembered what she did to Susan that first day.

"Hey Susan you want to come down and help me show these girls how to get out of a hold from an attacker."

"Now that is something I would love to do!" Susan chimed up as she stood and heading towards her.

Kaitlyn reminded the class that Susan had taken her classes before so she knew many of the things already, but Susan had been ready for this day for a very long time ago. Kaitlyn took Susan from behind, explaining the maneuver just like she had the first time, but this time, Susan knew what to do. Once Kaitlyn grabbed her, Susan stomped on her foot, elbowed her in the gut then turned and flipped her over her shoulder. Kaitlyn flew through the air and landed on her back on the mats and she looked up to Susan with a smile.

"Good to know I've been an influence on you."

Kaitlyn laughed as Susan smiled and held out her hand to help Kaitlyn up, but Kaitlyn wasn't going to lose her class that easily. With one swift move, she slid her leg under Susan, which knocked her over, and Kaitlyn spun upwards and leapt to her feet. Everyone applauded, and this time Kaitlyn held her hand out to help Susan up.

Suddenly Kaitlyn was having fun again, teaching her own class, using the moves and techniques for fight that Tom had taught her and she now taught others. It helped her feel complete and whole, and made her feel like she was doing something special with her life again. Like she had a place in the world, like she had a destiny, but after graduation, her classes stopped, and everyone moved on. Everyone, except Susan.

Susan and Kaitlyn moved in together. They became roommates to save money. Susan went on to college as Kaitlyn attempted to find herself in the working world. The problem Kaitlyn found, was that the working world was nothing like high school and the realization that she had to start all over again hit her hard. As she struggled with this new task she watched her friend Susan and the rest of the world move on. It had been four years since that grand day in the high school.

"Hey, did you take my sweater?" Kaitlyn asked, as she saw Susan walk into her room.

"No, but I do have something to tell you." Susan hesitated. Kaitlyn however wasn't paying attention to her friend, nor did she see the look of pure distress and torment on her friends face.

"What is it Susan?"

"Tom's dead."

To be continued...

Excerpt from:
Kaitlyn Jones "Surviving Death"

As Susan walked into Kaitlyn's room, she knew her task was going to be difficult. She had lived with Kaitlyn for the past four years and had learned her roommate's disposition. Knowing that Kaitlyn would be awake by now, and hopefully in a good mood, she prepared herself to tell Kaitlyn the horrible news. She trembled with the thought of having to do this difficult task. Finally, after watching her friend dive into her closet throwing clothing around, she spoke up.

"Kaitlyn, I have something I need to tell you."

"Have you seen my red sweater?" Kaitlyn asked her friend; whose second worst habit was going into Kaitlyn's closet and borrowing her clothes. Knowing that Kaitlyn wasn't listening to her, Susan began to shake, she was having a very hard time trying to form her words. The idea of having to repeat this ghastly news even once nearly made her sick to her stomach.

"Kaitlyn, I need to talk to you."

"What about?" Kaitlyn asked with her back turned towards her roommate, her attention was still focused on the closet. She didn't hear the quivering in her friend's voice, nor did she sense the anxiety that her friend was feeling.

"Kaitlyn, please!" Susan exploded. Finally, Kaitlyn turned to Susan. Her frustration at having to turn away from her task was evident on Kaitlyn's face.

"What is it, Susan?"

"It's about Tom." Susan said wearily.

"What about him?" Kaitlyn asked caught off guard after hearing his name after all of these years.

"He's dead."

As Kaitlyn stared at Susan, it seemed as if it took forever for the words to make sense. Kaitlyn's mouth dropped open as she slowly began to comprehend what Susan had just told her. With her eyes wide and shock beginning to fill her face, she scanned Susan's face for some shred of hope that Susan was just playing a horribly sick joke. But as she stared at her friend, seeing the sadness, remorse, and pity, Kaitlyn knew then that Susan was not joking. Tears began to whelp up into Kaitlyn's eyes. As she felt the burning sensation of tears forcing their way out, Kaitlyn refused to give in to the tears. She made herself remain calm and continued to stand there in disbelief.

"You're wrong. Tom's not dead." Kaitlyn said calmly.

"I got a call from his mother just a few minutes ago." Susan exclaimed.

"Well, it wasn't her."

"Yes, it was her. It was Marge McKinney and she sounded pretty upset." Susan stammered.

"Well, I don't believe it. I would know if Tom was dead."

"Kaitlyn, it's also here in the newspaper," Susan said as she showed Kaitlyn a computer printed copy of the newspaper article.

"What is?"

"The story of his death is on the front page of the San Diego Union-Tribune."

Kaitlyn stopped. Susan had printed the front page of San Diego's online newspaper to show the column and Tom's picture for proof. Kaitlyn wanted to simply doubt it since it was easy to create a fake article on the computer, but then she looked over Susan's shoulder and noticed that the computer screen was still on that web page. Kaitlyn took the paper from Susan and looked at it. She wanted desperately to prove Susan wrong, so she examined the picture. Looking for a flaw, anything, to prove that it was someone who looked just like Tom. Desperately hoping that it was a really sick joke and that the picture was a fake, Kaitlyn stared at the picture.

It wasn't the same man she had known from high school. This version of Tom was older and wiser and his hairstyle was different. There were now laugh lines around his mouth. However, as she looked at the picture and looked into his eyes, those eyes that had looked into her very soul so many times, the eyes that with a glance could tell her everything she had ever wanted to hear, suddenly Kaitlyn recognized this man. This was a man who was full of love and caring, a man who had so much to offer and to give. This man that she had loved so incredibly that it made her physically sick to think back to how horrible she had been to him. Suddenly Kaitlyn forgot how to breathe.

Kaitlyn's body begun an automatic shutdown. Her lungs forgot to breathe and her heart seemed to have stopped beating. Suddenly, tears filled her eyes. Feeling as if she were going to drown in her own tears, she closed her eyes. However, as she did, the room went dark and started spinning. She couldn't feel her legs or arms, she became light headed, uneasy on her feet. Feeling as if Earths gravitational pull was suddenly thrown off kilter Kaitlyn fell.

"Kaitlyn!" Susan screamed as she ran to help her fainting friend. Susan took hold of Kaitlyn's arm but in her haste to reach for her friend, she was pulled down also and landed on her instead. Susan began to panic. "Kaitlyn! Oh my God, Kaitlyn, wake up!" She slapped her friend on the face, wondering if she should get water or perform mouth to mouth. Kaitlyn's eyes then opened quickly which made Susan jump.

"Kaitlyn, are you all right?" Susan wanted to be there for her friend. She wanted to help her through this sad time and to give her a shoulder to lean on. But Kaitlyn didn't want any of it.

"It's a lie."

"What is?" Susan asked with shock.

"Tom's not dead." Kaitlyn said with so much certainty that Susan did not know what to think. Kaitlyn had fainted and now she was in denial. Susan knew that Kaitlyn was about to go through her worst life experience yet and she was grasping at ideas of how to help.

"It's in the paper…" Susan began trying to make sense of Kaitlyn's statement.

"I don't care if the pope said it! Tom is not dead! I know that I would feel it." Kaitlyn insisted.

"What do you mean you would feel it?" Susan asked curiously having heard this statement twice.

Kaitlyn had never told anyone of the telepathic link she had with Tom. She had never wanted to break the secret that he had sworn was so important for her to keep. They hadn't communicated telepathically with each other in four years, but once a connection like that was made, it couldn't ever be severed, could it? Kaitlyn began to doubt herself and to doubt the idea that she and Tom had really ever been close enough to know each other that well. But there was one thing she did know, even though they weren't as close as they had been in the past, her heart would feel slightly different if he were truly gone. She had to believe this, she had to believe that she would have felt differently the very second his soul left this planet. She wasn't sure why, but she really had to believe it or otherwise she would surely go crazy.

"Kaitlyn I'm so sorry I had to be the one to tell you this." Susan knew Kaitlyn was in denial, and she also knew Kaitlyn needed to go to the funeral. She needed to get closure, to see the body. She knew that with Kaitlyn's personality, she would believe it was a lie until she proved it wrong. So that night, Kaitlyn left with her bags packed for a weekend trip. Her heart determined to find the truth.

Continue Reading in:
Kaitlyn Jones "Surviving Death"
www.KathleensBooks.com

About the Author:

Kathleen J. Shields is a very creative, highly imaginative and extremely dedicated, hard working individual. She runs her own website and graphics design company, Kathleen's-Graphics, and has published various books; from fully-illustrated rhyming stories for ages 4 and up, children's chapter books for ages 8 and up, and young adult stories with plans for a few romantic mysteries stories as well.

Kathleen has been writing poetry and stories for years; both for fun and for hire in custom greeting cards and for local speaking engagements. She enjoys sharing her stories and talking with children and adults about how they too can write if they put their mind to it.

She has also started a blog with inspirational and educational posts both regarding her endeavors as an author as well as a business woman and Christian. Her views are always light-hearted and thought-provoking and are intended to get the reader thinking.

Her fully-illustrated rhyming children's stories, the Hamilton Troll Adventures, are inspirational as well as educational. These stories are engaging and amusing and provide informative descriptions of various animal characteristics, vocabulary words and definitions, all while incorporating real-life situations that young children can face. Each story introduces at least one additional character, presents new obstacles to overcome, teaches something new, all while imparting a positive impression. This is a terrific series for bedtime stories and young readers, as well as readers who are young at heart.

For more information about the author,
the various books she has written
and plans to write, please visit:
www.KathleensBooks.com
or follow her blog at **www.kathleenjshields.com**

www.ingramcontent.com/pod-product-compliance
Lightning Source LLC
Chambersburg PA
CBHW061613170626
46811CB00001B/415